INTO THE SKY

The Five Stones Pentalogy
Book 1

Erica Converso

Cover Design By
https://www.facebook.com/designforwriters/

To my family, for believing in me,
And to Chris, for everything.

Table of Contents

- CHAPTER 1 -

Rising

ALCIONE DREAMED OF flying. In her dream, she was a Talaria, proudly bearing the signet ring and sword, emblems of her office, a warrior of the sky astride her beautiful arion. The sun rose above the clouds, golden fingers reaching out to her—

She awoke with a start, throwing up a hand to block the light as the sun rose to breach the bottom sill of her tower window. She ran to the glass and squinted. Two black specks were silhouetted on the horizon. Was it them?

She watched a moment more, eyes wide. Once her suspicions were confirmed, a wide grin broke across her face. "It is!" she cried, running for the stairs. "Isaura, Kanase, wake up! Hermion and Father are home!"

She repeated the message as she dashed down the first flight of stairs into her sisters' room. She jumped on Kanase's bed and grabbed her shoulder, then went over to shake Isaura, a heavier sleeper.

1

"Wake up!" she shouted, bouncing on the soft feather mattress. "Father's back! Hermion too!"

Isaura groaned and threw a hand over her eyes. Her long golden-red hair spread out in a tangle on the pillow. On the other side of the room, Kanase sat up, dark hair tied back in a sensible braid. "We weren't expecting them for another week, were we?" she asked sleepily.

Alcie shook her head. "No, but that doesn't mean they couldn't have come! That's why I watched every morning – and see, I was right!"

Darting back up the stairs, Alcie wriggled out of her night shift. Yanking out a scarlet day dress – the first she laid hands on – she hauled herself into it, nearly toppling over in the process. She looped two small pouches onto her belt, taking care not to lose any of the precious leaves and pebbles from her collection within.

She came down just as her sisters' handmaid had begun to dress them. "Alcie," Isaura began, rolling her eyes. Her petticoats swished with her as she stepped away and came to stand before her youngest sister, pulling a hairbrush off the nearby nightstand as she went.

Alcie tried to stand still as Isaura brushed, but she couldn't help fidgeting. "It's not that important, is it?"

"Oh, Alcie," Kanase sighed. "You're forever running off somewhere. It's a lovely spring day – take a moment to enjoy it. And besides, Isaura's only trying to help. You know Mother will scold if your hair sticks out like it's doing now."

Defeated by sound logic, Alcie kept her hands at her sides. Kanase, serene and lovely in her dark blue dress, picked up her embroidery hoop and kit. As she passed them, she gave her sisters kisses on the cheeks.

As Alcie descended the stairs ahead of Isaura a moment later, she could hear her mother in the kitchen, chastising one of the staff. "I don't understand why you've been late every morning this past week. Honestly, it seems everyone's so giddy with spring that no one wants to work!"

Isaura's face grew tight, but Alcie was so excited that she barely noticed. "Come on!" she said. Unable to wait a moment longer, she sprinted for the door to the courtyard.

"Wait one moment, Alcione!" her mother called as Alcie's hand touched the door. "Don't think I don't hear you!"

"Drat," Alcie muttered. Isaura giggled from behind her.

Lady Montelymnë entered the parlor at a stately walk, the red-gold hair she'd passed to her daughters and son pressed back in a perfect bun. She shared Alcie's blue-grey eyes, but possessed none of her daughter's sun-deepened freckles. "I'll expect you back by midday meal at the latest. No excuses – Kanase is kind enough to help you practice your stitches, and Isaura will give you another dance lesson."

"She's hopeless, Mother," Isaura replied out of habit.

Lady Montelymnë's sharp gaze speared her daughters. "She will be, if she doesn't practice. Alcie, you will never be a lady—"

"—if you don't practice!" the girls chorused together.

"I know, I know!" Alcie replied. *But I don't want to be a lady! I want to be a rider!* "Yes, Mother," she said, knowing anything else would lead to an argument. "I'm going to see them now."

"Send your father in when you've greeted him," she called as Alcie bounded outside. "And remember, midday at the latest!"

It felt wonderful to finally be free of the constant winter rain and snow. Alcie turned her face to the light, letting its warmth bathe her as she ran. Her father's golden breastplate shimmered in the sun as he talked with Kanase, arm around the daughter who most resembled him. As Alcie raced to him, she could see that his dark beard had grown thick.

"Alcie!"

Hermion caught her first, wrapping her in a hug that lifted her off her feet and spun her around dizzily. She shrieked with surprise and delight. When he finally put her down, she looked him over head to toe, astonished by the changes eight short months had wrought.

4

He was taller than her, a fact that she noted with annoyance. His features were twins to her own, though he was a boy and a year older. But something indefinable separated him, some seriousness that infected her joy at seeing him. "What is it?" she asked.

He shook his head. "It's nothing." And then his smile returned, and he was the Hermion she'd always known. "Well, aren't you going to greet me properly?"

She stuck out her tongue at him. "Proper? Me? Never!"

Her father's booming laugh startled her. "That's my girl," Lord Montelymnë chortled. "I expect you're for the barn next. Does your mother know?" he asked, mock sternness drawing his brows down over his eyes.

Alcie nodded, coming over to hug him where he stood with Isaura and Kanase. "She said I have till midday. Will you come too?"

He shook his head. "We'll be in the study the rest of the day. Hermion and I have much to consider."

"Did something happen at the Talarinalia?" She spoke of the meet he had just returned from, where the King's protectors – the Talaria – met once a year.

"Nothing to concern yourself with," he said. He looked troubled for a moment, and she wondered what had happened. Then he smiled and patted her head, ruffling her hair a bit as he'd done since she was a little girl.

"Listen to your mother," he said. Dismissing her with a wave of his hand, he headed towards the main hall.

Isaura and Kanase greeted Hermion, then went inside as well. Hermion stayed a moment longer.

"Say hi to Romi for me," he told her. "I've missed him." He smiled. "Who knows? Maybe this could be the year he finally becomes my arion for real!"

Alcie nodded, feeling a pang of envy as her brother went to join her father. As a girl, she could never truly be allowed to be a rider like him. The feeling didn't last, though; nothing could mar the beauty of the spring morning. She made her way down to the barn at the edge of the walls of the Kayre.

The Stabler, her dearest friend outside of her family, waved in greeting as he rolled a barrow of dung to the compost. He always looked dour, but Alcie saw that he seemed unusually so this morning.

"Skipped morning meal again?" he asked without preamble.

She smiled. "You know me," she replied.

He looked steadily at her. "I do, lass."

She stepped past him into the barn. If he was in a bad mood, she'd let him be for a while. Eight heads poked from the stalls. In the near corner, old Thaia slept peacefully on her side. Alcie frowned. One was missing.

"Where's Romi?" she asked as she came back outside.

The Stabler scowled. "I been thinking on it all morning. It's as well yer father and brother are cloistered all day – it would've been my job if they found out."

Alcie started to grow nervous. "What happened?" Romi had been captured before Hermion left to train as a Talaria. The young arion was meant to be her brother's mount when he was tall enough, but he was still wild enough to cause trouble.

"Bit me and tore off for the woods in the wee hours when I tried to get him back from the outer paddock. Told yer father he shouldn't a grazed them outside the walls. I've been thinkin' how to tell him. Spero's helping his folks in the field, so there's no one to search for the beast."

"I could do it!"

The Stabler shook his head. "You, lass? Yer father would have my head. Come get the feed."

As they filled hay nets, Alcie pressed the issue. "Father would never have to know. I could find him and be back before nightfall."

"He might be deep into the Karya by now."

She grinned. "I could still find him."

In thirteen short years, Alcione had done much that girls were not supposed to do. Her brother had taught her about riding, and she had spent years toughening her muscles working in the stables alongside him. She had learned how to read an arion's ears to see its mood, and how to befriend them with carrots and apples. In secret, he had coached her on how to sit on an arion at a walk and, once, even at a trot.

And Alcie had sneaked out of the Kayre before, although only for brief afternoon walks at the edge of the Karya, the forest to the north of the castle. *I know I'd be able to find Romi and bring him back!*

"Romi's my favorite," she added. "He'd mind me if he'd listen to anyone."

She looked in at Moti, her brother's current mount. Although small, he was still graceful. *Arion are the most beautiful creatures in the world,* she thought. Four long legs gave onto hard, shiny hooves. They were the picture of nobility with their glossy coats of chestnut and black, grey or reddish-brown, and flowing manes and tails that danced in the wind.

But what set them apart from any other creature was their wings.

Arcing out wide from their shoulders, one on either side, they were the same rich color as an arion's coat, with hundreds of beautiful feathers.

On the ground, the wings tossed rider and arion off-balance as the breeze pushed them. But in the air, arion soared, powerful wings bearing them up to the clouds. It was a crime for any but the Talaria to ride them, as they watched the realm from above.

INTO THE SKY

Everyone knew the names of famous Talaria. They were the heroes of the realm. Alcie wanted to be a hero, and have songs sung in her honor. But more than that, Alcie wanted to ride.

As she boosted the last hay net onto a hook, gentle Inthys reached his dusty brown muzzle around her to begin his meal. Alcie took a treat from her pouch and fed him, her other hand stroking one wing. "I wonder what it's like to fly," she mused. "Men have all the fun!"

"Not all," Stabler said, coming to the stall door. "Ye help out as ye please. I do this and more every day."

"I don't do as I please!" she protested. "If I did, I'd be here every day too! And I'd be riding. I want to go on adventures, and have grand quests to conquer."

The Stabler sighed. "We all want what we can't have. But mayhap…"

He didn't speak for a moment as she ducked under Inthys's neck to exit the stall. "I suppose, just fer today, ye might have a quest. With the lads up doing the spring planting, I really don't have anyone else to ask."

Alcie brightened. "You mean it?"

He nodded. "Romi can't have got far – not past Karya. It isn't too twisty, if ye go straight up following the river. Could ye do it?"

"Of course!"

His gaze was sorrowful. "Ye need'na sound so gleeful."

Alcie scoffed. "Even if they found out I was gone, which they won't," she considered, already putting the lie together in her head, "I'll tell them it was my fault Romi got loose. They'd believe it. And that I sneaked out to make it right."

The Stabler huffed out a breath. "Always said ye could talk yer way out of anything. But don't go fallin' down or gettin' hurt!"

Clumsy as she was, it was a reasonable warning. Alcie shot him a cheeky grin. "I promise to be careful," she said. Her mind soared ahead with the idea of the journey.

Heading into the tack room, she reached for a dark bundle stowed in a corner, beside the trunk full of extra equipment. Her riding outfit. Taking it to Romi's empty stall, she laid her chemise and dress out over the stall door.

In no time, she had pulled a knee-length green tunic over her underclothes. She tugged on an old pair of her brother's leggings, and reached for her brother's worn pair of old riding boots.

She loved wearing the freer boys' clothes. When she went into town with her family, the ladies of the house were caged in a litter, and visits to neighboring estates were a long affair of itchy, high-necked gowns and wimples to cover her hair.

Now, she tucked her hair up into one of the round, puffy rustler caps that the stable boys wore, twisting it to make sure none of her long locks slipped out.

Only her locket remained. The silver was engraved with Montelymnë's crest: the sun rising over three mountains, a waterfall rushing down the center. It was a symbol of her heritage, and of lessons learned. After her father had given it to her on her last birthday, it never left her, even in sleep. She tucked it under the collar of the tunic.

"I'm ready," she called, and stepped out of the stall.

The Stabler inspected her. "Ye'll need a halter and lead," he said curtly, handing her the rope head collar. "Romi'll not be half as easy as he is in a stall. Ye remember how to catch 'em in the paddocks?"

Alcione recited, "Don't look like you're afraid, and do it quickly. Over the nose, over the ears, loop under the chin to cinch, and hold tight once they understand what you've done."

He nodded. "Just so. A belt, and that'll do it," he said, and gestured to her gown.

Alcione stripped the belt from her dress, grateful for its plainness. She looped it around her waist, shuffling her treat and treasure pouches to the front. The candies, stones, and trinkets she stored jingled against her body.

"One more thing."

The Stabler went into the tack room and returned with a small rucksack and a drab green cloak that had faded nearly to brown. He clasped it around her neck. "To keep ye warm," he said.

Thanking him, she hefted the sack over one shoulder. "There's food," he said. "I had it ready fer this afternoon, if I could find some way to get out and look for Romi. I am sorry, lass."

He looked sad, and she wondered if he was worried about being let go. "I'll find him," she promised. "No one will even know he was gone. Don't worry!"

It didn't seem to ease his mind. But then, Alcie supposed, probably nothing would until Romi was back. She was so excited, she had to fight not to skip towards the gate. The clothes were dusty and stained and there'd be plenty of trouble if she got caught, but it was worth the risk.

"Don' stay out too long," he warned her. "And don' get lost neither! Just go straight. Ye've a good head on yer shoulders. Ye'll be fine. Now follow me."

As they approached the gate, he called out to the guards stationed atop the ten-foot stone wall that surrounded the Kayre. "Hail the gate! I'm down to the village, the boy into the woods to help me find some marshwort and such fer the arion. Pass-right?"

"Pass-right granted!" one of the men shouted down to him. "Who's the boy? Is that young Spero?"

"Spero's in the fields, clearing stones. This is me sister's boy, Alcion. Fine lad."

Looking down, he gave Alcie a small smile. "I told Spero to send him up when he went out earlier."

Alcione smiled back, knowing the guard would think she'd come in from the west gate. Perhaps she could try this trick again sometime, and go into the village instead of the woods. Her normal way out was through a servants' entrance in the west, but the north gate was the quickest way to the Karya.

"Are ye in fer tonight's game o' chance?" the other guard asked.

The Stabler's face darkened for a moment. "Aye," he replied, smiling tightly. "See yer at sundown!"

Alcie looked at him questioningly. "Hard to risk coin where you might have none on the morrow," he replied to her unasked question.

Even more determined to get Romi back, Alcie nodded.

The guard gave a short salute, and looked down at Alcione. "It'll be right grand come sundown, eh lad?" he asked. "Them nobs—"

"Won't be as rich as me when I've done with our game!" the Stabler interrupted, giving the man a cautioning glare. "I'll see ye tonight, friend."

Alcie wondered what the man might have been about to say. Likely, the Stabler had been protecting her from a slur against her family. Folk were always saying things because her family lived in the Kayre while they lived in the villages. Inwardly, she thought it was a bit unfair, but she wouldn't have liked to trade places, either.

Men moved to the chain levers and slowly the first portcullis, then the second, rose a few feet into the air. Ducking under and walking fast to make the men's job easier, the Stabler strode out, Alcie trotting behind him. The gates closed behind them with a resounding thud.

The planks wobbled a bit as the two strode across the narrow drawbridge to the other side. The shallow moat beneath them moved sluggishly, small chunks of ice still mixed with the chilly water. Outside the Kayre, the sky seemed wider and bluer than Alcie remembered.

"This is where I leave ye," Stabler said. He gestured to the woods that appeared as a misty green blur at the edge of the pastures. The trees there were evergreen; they kept their spindly needles all the year round.

Malim and barra grazed the pastures, piebald and dappled splotches scattered amidst the tall grass. Alcione's heart leaped into her throat. This was it! Her very first quest! Her heart fluttered in her chest like feathers, beating light and fast.

"I'll be back by nightfall," she promised. "See you then!"

"Take care, lass," he told her. "I—I'll see ye when ye get back."

His face looked older then, lined with worry. She had a vague feeling of uneasiness, like something more was wrong. Squelching it, she turned away from him.

The countryside unfolded before her, a wide expanse of fields and scattered thatch huts, the Karya beckoning beyond. As the sun rose into the sky, it seemed the horizon went on forever. She began to walk, a wide smile spreading across her face as she set off for adventure.

- CHAPTER 2 -

A Strange Creature

ALCIONE STRODE PURPOSEFULLY across the wide expanse, glad to be walking across the fallow fields, empty of both crops and people. She tried to imagine where Romi might have gone. If Welm had gotten loose, she'd expect him to be rolling about in the dirt. Thaia would have stood at the gate of the Kayre, waiting to be let back in. Not Romi. *He's like me. If I was going to have an adventure, I'd do it right!*

In the distance, a farmer raised a hand to her in greeting and she responded in kind. Arion were smart in a tricky sort of way, and Romi more than most. His heart was still with his radiance, the wild arion who lived in the Brakehills beyond the woods. Perhaps he'd tried to return to them.

The light dimmed as Alcie entered the woods. Stones and branches littered her path, tripping her. In the first hour, she accumulated a wealth of scratches on her hands and tiny rips in her leggings and sleeves.

INTO THE SKY

Animals darted between tree trunks and through the underbrush. Alcie grinned, trying to spot them, and stopped whenever one stayed still long enough to watch. There were bright blue birds, and birds with yellow wings or scarlet breasts. Furry brown ketcha chewed nuts and leaped, gliding from tree to tree with webbed forelegs stretched like wings. As she walked, she gathered interesting stones and leaves for her collection, nearly filling her pouch to the brim.

After some time, Alcie sat down by a small stream to rest. She checked the pack and found a water skin, a loaf of berry bread, and a hunk of brynza cheese. As she was eating, a flash of white darted past her feet to hide underneath the raised root of a nearby tree. The white ball of fur squeaked, then let out a yip as she broke off a piece of bread and offered it.

With an excited bark, the creature ran forward, tripping over its paws. As it came over and licked up the crumbled bread from her hand, she got a closer look. It was small – but perhaps too large to be a baby – and streaked with lavender and indigo and dusky blue tufts of fur, like a twilit horizon. If she tilted her head, it almost seemed to glimmer.

It looked like an ysrei pup, but taller and skinnier. Its face was narrower, and its ears weren't half so large. She had read about the creatures of the woods, and asked the Stabler for details whenever he went for berries, but this was nothing like she had heard or read. *Perhaps,* she thought, noting how tame it was, *it's someone's pet. Stabler said a few folk live out this way, on the edge of the woods.*

It slobbered on her until her hand was dripping and the bread was gone, then plunked itself down at her feet and looked up at her, tongue lolling to one side, then back where it belonged between a jaw full of sharp, jagged white teeth.

As Alcione looked into a strangely human-like pair of wide, lake blue eyes, she had the oddest sensation of being judged. Slowly, she put out a hand to the creature as it stood still and continued its perusal of her. Her fingers gently reached to touch the soft white fur.

She scratched under its chin, and the spell was broken; a short, rough pink tongue came out to lap at her hand, and then a wet black nose was being thrust against her chest as two big paws planted themselves on her legs. "Down!" she told the creature with a giggle, gently nudging it away. Obediently, it returned its feet to the ground.

"What are you?" she wondered aloud. "You're not like anything I've ever seen before." As it sniffed her, she glanced under its belly. "I hope your mother isn't looking for you, boy." *Or your owner,* she added silently. *I want more time to play with you!*

Strangely, the creature shook his head, as if he knew exactly what he was being asked. Alcione knew that animals liked her, but this was ridiculous. They didn't come up to you in the woods – at least, she didn't think so. They were supposed to be scared of people. But this creature almost seemed *human*! They sat there in companionable silence for a few more moments, and the creature didn't budge.

"Well, boy," she asked, shrugging, "do you want to come along with me? I'm looking for my friend, Romi. He's an arion, and he's lost."

The whatever-it-was barked happily, and Alcie fed him another piece of bread. Getting up, she put the rest of her food back into the pack and dusted the crumbs off. The creature's hungry mouth was waiting to snatch them up.

After a few steps it was obvious that whatever the creature was, he didn't intend to leave. In truth, she was glad of the company. The woods were bigger and darker than she'd thought they'd be. Keeping alert, Alcione continued her walk, calling out Romi's name every so often. With the creature at her side, she walked on, kneeling occasionally to stuff an interesting pebble or twig into her pack.

Hours passed. There was no sign of the stubborn arion. Alcione had been careful to stay in a straight line, and she took time as she walked to rearrange nearby branches in patterns to mark her path.

She was having a fine time, every once in a while taking a stick to toss for her new friend to chase after and bring back. She had named him Sola, the ancient word for "dusk," and he seemed perfectly happy to stay by her side, only leaving every so often to mark the territory or investigate an interesting tree stump.

As he skittered ahead, all scrabbling claws and waving, fluffy blue-purple tail, Alcie heard an encouraging sound: a surprised bark and an even more surprised whinny. Running forward, she burst into a small clearing.

There was Romi! His fiery bay coat shone even in the dim light that filtered through the treetops, and his thick black mane and forelock streamed around his head and neck like shimmering curtains. His wing feathers were reddish, flowing to dark brown, and finally black at the tips. But for all his arrogant, royal presence, there was an unmistakable, charmingly crooked blaze streaking its way down his nose to soften the look.

Here, in the dimly lit woods, the mischievous spirit that blaze suggested seemed to have all but deserted Romi. His eyes wheeled, the whites of them visible. When Sola came close, Romi didn't run away as Alcione expected, but tried to kick at the pup, hooves flailing.

Or rather, three hooves did.

Coming closer, Alcione saw that the arion's right hind hoof was caught in a patch of dusa. The dark green plant had long, thorny tendrils that grew in shallow dirt and could trap unsuspecting animals if they stepped in the wrong place. Romi's hoof was wrapped in its thin vines. Blood dripped down his leg where the thorns had pierced his skin.

INTO THE SKY

"Oh, poor Romi," Alcie whispered. The arion's head snapped up to look at her as Sola scuttled back to her side to hide behind her, whimpering. "Easy, boy," she said, speaking to both of them. Moving slowly so as not to scare Romi, she put down her pack.

She reached into it and took out some slices of guara, a small fruit with burgundy skin and peach innards that all arion seemed to love. Carefully, she proffered one with outstretched palm. In her other hand, she clutched the halter behind her back. She advanced towards him, and saw with relief that Sola had decided to guard the rucksack instead of her.

After a moment of indecision, Romi's neck snaked out and he snatched the guara from her palm. He bared his teeth at her, but didn't try to bite. "That's right," she said soothingly as she fed him another slice. "I'm here to help you. You remember me, right?"

She left a few more slices of guara on the ground and waited for him to stretch his neck down to lip them up. As he did, she crept up close, took a deep breath, and reached out with her other hand.

Romi, sensing her nearness, threw up his head and banged into her. She careened backwards, nearly tripping over Sola. She grabbed a nearby tree to keep her balance. More irritated than hurt, she stood to try the halter again.

When she reached him, Romi craned his head around as if to scare her away. Gently, she nudged his nose back to the guara on the ground. "Don't you try that with me!" she told him sternly, mimicking the Stabler's usual reprimand. "I know your tricks."

She sidled up to his neck and reached one hand under it to hang onto him. For a moment she didn't move, watching him eat and waiting for her chance. The moment he lifted his head, she slid the halter over his nose and one ear as he threw his head up again in protest. Alcie was left sprawled on the ground, the halter dangling over one of Romi's ears. *You look lopsided, boy!* Alcie smiled wryly. *I should have known it wouldn't be this easy.*

It took her another few minutes and nearly all of the guara in the pack, but she at last got the halter over the other ear, and the loop under his chin tied. She took the dangling lead-piece and tied it to a sturdy-looking, low-set tree branch. She knew it wouldn't hold if Romi really got scared, but it would have to do. As he began to search for more guara, she bent to examine his wounded leg to find the best way to set him free from the dusa.

She remembered the Stabler mentioning that the vines weren't all that strong. He'd rid the paddocks of some the year before. She thought back to his actions. If she could break the vines apart, she could pull them free from Romi's leg.

Starting far away from his leg, she avoided the thorns and quickly broke the vines off from the ground. Now the arion could move away from the dusa, even though some of the dying vines were still tangled around his leg.

Getting up, she checked to make sure there were no more visible vine traps on the ground, and then took out another slice of guara. "Come and get it," she urged, as she held it out and took a step backwards.

Romi's eyes widened even more, not trusting this new trick. Cautiously, he hopped forward on three legs and dragged the fourth, then pinned his ears back at the pain. "Sorry, boy!" she exclaimed as he tried to bite at her hand. She snatched it back, and put the guara on a flat rock nearer to the end of the lead-piece attached to the tree.

Stepping back to where Sola watched with wary fascination, she let Romi take a few more hop-steps away from the dusa patch.

When he was occupied with another few slices of guara, she drew near to his injured leg once more. There were only three or four vines left. Deciding the quick way was best, she reached for a piece without any thorns, and yanked.

It was a full moment before she realized what had happened. The first sensation was pain. Romi's kick had caught her squarely on her left side. There was a searing burn in her gut, and she bit her lip hard to keep from crying out. Romi snorted and backed away, his ears flat back against his neck, his eyes rolling with fear and pain. Sola growled, standing between Alcione and the arion protectively.

Alcione tried to move, then gasped as a line of fire shot from her toes to her scalp. Her cap had been lost in the scuffle, and her long hair was spread out against the hard ground in all directions. Her hand was bleeding where some of the thorns had caught it as she tossed the dusa away.

"Ow!" she wailed. "Romi, you great bully, that hurt!" As she lay on the ground, she tried to see whether she had gotten all of the dusa out. From what she could make out, only one small vine remained, two thorns embedded in Romi's leg just above the hoof.

Lying on her back, she considered what to do. Sola was sitting down now, glancing back and forth between her and Romi with what looked very much like worry. She could try to get the last piece of dusa out, or hope that it came loose on its own. *Romi, you'll have to do for yourself,* she decided. She didn't feel like she could get up just yet.

The blood on Romi's leg was already drying, so he would probably heal just fine once she got him back to the Kayre. But, she thought with an uneasy feeling at the bottom of her stomach, could she get him back with both of them now hurt?

Slowly, taking great care not to bend in either direction, she tried to sit up. Even so, it felt like forever before she could even manage to get upright and drag herself over to lean against the trunk of a tree. Sola tried to help, standing close so she could lean on him, but he was too short for her to do much but put the tips of her fingers on top of his head for comfort.

At last, she was propped against the tree, Sola at her side, staring at Romi. The arion stared back, a mixture of remorse and resentment in his eyes. He seemed to want to come closer, his head cocked to one side, but he stood as if fixed to the spot. His wings were bunched in tightly at his sides, shivering with tension.

"You're trouble," she said to him, sighing. "It's the word you're named for, and it's what you are."

She looked up at the sky, noting the orange sunbeams with another sigh. Sunset was nearly here, and there was no way she was going to make it home before nightfall. If she tried to go now, she'd only be hopelessly lost in the dark. It was no use; she was stuck here tonight.

Shivering, she tugged the Stabler's cloak close around her and hunched in on herself. Her side still hurt, and she didn't look forward to the long night ahead. *I suppose my father will be very angry,* she thought glumly. *I'm sorry, Stabler! I truly tried. Now I'll just have to make the best of things out here.*

She looked into her pack and saw that there was still a bit of bread, some cheese, and some sticks of kert left. Beneath them was a gummy blob: sweet toffin. She supposed she was lucky the Stabler's nephew shared a love of Alcione's favorite snack. She would manage for a night.

What to do to pass all these hours, though? Next to her, Sola lay down and whuffled softly. Romi had made up his mind, and had shuffled close to her as well. He touched noses with Sola as if to apologize for his earlier behavior, and then settled, holding his wings loosely just off his flanks, as he might do at rest in his stall.

Alcione settled back to do what she always did when she was bored: tell stories. "Sola," she said to the creature, rubbing his silky fur with one hand. "I'm going to tell you all the stories I know until I fall asleep. All right?"

He looked up at her, whimpering. "I know, I know. You'll get bored. But you'll get your turn to talk, too."

She grinned, thinking of all the times she and her sisters had stayed up late into the night, Alcie weaving stories, and Isaura and Kanase chiming in with additions now and then. It was one of her favorite things to do. "All right," she said. "Now listen up: I'll tell you the tale of Prince Orfel. He was brave and strong and true, all the things a hero ought to be. He was the hero of the Riders of his age – he even slew the Great Beast of Nyxe!"

She stopped to swallow a few bites of bread. "But everything changed when he met the beautiful maiden Geyende. That part's kind of boring. They say she was the loveliest girl in the land, but they never say if she was smart or kind or if she could have saved herself."

Caught up in the tale, she embellished. "I think she had to have been more than pretty for Orfel to like her so much. Maybe she couldn't go outside because her parents worried too much." *Like mine,* she added silently. "Anyway, when he met Geyende, Orfel simply had to marry her. But Geyende's father didn't approve.

"They say he built the tower at Howlingfort across the Karya. He made it to lock Geyende up where Orfel could never see her. And that's where she died. That's why they call it the Sorrowful Tower."

Sola barked. Alcione looked at him and tried to read his face. "No, that's not the end of the story, silly," she said. "And yes, you can have more." She tipped the bag of kert onto the ground and let him forage. "You should be sadder, you know. You'd feel bad if I died."

Sola didn't look very much as if he'd feel bad. Neither did Romi, who was grazing nearby and listening with one ear tilted to her. *I always make too much of their faces.*

"Orfel was brokenhearted. They buried Geyende, with him watching from afar." At this part she winced. "But before they did, Orfel made her a promise. 'I'll get you back,' he said to her, 'even if I have to go to the Land of the Dead to do it.'"

Before long, the sun had gone beyond the mountains and the wind had picked up. Alcie continued telling stories as the stars appeared the sky.

She had always found it easy to talk to animals. In a way, their body language was like talking back. Romi paced, ears flicking to her as Alcie raised her voice at the good parts, excited. Now and again he stopped, tail swishing, and she felt a need to elaborate. "Oh, so you wanted to know more about the Old North Fort, boy? Well, this is what I remember…"

In time, pauses between tales turned to yawns. Breaking off a piece of toffin, she saw that both Romi and Sola were falling asleep. It was cold, but she was warm enough in the shelter of tree, cloak, and furball. She swallowed the toffin with a smile, and let her head drop onto one shoulder. It wouldn't be comfortable, but she would be safe with her friends watching over her.

Before trying to sleep, she said her evening prayer to Tanatos. She said the formal words of worship first. "Tanatos, father of all, thank you for your gifts. Bless your children as you blessed their ancestors before them."

She thought hard about what to add. She didn't really think about the gods much from day to day, and she rarely asked them for anything. So she simply said, "Thank you for watching over me. I hope I don't get home too late tomorrow. Please tell Father to be kind to the Stabler until I get back. Oh, and please don't let it snow on me!

"I hope I don't make my family too worried, either," she added belatedly. She complained a lot about her parents and siblings, but she loved them and knew that they loved her, even if she was different from them. They would miss her if she wasn't home soon. But at least for now, she could pretend that she was in one of her stories, out to rescue the fair maiden with Romi and Sola at her side.

I may be cold and scared, but I'd still rather be here, she decided as she closed her eyes and willed herself to stop thinking and dream. *After all, it's an adventure! And everything will be fine in the morning.*

- CHAPTER 3 -

A Stain on the Air

S HE WAS LOST. She could hardly see, the unrelenting black sky hanging like a shroud. The moon was a round eye, pale yellow as it beamed coldly down on her. There was no wind.

The stars were cold and harshly bright. No, not stars. She squinted, watching the silver lights wink in and out of existence. Fulgora. The malicious little spark bugs whose sharp bite stung her arms in summer were beautiful at night, blinking here and there like a moving cloud of starlight.

They drifted slowly away, a swirling mist like a slow-moving arrow. Alcione followed. Her breath on the air came in white clouds. It hung before her, brushing past her face as she moved forward.

Something's wrong.

The feeling was sudden and certain. The mass of fulgora began to buzz, a persistent humming that grew as it expanded, building a silver wall in the air. The winking lights formed shapes: a whirlwind spiraled upward into a tall turret, a rippling wave became battlements atop stony walls and a bastion at each corner. The fulgora were building Kayre Montelymnë right before her eyes!

Alcie ran forward, wanting to get inside, to go home where it was safe, but the drawbridge and portcullis were closed. She stood at the edge of the moat ditch and called up to the guard tower. "Let me in! It's me, Alcione! Let me in!" The buzzing in her ears had become a roar.

She coughed as the smell of fire reached her. The fulgora sped in a line down the water, turning everything to flame. A wall of smoke rose to obscure the castle. She screamed, and heard the sound echo. She stumbled back and tripped over her heels. The ground rose to meet her, and knocked her breath away.

Looking up, she saw a lone tower, and four faces crowded at the window. Her father, austere features transformed into a gruesome mask of terror. Her mother's face streaked with tears such as Alcione had never seen in her waking life. Isaura and Kanase clung to each other, sobbing. But where was her brother?

"Hermion!" she cried. "Where are you? We have to save them!"

She dragged herself up and began to run through the smoke, through the fulgora as they nipped at her arms and face. The moat beneath her was gone, turned to an icy, insubstantial path that

Alcie could feel through her boots like the touch of fresh snow.

Thunder crashed. Lines of lightning tore the sky. Alcione tried and tried, but couldn't find a way through the fire. Steeling herself for the pain, she dove into it. But unlike true fire, it didn't burn her. The wall of flames seemed endless as her family's continued cries for help came down to her. Where was Hermion?

"Alcione!"

Her head snapped up and he was there, standing atop the battlements by the chain-lever. "Pull the chain, Hermion!" she yelled, running to him. "Pull the chain so I can get in!"

But he simply stood, tears cutting lines through his ash-dusted cheeks. "It's too late," he whispered, and somehow she heard him.

No!

"Hermion, please!" she begged him. "They're in danger! We're supposed to save them! That's how it works!"

"Not this time," he told her. "See?"

He raised an arm to indicate the sky, and as he did, Alcie's world tilted on its end. The grounded lifted and thundered through her. The fulgora pinched at her eyelids. The fire circled her, pulling in so close she couldn't breathe. She tore at her throat, frantically trying to escape.

With a crack of lightning, the fire shattered into a burst of falling feathers, and as the glittering image of Kayre Montelymnë toppled, Alcione saw the sky beyond it. There was a streak of red across the moon, as if someone had taken a brush and painted it: a stain on the air.

She woke to the sound of screaming.

- CHAPTER 4 -

Ruin

BOLTING UPRIGHT, hissing at the pain in her side, Alcione looked around. Sola stood nearby, head thrown back as he howled. The scream was real, and it was coming from Romi. Alcie lurched over.

"Romi!" Grabbing his lead, she untied him from the tree. She had to get home! Something was horribly wrong. She could feel it like a river churning in her gut.

As she tugged Romi forward, she was stunned when the arion nearly toppled as he took his first steps. She turned to look at him, to see if the cuts on his leg were bleeding. The shafts of moonlight through the trees were thin, and she squinted. When she finally saw, she gasped and dropped the lead rope.

His wings were gone!

Alcie stared at the arion. It just wasn't possible. It was like...like losing your arms without any reason! There wasn't even a sign that Romi had ever had wings in the first place. No bones, no feathers, not even the nubs where the wings began, at the tops of his shoulders. Just…nothing.

"What in the name of Tanatos…?" she breathed. Nothing explained this. In seconds, the world had turned upside down and all its rules were changed. *What's happening?*

"We have to go home," Alcione said, images of the dream fresh in her mind. "We have to go now! Romi, Sola, come on!"

She wasn't sure if they would follow as she gathered up her things. But when she took hold of Romi's lead once more, he came without an argument. It was as if he, too, was in shock at what had occurred. His gait was weaving, wobbly. With her weight distributed unevenly to minimize the pain in her side, Alcie knew how he felt. It was as if the entire world were off-balance.

The moon was veiled by the dense foliage. She didn't know the way back, but Sola ran ahead. She had no better guide, so she followed the white figure as he darted through the trees like a ghost. For hours she fought her way through the woods, leaning on Romi when she got tired. When they paused to take a breath he leaned into her, ears pricked back with fear.

They pushed forward, never stopping for more than a moment. Neither of them were in any shape to run, but terror urged them on as quickly as they could go. When they faltered, Sola yowled as if to say, "Something's wrong! No time to waste!"

The sky lightened as they went, and in the faint glow of dawn Alcione began to make out the trail she had laid before. Her stomach growled, but she forced the feeling away and kept going. Finally, the woods began to slope down and thin out.

Lips parched, cloak muddy, and hair straggling out from beneath the dirt-streaked rustler cap, Alcione tumbled out of the forest and fell to the soft bed of dirt at the edge of the pastures. Behind her, Romi stood quivering, his lead rope tingling in Alcie's hand. In terror, she looked up at Kayre Montelymnë.

The nightmare had come true. The fire was over, smoldering only in small patches. Even from afar, the destruction was clear. The inner and outer walls of the Kayre had collapsed, leaving giant piles of rubble scattered about. There was no sign of the outbuildings – the kennel, the falconry. All of it gone.

No fire would burn all this. Not without help. This can't have happened. It can't!

Looking up as the tears formed in her eyes, Alcione saw the fading moon. A crimson smear tore it in two. She didn't know how long she sat watching it, Romi behind her, Sola at her side. She gazed with empty eyes until the sun broke over the horizon.

Standing up, she began a somnolent march over the fields. Smoke drifted up in lazy trails, and there was no one in sight. Nothing stirred as the three lonely figures made their way to the edge of the moat.

Her dream hadn't come true entirely, she thought, noting the splintered, yet still intact, drawbridge. It had fallen crookedly, as if someone had tried to pull it up and dropped it midway in the air. The entrance was twisted and charred into a stony hill covered in strips of cooled iron.

Alcione stopped, then saw something move on the far side of the ruined Kayre. "Wait!" she cried.

She ran across the bridge, heedless of arion and pup behind her, the wood creaking and swaying beneath their weight. "Wait, please! Father, Mother! Hermion! Anyone, please!"

She dashed into the Kayre, stubbing the toe of one boot on a pile of still-hot rubble. She tried to stamp out the fire while still pushing forward. Piles of debris, the remains of tapestries and tables, chaises and cookware, lay where they had fallen. Nothing had been left untouched. Alcione's heart wrenched. She hardly realized that she was sobbing as she continued her quest.

When she was just out of breath, she came around the far side of the Kayre, where the barn was supposed to be. All that remained was a hollow shell where the straw roof had caved in. A lone figure sat facing the sad structure, his back hunched in.

Alcione threw herself down beside him and grasped his shoulders, looking into the man's haunted face. "Stabler," she begged. "What happened? Who did this? Where are the arion? *Where is my family?*"

For a moment, he said nothing. Then he started to his feet, and whirled around. He looked at Romi, lead rope dangling, and Sola, the other end clutched loosely in his jaws. The Stabler turned to Alcione with an awful look.

"I din' have no choice," he said dully. "No choice, lass."

Alcione's look hardened. "You mean you were a part of this?" She wanted to scream, and go on screaming, but she forced herself to talk. "What did you do? What happened?"

He said nothing, looking away from her to the desolation beyond. The worry that knotted her stomach clenched at her like claws.

"The rebels, my girl," he said finally. "What d'ye know about the situation in the capital?"

She couldn't follow his train of thought. "What does it matter?"

"It'll…" he sighed, and the awful look got worse. He wouldn't meet her eyes. "It'll make more sense if ye know."

Alcione sat down on the ground, suddenly so tired she wanted to sleep forever. It was unthinkable, unfathomable, and yet she knew. "Just tell me. Are they dead?"

"Yer family?" Another great sigh. "Yeh. They…there was nothing to be done."

INTO THE SKY

Her body felt too tight, like the world was pressing in on her from all directions. *No, no, no* – it was a long, shuddering refrain that she could do nothing to stop. She was breaking, a million pieces of her crumbled into ashes.

"Leave me alone. I don't want to know any more."

The Stabler turned at last to face her. "Ye have to, miss. And I need t' say it, so's ye understand."

"Then say it," came the flat reply. "And go away."

"Aye. The rebels, they been angry at the King fer a long time, on account of the taxes goin' so high an' their children starvin' in the fields. Little bairns no bigger than yerself. They had a right t' be angry."

The cajoling tone ripped at her. "They didn't have a right to kill my family!" she snarled. He shook his head. Alcione shut her eyes as he continued, struggling to hear him through the scream that still would not stop.

"There was a man," the Stabler said, as if beginning one of the old tales he used to tell her. "Name of Trienes. He told the men that the King needed t' be stopped. But the only way t' do that was t' get rid of his guards first."

"The Talaria," Alcione whispered. Tears wet her cheeks, twin burns at the corners of her eyes.

"This Trienes made hisself a plan. He tells the men: kill the Talaria an' yer wives an' children will never be hungry again. He even got a magian out from exile to prove how far he meant to go. So they set a date, and folk rode out from Ianthe t' tell the country what t' do. They kept it close, an' shut up anybody who dared t' spill. It was the land's best-kept secret.

"Yesterday was that day. On'y I din' want ye dead. So I let Romi loose."

Alcione stared at him in uncomprehending horror. "But...you mean...you sent me out there and then let the rest of them die? What about Hermion? What about my sisters? My parents?"

"I couldn' save 'em all, lass! I did the best I could!"

Getting up, she backed away from him, trembling. "You monster!"

Her bones felt as though they might crack. If a person could freeze from inside, surely this must be what it felt like. "Get away from me." Each word was bitten off like a chip of ice. "If I ever see you again, I swear by Tanatos and all the rest of the gods, I will kill you myself."

"Alcione, I—" The Stabler broke off. His face was worn, broken. She had no pity left. "I'm sorry. I'll leave. But what will ye do?"

"Why? So you can kill me too?"

He flinched as if she'd struck him. "Alcie..."

She shook her head. "No. Don't. I don't care anymore."

Silenced, he left. Alcione staggered to Romi and put her arms about his neck. He nudged her with his nose, almost like a hug. Sola huddled close too, strange blue eyes shining and moist. They stood there, three shadows merged into one, long after the sun had risen into the sky over the barren wreckage that was once a castle.

- CHAPTER 5 -

Five Keys

WEEKS PASSED. The sun rose and set, and the scarlet stain left the moon. After a last light fall of snow, winter surrendered to spring. Wildflowers blossomed. They wound through the ruins of Kayre Montelymnë, bringing splashes of color to the dead landscape.

Alcione survived. She had discovered a small alcove in the ruins, a pit that had once been part of the cellar and still had a ceiling. The debris had crumbled in such a way as to make a shallow hill that she could easily climb as an entrance. Moving the rocks at night kept the wind from snaking in.

She slept, haunted by nightmares of her family pleading with her to save them. When she awoke, Sola stood over her, whimpering. Romi slept outside, sheltering where he could. Alcie had taken the lead rope off. He showed no inclination to leave, reinforcing the drastic action the Stabler must have taken to coax him to run all the way out into the woods.

The first morning was a haze of tears. Sola nudged her with his wet nose and she pushed the rocks away to let him out. Mixed scents of wood smoke and pungent cheese wafted towards her. She emerged from the cavern chamber to see three piles of food on the ground: one of hay, one of kert-sticks, and one of bread, brynza, and snow berries.

The meals seemed fresh laid, the berries wet with dew and the bread crisp and not moldy. She drank water from the well, so far on the edge of the Kayre that it had survived demolition.

There was a careful block on her thoughts. She saw, heard, smelled, walked, but nothing beyond. The surroundings were foreign and forlorn. As she ate, she watched Romi wander the ruins, Sola at his side. The strange pup darted often between the arion's hooves. Distantly, Alcie wondered if she should shoo him away, but Romi appeared to understand that Sola meant him no harm. If the eager multicolored furball got too close, the arion simply bared his teeth and whinnied.

When they tired, they came to stand beside her. In a hollow voice, Alcie told them stories, reciting old bedtime tales she knew by heart. Lost in tales of the great heroes, silent tears rolled down her face.

Slowly, Alcione began to create a shell for herself, a little world to hide away in. Her family wasn't dead, only gone away for a while. They had just vanished. She was on an adventure, and she occupied the hours telling Romi and Sola how they would go and find the tyrant who had taken them and force him to give them back. It was only a matter of time.

She took to wandering the abandoned Kayre, her friends at her heels. They saw no one, and there was no other shelter – save for a small mud-thatch hut just outside the wreckage of the walls, where a farmer might have once lived. She went only to the edge of the moat, but she could recognize the tall, lanky silhouette that stood motionless, watching the sunset every evening.

She grew thinner on only one meal a day – but the same meal was always there. And when she found Hermion's old dagger, protected in its tattered case and preserved within a blackened pile of rocks, she used it to cut her hair to the level of her ears, as some women did in mourning. She took to carrying the knife with her everywhere, just at the side of her collector's pouch.

Her skin deepened to a pale brown in the healing rays of the sun, and every day she cried fewer tears than before. Her nightmares remained, scenes of the tragedy and of the horrible warning of it, reality mixed with dream in a gruesome caricature of the truth.

She often awoke screaming, and gripped Sola tightly until the shuddering fits of tears stopped. She took to napping by day, in the sunlight that kept the worst at bay. Her tunic had become ragged and worn, the green faded to a murky brown-grey. There was a hole in the toe of her right boot.

She'd planned to burn the Stabler's cloak, or rip it to shreds, but as she'd thrown it to the ground in anger, her gaze was drawn to a flash of blue buried beside it. She dug out the battered book and saw it was the Book of Tanatos. Written in the ancient language, it told stories of the past. Tracing the letters with narrow fingers, she read aloud to Romi and Sola. And each night, the cloak grew shabbier as she wrapped it around the book for protection.

One morning, in the pre-dawn light, she awakened to Sola's tongue licking her face. She had finally begun to sleep through the nights again, now that they were warmer and shorter. In the distance, she heard footsteps. Moments later, the crunch of gravel signified someone trying to find their way into her cavern.

"Who's there?" she asked, trying to adjust her sight in the darkness.

"'Tis meself, lass. I've come t' talk."

Alcione scoffed. "And not to kill me as I sleep?"

The Stabler's face came into view, looking haggard even in the misty shadows. "If I'd wanted to, I could've," he said frankly. "An' ye know fair well who's been feedin' ye, jest as I know ye've been eatin' it."

"How do you know it wasn't Romi or Sola who ate it?" she asked stubbornly.

"'Coz no one yer size survives a fortnight wi'out a meal," came the logical reply. "Now come on out. We've got t' talk."

Alcione followed, Sola scrambling up beside her. Romi was outside, fast asleep. He swayed back and forth like a rolling wagon, as if feeling a ghostly wind ruffle the feathers of wings no longer there. He had gotten the trick of running without them, but whenever he leaped in the air, he would skid to a stop, looking heartbreakingly bewildered.

Alcione knew just how he felt. It was just the way she herself felt a thousand times a day, when she turned to go find Hermion to tell him something funny, or went to see how Isaura and Kanase were progressing with their sewing. When that happened, she simply sat down wherever she was and took big, deep breaths until she had blocked out the tears, the memory, all of it.

She looked at the sky, soft reds and pinks. The Stabler was a withered shadow of himself against it. He waited for her to come stand beside him.

"Ye mus' know I can' feed ye much longer, lass," he said without preamble. "Tisn't that I don' want to, but there's little enough food here for one since the others left."

"I thought your leader said when the King and all the nobles were dead, no one would ever go hungry again," Alcie spat bitterly. "What happened to that?"

"So he did," the Stabler agreed. "But he means to rule a much smaller land than the kings before him. Folk were asked to come nearer the city, and none liked it up here in the cold so much that they stayed. Took what they could to sell, and went to find a new life in the capital. I don' know as they ever made it, but none came back."

He shrugged. "I'll be leaving meself soon enough. I've word this morn that the traders arrived here from the north. They're on their way to Ianthe. Best ye go with them."

"What could I do?"

"Ye're as good as any hired hand I ever had. There's a man buying up the rest o' the arion, and like as not he'll need help. Anyhow, ye've no choice unless ye plan to feed yerself from now on."

For the first time in days, Alcione began to feel something. "You mean...the arion...they're not dead? But I thought..."

The Stabler snorted. "Ye thought I'd leave 'em t' die. First, they're valuable. Second, they're me family, as ye are. Aye, they're all alive..." He halted. "All save ol' Thaia. She wouldn' leave even when the fires took the barn."

Torn between relief at finding some friends returned to her and sorrow at the loss of an old, dear companion, Alcie returned to silence.

"The traders are a tricky lot, full o' strange folk," the Stabler was saying, "but they'll pay fer a gift like yers, and fer the arion." He indicated Romi.

Alcie hesitated. "Did they all lose…" She looked at the arion.

He nodded. "No one knows why. Mayhap t' death of the Riders, mayhap Tanatos wants it this way. Who can say? But it's good fer ye, lass, so don' complain. Ye'll have it rough enough handlin' them wi'out wings. Don' borrow trouble.

"Go t' the capital an' make yer fortune like the rest o' us. Ye can learn t' do somethin' useful, jest as ye wanted."

But not like this, her mind protested. *Not like this.* "How would I convince them to take me?" she asked uncertainly. "And how long will I have to…to say goodbye?" The last words came out in a whisper.

"They'll be here for a day or so. I told 'em ye were me nephew Alcion, come from Ianthe wi' the message for freedom, an' now ye've a wish t' go back."

"That—" Alcione spluttered. "You as good as told them I was the herald bringing my family's death sentence!"

"Aye, so they'll never suspect ye. 'Tis good ye cut yer hair. Ye'll look a boy, in that getup. Actually, ye look like yer brother."

"Don't you say that!" Alcie warned him. "You aren't fit to! You act as if it's nothing, what they've done. What *you've* done."

The Stabler stamped a foot, harrumphing and looking very like one of his beloved arion. "Don' say things when ye've no notion of the truth."

"The truth is that you're murderers, all of you!"

"An' they weren't?" he thundered back. "When they denied our children food? Me own girl would've been yer age, if she'd lived. She died fifteen years ago, thin as a post. Starved to death. Me wife died o' the heartbreak. I've never forgotten." His face was harsh, twisted beyond recognition.

"Yer family's dead now too, an' there's nothin' ye can do. Ye can' bring them back, so wake up an' move on." He scuffed a toe against the ground, and cleared his throat. Suddenly he was the familiar Stabler again, only much, much older and terribly sad. "I did."

Alcie bit her lip. "I didn't know. And I'm sorry. But that doesn't make it right, what they did."

"I know it. But it's done. What's dead is dead. And ye're no Orfel."

"What?" It took her a moment to understand. Stunned, her mind caught at the notion, frightened and thrilled and spinning. "I – I need to think," she murmured.

"Aye." The Stabler reached out to touch her shoulder, then halted. "If ye decide t' go, come down to the village. I'll wait fer ye there." Abruptly, he turned and walked off, a thin, stooped figure receding into the distance.

Orfel!

Sola nudged her knee. Alcione saw that the Stabler had left three packages of food near the entrance of the cellar. Romi had already begun to nibble at his, and Alcione walked over to take the two smaller bundles with her to sit in the dirt, as the grass was still damp.

"Sola, I never finished telling you about Orfel, did I?" she asked, feeding him a half-stick of kert. She needed to say it aloud, to make sense of it.

The Land of the Dead. Its true name was Astraea, but it was also called Land of Mirrors, Land of Crossroads, Land of Dream. The belief was that all spirits found peace in Astraea, that they lived there as here, only with no evil. All choices led to good ends, and there was no intent to harm in those who abided there.

It was the perfect other side of the mirror. But people only went when the gods said it was their time to go. Alcione was certain that in this case, whoever was doing the choosing – even if it was Tanatos himself – had made a terrible mistake.

"After Geyende died, Orfel traveled every pathway, up and down each road, searching for a way into Astraea. In the farthest, coldest corner of the world, he found an old oracle, who told him this:

"Five gems there are to act as keys,
For the gate to the land of death,
In silver, over mountain, beyond the trees,
At journey's center, across the seas,
To pass the door where no man draws breath," she
recited.

She took a deep breath. "Orfel was determined to go, no matter what. He asked the oracle how to find the stones. She told him to follow his heart. He found the first stone in the Sorrowful Tower. That led him to the next, and the next after that, until he had all of them in his possession. Then he returned to the oracle.

"This time, the oracle gave him another song, this one to tell him how to reach the Rift-Door, the Mirror to Astraea at the edge of the world." She grimaced, and looked down at Sola apologetically. "The books I read never had that song. It was missing by the time they were written.

"Orfel followed the directions, and brought the stones to the gate. He went to Astraea and bargained with Makaria, the Fateful One, for the life of his dear Geyende. She was so moved by his plea that she let Geyende go."

Alcie rubbed her arms as the chill wind rose. "Her father had started a war against the King, blaming him and Orfel for his daughter's death. They came back across the Mirror and returned to Ianthe to stop the war. Geyende's father was so happy to have his daughter back that he let Orfel marry her. And they lived happily ever after."

Alcione considered. If she could find the legendary stones, she could enter Astraea and bring her family back home. Makaria would have to listen to her. It wasn't right for a girl to be alone in the world without a family, even if she did have an arion and a whatever-he-was-pup for best friends.

If the gods are real, then there must be a way to get to them. And if there's a way, there's no reason I can't find it!

Sola sidled over to her lap and started sniffing for crumbs. Leaning back, Alcione let him lick her clean. "They lived happily ever after," she repeated, and tried to think if there was any more of the story. "Ah! Sorry!" In her excitement, she had flung out a hand and neatly whapped Sola on the chin. He huffed his displeasure, then went back to work on her tunic.

"They lived happily ever after, and in Geyende's honor, Orfel placed the stones into Geyende's crown for safekeeping. And that crown, if I am not mistaken," she said, her voice rising, "should still be in Ianthe to this very day."

At long last she had a direction. Clearly, she needed to go to Ianthe to find the crown and the stones to get her family back. It would be a great adventure, the likes of which hadn't been seen since the days of legend. Alcie knew that she mustn't fail.

*The gods have to know how important this is! They took my family to test me. If I'm brave enough, strong enough, I know I can get them back! I **need** my family!*

But the first step still lay ahead of her. She would have to leave with the traders. Romi and Sola would come with her, and somehow they would do this great thing.

The part of her hidden deep within her shell said, *what's dead is dead. A story is just a story.* And though she denied that little voice inside, though she believed the story of Orfel with all her heart, she wasn't ready to leave. Even though she had to find her way to those stones…

Could she really leave Montelymnë, forever?

- CHAPTER 6 -

The Caravan at Lymnoi

A FEW HOURS LATER, Alcione walked down the road to the small village of Lymnoi. Romi plodded along behind her on his lead rope. Sola gamboled back and forth, circling around Alcie and ducking under Romi's legs, causing the arion to nip playfully at him as he passed. Her pack was filled with reminders of her life before the fire; reminders of home.

Isaura's favorite dancing slipper was a tatter of pale pink. A handkerchief Kanase had embroidered had survived almost unscathed, delicate flowers curling up from the corners. Her mother's gold band was charred nearly beyond recognition. Her father's drinking pouch hung on her belt next to Hermion's knife, and her beloved locket lay close against her heart.

The rest of her pack was filled with assorted debris she thought she might sell to the traders. The book – too heavy to carry for long – she'd left in the corner of her cavern after kissing the cover in one last farewell.

The woods of Karya bordered the fields to her left, and a small stream ran along the path to her right. The town would soon be in view. Alcie took a deep breath, preparing herself.

Lymnoi was tiny, a cross section of two roads around which a scant nine or ten buildings were clustered. To the west, brown lines indicated longhouses and tenant farms. Thatched huts were scattered along the two roads. At the edge of the woods beyond the town was a cluster of brightly painted shapes.

The Stabler had told the truth: no one had remained behind but him. There were no yeomen working the fields and farmsteads. Huge tracts of barren earth were speckled with patches of green, the first of the spring crops. The fields looked messy, as if someone had dug them up. The villagers must have taken all they could and left the rest.

The bright shapes grew larger – a circle of wagons. Alcie and her family had gone to visit the Trifira trader caravan twice a year, when they came south in the spring and north again in fall to spend the winter making crafts and gathering resources in the mountains. They were named for the river Trifira, of which the nearby stream was a tributary, and whose path they followed.

Alcie remembered the loud, repeated calls as they hawked their wares from makeshift booths in the main square.

"Look at those scarves, Alcie!" Isaura's voice was a ghostly echo in her mind. "Such bright colors! Let's get three matching ones so we can wear them together!" Biting her lip, Alcione forced the memory away and looked around.

Traces of the market were in evidence now. Three or four empty stalls were stationed in front of the smithy shack. But instead of the usual twenty or so wagons that made up the caravan, there were only eleven. The carnival atmosphere was gone, leaving only a quiet, murmuring bustle.

People milled about – she recognized a few who had once lived on Kayre land wandering with the rest. Adjusting her cap so that it came down more snugly on her head and shaded her face, she squared her shoulders and hunched into herself the way the Stabler did.

To her relief, she found no one looked at a drab stable boy. The animals, beautiful and rare, were a far more interesting sight. Her tunic was worn and ragged compared to the clean-pressed aprons and patched outfits of the people she passed. *I look even poorer than they do,* she realized.

"Alcion!" the Stabler called. He hustled out from the center of the ring of wagons to meet her. "Here, lad!"

He took Romi's lead from her hand. Sola started to follow, but the Stabler's wary look had the pup slinking back to shelter at Alcione's side. They followed him back to the wagons, where a man and a woman leaned against a garish red and gold monstrosity with rickety wheels and a crimson and yellow striped felt top.

The man towered over them all. The shadow he cast engulfed Alcione. His eyes were muddy brown and squinty, and his hair thin, blond, and not quite able to cover his wide, square head. His skin was bronzed by the sun, his hands hard from work. He stared stonily at her. Alcie fidgeted, feeling as if she'd done something wrong, and how dare she not know what it was!

The woman was dark-haired, with skin the color of maple bark. She wore a beautiful scarlet blouse beneath a burgundy robe. Her skirt and the kerchief covering her head were grey cloudspun. The few curly tendrils that escaped were a shiny black.

She stood serenely, and Alcie thought she had never seen anyone so beautiful. *This must have been what Geyende looked like,* she thought. But this woman's eyes, though beautiful, were not vacant and dull as Alcie imagined Geyende's to be. Dark and crinkled with a hint of laughter, these eyes were kind.

At Alcie's approach, the woman offered a gentle smile and reached out to pet Sola. The pup sniffed her fingers. He consented to let her stroke his fur, his head erect and looking only at Alcione. "Aren't you proud of how well I behave?" he seemed to be saying.

"This is me nephew, Alcion," the Stabler said to the tall man. "Better hand wi' arion ye'll not see. This one's attached to him." He jerked a thumb to indicate Romi. "An' ye'll not get him tame wi'out the lad."

"Sell well enough in th' cap'tal," the man commented, his accent thick. He looked Alcie up and down, assessing her.

"Fair deal, Mat Stabler," he said, using the short version of 'master,' as common men referred to each other. "I'll take yer lad on. If he pass'n a simple test."

"What kind of test?" Alcie asked warily, deepening her voice to sound more like a boy.

"See if yer oncle tells truths," he responded, folding his brawny arms across his chest. "Round up them arion thar, an' bring 'em t' me." He turned his head, and Alcie followed his line of sight to eight arion hitched to a post beyond the caravan circle. Not one had wings.

Alcione's eyes widened, and she gave a broad smile. "Aye, sir," she said, in her best imitation of the Stabler. One by one, she took her old friends, Adrie and Inthys, Moti and Ocne and all the rest, and brought them to the tall man and the Stabler. They behaved well enough, although she had to tug for a few moments before stubborn Welm would listen to her.

"Come on, you oaf!" she hissed under her breath, yanking at his lead rope and digging in with both heels. "You're supposed to be lighter without all those feathers and bones!" Unfortunately, Welm had rooted himself to the ground, and they hadn't named him after the old word for Great-Hooves for nothing.

"I'll stomp on you!" she threatened, and gave him her fiercest look. She couldn't possibly do a thing to hurt him, and hoped the arion wouldn't realize it. He snorted, but lumbered forward when she gave another sharp tug, nearly plowing through her as he went.

When they all stood before the tall man, he went one at a time down the line to remove their halters. The Stabler scowled. "You wouldn't..." he breathed.

The tall man grinned. "I'm no poorer for it, Mat Stabler. I'm taking 'em as a gift fer t'Arkos if'n he wants. No one else has use fer 'em. You!" He jabbed a finger in Alcione's direction. "Git."

With a wild yell, he flapped his arms, startling the arion she'd just rounded up into a panic and sending them off in various directions. Alcione immediately realized his intent and barely managed to grab hold of Adrie's mane. Sweet-tempered and lazy by nature, he stopped and turned to stare at her. Grabbing a halter, Alcie yanked it over his head and handed him to the Stabler.

"You want me to get all of them?" she demanded.

The tall man shook his head. "*You* wan' you t' get all of 'em. Or ye'll not be joinin' me on th' morrow. Y'want t' go along, show ye'll earn yer keep."

Alcie spent the afternoon dashing through fields, across the little stream, and in and out of the thin woodland at the edge of the Karya, halters in hand. Sola helped where he could, backing the arion into corners and growling to corral them. By evening, Alcione was exhausted. Her feet ached and her lungs burned from the exertion. But Romi and little Moti were still out there.

As the sun went down, Sola bounded back to her with a short coughing yip-yip that meant, *Come look! Something is nearby!* She followed him to where Moti had plopped down on the banks of the stream. Alcie groaned. She had already waded through a thousand times, she was sure, and tripped at least half as many. The fur lining her boots was so wet that if it had been alive, it would have drowned. Moti looked at her with deceptively innocent long-lashed eyes.

"Hi, buddy," she called softly, so as not to startle him across the water. He wasn't near the shallow part she'd crossed earlier, and Alcie didn't know how to swim. "Let's go home now. It's time for supper, and I know you're hungry from all that running."

Moti lay where he was, and she knew a moment of worry for the short, stout mischief-maker. "Moti? Are you all right?"

She walked over to him, footsteps light to keep from making too much noise. When she reached him, she put a hand on his neck. He turned to nuzzle her, and she easily slipped the halter over his nose and ears. "Good boy," she praised, then sat down beside him to take a rest.

It was odd seeing him without his wings, but now at least she could lean against him without feeling all the grooves and joints and bone. Leaning against his shoulder, she sighed. *It must be horrible for him not to be able to fly.*

She had only closed her eyes for a moment to lean back against Moti's withers when she felt him surge to his feet. She rolled to get clear of his hooves, but in her haste she didn't realize until she opened them again that she had rolled the wrong way, right into a patch of mud on the banks of the stream. Moti's eager whinny as he began to trot towards the shelter of the village sounded eerily like laughter.

"Good-for-naught, pudgy, poxy, rotten, fulgora-bitten mongrel!" she yelled after him as he faded into the distance, using the language the Stabler did when he was mad. "See if I feed you treats again anytime soon!"

Something nudged her shoulder and she stilled, afraid to turn around. When it uttered a low rumbling nicker, she breathed a sigh of relief.

"Romi." Turning, she put the last of the halters on her friend, and rolled her eyes at him. "Where were you?" she asked.

Leaves were tangled in his mane. Obviously he had been in the woods. "Your last adventure didn't teach you anything?" she chided. "You just healed from that dusa. You wouldn't like it if it happened again."

Romi shook his mane. *Wouldn't bother me. Didn't hurt much.*

"Sure it didn't," she replied. "That's why every time I tried to clean and bandage it I nearly got kicked, eh?"

It hit her a moment later that in all the years she had worked with arion, she had never understood a thought so clearly. "I'm going mad," she said aloud. "You didn't just say that to me, did you?"

Alcione looked in his eyes, willing him to speak again. But he was silent. Whatever she dreamed she could read in their movements, whatever questions she asked or stories she told, never before had she actually heard a vocal reply. Romi's was just as she had imagined, a brave little boy puffing up to hide his fear.

"No." She turned away. "No, I'm just wishing you sounded that way. You're an arion, and whatever I may think I hear, you don't talk! And...and even if you did, it wouldn't be like me!"

Taking his lead, she returned to the caravan. The traders were gathered around a fire. A large cauldron sat on a slab of rock, simmering in the center of the circle of fire-eaten logs. The tall man glanced up when she returned with Romi. He didn't say anything, only nodded and handed her a wooden bowl filled with stew. The Stabler threw her an encouraging smile. She gave him Romi's lead rope and scuttled away.

As she sat by the fire with her stew, Alcie looked around at the rest of the traders. There were perhaps fifty of them, scattered around the campsite in small groups huddled beside smaller fires. The kind-eyed woman sat on a log between two girls, chatting merrily.

One girl looked near to Alcie's age, and resembled the dark-skinned woman. The other girl was older, with the same pale blond hair as the tall man. But where his features were harsh, hers were round and rosy, her eyes lit with merriment.

Outside the firelight was a short figure whose features she couldn't make out. He ate his stew without a word, looking off into the distance. Alcione liked him best. She didn't want to talk to these people either.

So she sat at the edge of the fire, Sola by her side, and ate in silence. The stew was grainy and thick, like nothing she had ever tasted. But though strange, to her grumbling stomach it was wonderful.

After the meal, the Stabler drew her away from the others. He handed her Romi's lead rope, and she took it gingerly, half afraid and half eager to hear if the arion would speak again. Still there was nothing.

"Ye're t' go wi' him," the Stabler said, nodding to the tall man. "Master Goso Mopsus. He sells animals of all sorts. Ye'll do well enou'. I'm fer me brother's in Elpis."

He paused. "Ye may not like it, but I'll say it anyhow: I love ye like I loved me own girl. Be safe."

She looked up at him, tears trembling at her lashes. "I don't forgive you. Still, I'm grateful not to be…" She faltered.

He gave a sad half-smile. "I know it. Someday." He reached out tentatively, and put a hand on her shoulder. "Courage, lad," he said, loud enough for others to hear. And he went, leaving her alone with the traders.

The man named Goso walked over to her. "Come along, boy. I'll introduce ye t' the rest of the wagon." He led her to where the three women and the shadowy figure were sitting.

"That thar is Middy Huin Woodrush. She's a fine tailor. 'er niece, Raka," he pointed to the dark girl, "makes dolls to sell out th' scraps." Both gave quiet smiles as Goso named them.

Indicating the blond girl, he said, "That's m'own girl Deena. Works wi' our birds and beasties. She'll help ye wi' the arion on the road, and once we're in the cap'tal. Ye needn' fret o'er yer friend once y'sell."

When she realized he meant Romi, she shook her head. "I'm not selling him, sir. He's mine."

64

Goso's shaggy brows rose. "Oh, really? News t' me. Ye've no money t' keep sommat as fine as that. D'y'expect me t' pay fer his keep in the city, then? I does yer oncle a favor, I does, takin' y'on like I do."

Alcione backed up, standing protectively in front of the arion. "You can't have him," she repeated. "Not you or anybody else."

"Let it be, Goso," came a voice from below her. The figure in the shadows. "T'isn't worth the trouble. The lad's serious. You see it well as I."

He walked to them, emerging from the shadow of the wagons to stand by Goso. His hair was pale and brownish, but she couldn't make out the color of his eyes. Like her, he wore a tunic with a cloak over it. He wasn't tall enough to be much older than she, but his assurance in calling the older trader by his given name told Alcione that this was someone who demanded – and got – respect, wherever he asked for it.

"What do I care fer that, Tremi?" Goso growled. "T'Arkos won't like havin' e'en one o' them beasts in any hands but his own. T'ain't worth earning disfavor over."

"T'isn't you who'd be losin' favor. T'would be the boy. What's it matter if he gets hisself tossed in the dunge?"

Goso grumbled something under his breath. "An' how d'ye plan t' pay fer his feed, boy? I on'y took you on fer as much as would feed yer own mouth."

Alcie looked to the boy. He shrugged a shoulder, unconcerned. "Well, boy? 'Tis your arion, for the moment."

"Um…" Scrambling frantically for an idea, Alcione thought of everything she owned, from her feet up. Boots, leggings, tunic, rucksack – sack! "I've got things I was going to sell in the city. I can give them to you, only don't take Romi!"

Struggling out of it, Alcie knelt and spilled the contents of the pack on the ground. Goso squatted to examine them. His blond brows drew together. "Scrap and tatters," he pronounced succinctly.

"I've a liking for that blade," Tremi said, kneeling beside them to look at a kitchen knife she'd wrapped in an old rag. "Could melt it, use it for a frame," he mused.

Coming over with the two girls beside her, Huin said, "Raka, that slipper would make a fine dress for a doll." Her voice was as peaceful as the rest of her, a dulcet tenor with a very slight accent that Alcie couldn't place. "And those scraps of fabric as well." Alcie watched with dismay as she pointed to the remains of Kanase's handkerchiefs.

"I want some too, Papa!" Deena cried. "They're beautiful! I bet the nobles wore them!"

"Stole them from the ashes?" Raka asked, glancing back in the direction of the ruined Kayre. She gave Alcione a dark glare. "Stealing from the dead is a sin."

INTO THE SKY

Tremi nudged Raka away from the pile. "You're in my light, an' who're you to talk? Stealing from the dead's not like stealing from the living."

"Grey Folk are not thieves!" she hissed. "Take it back!"

Tremi nudged her again, hard enough to shove her back a few steps. "I never said it. What's to take back?"

Muttering several words in a strange language, she stalked off. Huin followed her, slipper in hand. Deena had her arms around her father's waist. She whispered something in his ear and giggled, then reached down to take a handkerchief. Helpless to protest, Alcione watched as she took the cloth and held it to her cheek, a flower winking at her in the firelight.

"We'll split this between ourselves," Goso announced. "T'won't make up the twelve dagats t' feed 'im all the way to Ianthe, but t'will make a start." He took a handful of things in one meaty fist. "We can figger out the rest later."

Tremi's thin, nimble hands picked through the objects, selecting bits of metal with the eye of a professional. *But a professional what?* Alcione wondered. With a mix of sorrow and relief, she watched as the others selected from what remained. When she was done, there was only her locket, water pouch, and Hermion's dagger left, concealed by her cloak and tunic. Sadly, she took her now-empty sack and held it to her.

"Come on, boy," Tremi invited her when they were done. "Girls get the bed." He waved a hand at the arched felt cover. The words reminded her that she was a girl no longer. "Goso sleeps fine under the wagon, but meself, I like the sky."

He led Alcione to the far side of the wagon, where the arion were tethered. Unsure, she tied Romi's lead rope to one of the deeply rooted posts set up to secure the mullers, horned malim who pulled the caravans.

"Not that way!" Tremi exclaimed. "Not if you want him to stay till morn. Here." He snatched the rope from her hands and wound it deftly into a strong knot that wouldn't be easily unbound. "Like this!"

"But he won't be able to get free if there's an emergency!" she objected. "I was taught to –"

"Forget it," Tremi dismissed the thought and turned away from the posts. "And forget any else they taught you too, if you want to live." He walked back towards the wagon, and Alcie followed.

"They?" she asked, confused.

"The Riders," he said, as if it had been obvious. Alcione tried to speak, but no words would come. "You're one of 'em, aye? If you want to survive, you'll learn to mask your accent. Won't do. You'll 'ave to learn to talk like me."

"I'm not one of them!" she hissed.

"Suit yourself. I'll not say so. Your voice'll give you away soon enough. 'Tis a miracle Goso hasn't noticed yet, but 'e always was thick. Huin may have, but she wouldn't say." Turning away, he lay down beside the wagon and wrapped himself up tightly in his cloak. His head lay directly on the dirt, but he didn't seem to mind.

Alcione swallowed hard, then copied him. Looking uneasily at the dirt, she took off her cap and put it beneath her for a pillow. Her hair was short enough that she didn't have to worry about removing it anymore. Sola curled up at her side.

"H-how can you tell?" she whispered after a while. "I mean, how *could* you, supposing I was a noble? I don't sound that different from you."

"The things you say, the way you say them. I..." He struggled to explain. "You just know," he said finally.

The words were familiar. It was what Alcie had always said when her parents asked why she thought she knew what animals were saying. "Could you teach me how to be like you and Goso and the rest?"

There was a muffled sound that might have been laughter. "I don't think you want to be like Goso," he said finally. "Don't think you could, thank Tanatos. But I can teach you to be like me."

As the exhaustion from the day's work began to claim her, she had a last question. "Why would you do this? Why not turn me in if you know?"

"You're just a kid. Ain't right, what they done. Kids are too young to get punished for what their parents do. 'Sides, I ain't got no liking for the Arkos.

Kings is kings, born or made. The people should run things, that's who. But your sort wouldn't understand."

"What's that supposed to mean?" Alcie demanded in a whisper.

"Nothing," he muttered. He seemed to want to say more, but fell silent. Alcione didn't press him. After a while, his even breathing told her that he was asleep. Twisting and turning on the scratchy cloak, Alcie fell into a troubled slumber.

- CHAPTER 7 -
New Words

"WAKE UP!"

Alcione was caught in a nightmare, the flames tearing at her clothes, her family's voices screaming in her ears. "No!" she cried. "No, let me go!"

"Oy, fine! Don't wake up. Take all the time in the world."

The practical words were like a dousing of cold water. Alcie opened her eyes and threw up a hand to ward off the bright sunshine. "What?"

Tremi, sitting up and munching a crust of berry bread, grinned at her. "So we're awake, are we? We're for the road as soon as we form up."

"Form up?"

"What are you, my echo? It means putting the caravan into a line. We're last, since we've the animals. The wind catches their smell and it reeks for miles down the road. Up at the front, t'would be a right mess."

Alcione sat up. The market stalls had been taken down, the caravans packed and slowly moving out of their circle. The mullers were hitched six to each wagon, except Goso's, where six of the arion were harnessed instead. The remaining three – Moti, Enno, and Romi – were piled with bundles attached to pack saddles. They would follow just behind the wagon. Moti and Enno stood quietly, but Deena held Romi, who continued to fidget.

Tremi followed Alcie's gaze, then stood up and held out a hand to her. In the daylight she could see that his hair was sandy brown, and his cloak was the same dusty roan color as an arion's coat. His tunic, though, was a pretty blue-green shade that she had never seen before. As he helped her to her feet, she asked him about it.

"It's called dipthyonis," he told her. "It's a poison plant. It won't hurt you to wear somethin' dyed in it, but it could kill the person making it, so there aren't many."

"How did you get it?"

He hesitated. "A friend made it for me. He died, but not of poison."

Alcione didn't ask, but the question was poised on her tongue. Tremi sighed.

"Bandits," he said flatly.

Hermion always used to smile thinking of bandits and thieves and pirates. He thought it would be grand to take them on, or even more exciting to be one. But Tremi didn't look the least bit amused.

They walked to Deena, who was still struggling with Romi.

"Can ye make him stop?" she asked as they approached. "He won't listen to me."

Tremi gave her an approving nod as Alcie moved to Romi's side. "Hey, boy," she greeted him. "What's wrong? This is nothing to worry about." She tugged his head around so he could look at the pack saddle and see that it was no threat to him.

Unappeased, Romi shook his head, his mane spraying in all directions. *It itches.*

Alcione's eyes widened. There was his voice again, petulant and stubborn. "I think the saddle might be on wrong," she said to Deena as the blond girl gave her a quizzical look. "I think it's itching him."

Deena looked doubtful, but checked his girths, the belts that looped around the saddle to tie it in place. "There's nothin' there."

But Alcie felt a buzzing in her mind. Romi still wasn't happy. In fact, she almost felt an itch on her own side, thinking of it. "He doesn't like it," she insisted.

Goso strode up to them. "What is it?" he asked, frowning at Romi. "This 'un again? Let th' boy carry some o' the packs and toss the rest in t'wagon. Boy, sit on 'im an' keep an eye on t' bundles."

He and Deena removed the heavy sacks and packages, moving as many as they could to the wagon. Leaving some on the ground, Deena tried to take the saddle from Romi. When he bared his teeth, Alcie stepped forward to tap him on the nose.

His ears stayed flat as he eyed her, but he let her remove the saddle.

"What do you know?" Tremi said. A patch of prickly hay from the arion's breakfast had come loose with the saddle pad. "There was something bothering him. Good instincts," he told Alcie approvingly.

After a check for other irritants, they put the pads and saddle back on. Goso looked at Alcie expectantly, and it was then that she realized he meant for her to ride. Before the Arkos had come to power, a groom would never have been allowed to ride, yet it seemed they thought she'd know something of what to do.

Her secret lessons would help her stay aboard, but she'd never considered how to get on without the wooden mounting block she used at home. Heart in her throat, she debated how best to climb up.

"The backboard's a good bet," Tremi said under his breath, watching her eyes dart around for things to stand on.

"Backboard?" Goso muttered, overhearing. "Why bother?" One hand on the saddle, he reached down and boosted Alcione up over Romi's back. Completely unprepared, she grabbed for purchase, found none, and toppled to the ground.

Looking up, she found Deena giggling, Goso grumbling, and Tremi eyeing her with barely veiled amusement. "Din't go so well," Tremi murmured. "Mayhap the backboard?"

With a sigh, Goso unhitched Romi and moved him parallel to the back of the wagon. Alcie clambered onto the backboard, then nearly lost her balance again as Sola jumped up after her. Near the front of the wagon, Huin set aside a cream-colored dress and gestured to Sola. "He can ride with us," she said.

Nodding, Alcie turned her attention to Romi, whose lead rope had been looped over his head and tied to the other end of his halter for a makeshift set of reins. This time, she boosted herself onto his back without any problem. Goso took another lead and hitched Romi to the back left corner of the wagon. Moti he tied to the center, and Enno to the right. He handed Alcie the remaining few bundles to hold on her lap and left.

As the wagon began to move, Tremi bounded into a corner of it. He sat facing her, slouching against the discarded packages. He'd told her he was fourteen, a year older than she. As they were the same height and equally skinny, Alcie never would have guessed. Up close, his skin was tanned but not brown, and his nose was slightly bent. His eyes were a murky greenish-blue, more the color of well water than of his tunic.

It was a friendly face, she thought, and a strangely honest one for someone intending to teach her how to deceive the world.

"All right," he said without preamble, "time to start your lessons."

Alcie looked at the rest of the wagon. Deena was with her father, who was driving. Behind them were Huin and Raka, fabric in hand. For a moment, Alcie had an image of her mother and sisters and wanted to cry. She remembered them a hundred times a day, it seemed, and the pain never lessened. *They're in Astraea, and I'm going to Ianthe to get them back,* she reminded herself. *Just as soon as I find that crown!*

"Right, then," Tremi said. "First things first, you got to learn to keep your mouth shut."

"That's rude," Alcie told him, frowning.

"That's right," he agreed. "But it's true. If you're quiet, nobody can tell where you're from. And you'll learn in ways you don't from being talky. When you can speak right, then you can say more."

"Oh," Alcione said, feeling foolish. *Well, that's a good reason to keep quiet,* she thought. *I'm less likely to say the wrong thing. Besides, why would I even want to talk to these people? They hate me, all without ever knowing what my family and I are really like!*

Over the next few hours, Tremi taught her about different cants, the styles of language people spoke in. Raka and Huin were Grey Folk from the Fens in the southwest, so sometimes they stumbled over words, or mixed up phrases because the order of the words wasn't the same in their own language.

Goso and Deena were originally from the east, and their words came from deep in their throats, as if each syllable went through a gauzy web first, and came out thick and guttural. Tremi helped Alcie to form the broad vowels that people used in the eastern countryside.

When she tripped over them, he laughed. That frustrated her, so she tried harder until she got better at it. "If arion could speak," he said cheekily, "I think they'd sound like you."

Tremi himself was from Ianthe, so he mostly taught her that cant. "We don' use so many words out here," he explained. "We say what we mean, and no beatin' about the point."

He taught her how to say what she meant without sounding like a noble – to say "aye" instead of "yes," as he put it.

Plain folk didn't speak formal, he said. They didn't need words to describe possessions they'd never own. He made her forget words like "goblet" and "splendid," and taught her new ones in their place.

"Try a pint o' the good man's vice," he instructed. He made a motion like he was lifting a flask to his mouth.

"What's vice?" Alcie asked.

Tremi grinned at her. "'Tis a drink, lad. The kind men have when they feel like havin' a fine night at the tavern. And here's another thing.

"Medka are drinking songs," he told her. "Like this: Sal has got a little spot, off my street just a hop.

And all the boys in town rejoice when she takes off her –"

"Stop!" Alcie cried, taking a hand off the reins to halt him. She could feel herself blush.

Tremi smirked. "Come on, lad, don' turn all red. They'll think you're a girl, they will."

"Me?" Alcie squeaked. Dropping the reins entirely, she covered her mouth with her hands. "That's ridiculous!" She lowered her pitch – trying not to sound as if she'd lowered it – and picked up the rope-reins again.

Tremi grinned. "We'll 'ave you singing it in no time," he said, and winked at her. Up ahead, a voice called out something Alcie couldn't hear.

"That'd be hold-meet," said Tremi. "Means we're stopping for dinner. You do know dinner's midday meal, aye?"

Mesmerized by all the new things she was learning, Alcione had completely forgotten about food. Feeling her stomach grumble now, as it probably had been for a while, she smiled at him. "Aye."

- CHAPTER 8 -
The Way of the World

ALCIE'S EDUCATION RESUMED after dinner. The caravan had entered the southern stretch of the Karya more fully and Goso's attention was on navigating the unsteady stretch of road that ran through the forest. Huin and Deena had gotten off to walk beside the wagons, talking with friends up ahead while stretching their legs. Raka was still sewing.

The woods were lusher and greener than the ones near home. Winter was shorter here, so the trees had seen more spring than the ones nearest Montelymnë. Tremi drew her attention to a spot in the distance.

"D'you see that rotting log there? The one tipped o'er into its brother?"

Alcione nodded.

"That's a fair place to look for halay," he said. "Wait here."

Holding up a hand to forestall further questions, Tremi hopped over the side of the wagon and slid along the backboard until he was at its edge. Ahead, he waved a salute to Goso before disappearing into the trees.

Seeing the vacant spot, Raka moved to the back of the wagon and sat down beside Sola, who was dozing contentedly. Alcie eyed her nervously.

"Just because he likes you does not mean I do," she announced.

Alcione nodded. Her knuckles whitened on the reins. Romi protested the added pressure with a short toss of his head that yanked the rope straight out of her hands. Raka laughed, abrupt and cold.

"You are not foolish, that much is clear," she stated. "But if you are foolish enough to think that his teaching will keep you safe, rich boy, be warned. You are not so protected as you believe."

Alcione's lips pressed into a thin line. *She must have overheard Tremi talking to me, or guessed from my accent the way he did.* "Will you tell?" she asked finally. It would do her no good to lie. Raka was too angry, too sure.

Raka cocked her head to one side and tapped a finger rhythmically against her cheek, a strange-looking gesture. Tremi had told her the Fen people moved in different ways. Alcie wondered if this was their way of thinking.

"Who would I tell?" the darker-skinned girl replied after a moment. "These followers of the

Arkos are no more my friends than the followers of the King before him. Grey Folk do not speak to outsiders, except in trade."

She could bear it no more. This girl had more arrogance than any noble Alcie had ever met. "Then why don't you go speak to someone else? Why come here to warn me?"

"I did not come only to warn you," said Raka. "I came to remind you. Here, in this caravan, you are no better than me. You are low as the dirt here. I do good, honest work. So does Tremi. If you made a mistake and revealed yourself, he might be harmed. There is nothing I would not do to prevent that."

Her meaning was clear. Alcione could only nod. Her own cowardly wish to promise this wretched girl that she would never hurt Tremi, to promise her anything if she would just leave, humiliated her.

Ducking her head, she focused hard on the texture of Romi's mane, her chapped hands gripping the rope-reins. She heard Raka move back to her side of the wagon just as she saw Tremi returning from the corner of her eye.

"Look up, you!"

Swinging his battered rucksack into the wagon, Tremi sprang in after it. He shifted his weight to avoid Sola, then settled into his corner.

He opened the sack and took out a small, round object. Alcie forgot her anger and worry for the moment and leaned in to look. From different angles, the object changed colors, going from misty black to swirling silver, and a dozen other glittering shades. "What is it?" she asked, enraptured.

"S'called halay. Poor man's gem," he translated.

"I've never seen any stone like it," Alcie marveled.

Tremi handed it to her. "Because it's not a stone. It's a bug."

Alcie smiled. Her sisters would have let out a shriek you could hear miles off. But she was fascinated. "And it lives in rotting logs?"

"Aye. They live in colonies. If you pour this on them," he dug around in his pack for a murky vial of powder. "'Tis crushed bloodthorn, the white flower growing by the foot of these trees, with the dark red spots in its center. Pour it on halay, and they can't breathe. Die instantly."

"Isn't that cruel?"

Tremi raised a brow. "You eat meat, aye? And fish? No more cruel than that. Halay are for cheap jewelry, for ingredients in potions, and some folk use 'em as good-luck charms. They're easy to catch, easy to breed, and pretty."

Alcie asked the question Tremi had taught her to ask. "Why do I need to know about them?"

He took the halay from her hand and popped it into his mouth. He chewed and swallowed it with a loud crunch while Alcie looked on, impressed. "Safe to eat, too, if a bit tough. Good to know in case you're lost out here. You need to know what you can and can't eat on the trail, how to find good water."

"Isn't all water good?"

"You'd drink the water in the farmin' ditches? Or near to the latrines?"

"Yuck!" Alcione thought of the pits on the far low side of Montelymnë, where the servants went to empty her family's chamber pots, or to relieve themselves. "I guess not," she conceded.

"Right, so you need to know how to find good water. First, follow the animals. They have to drink too, and they know the best places. Second, the water should flow fast, best o'er rocks but not through mallow dams – they'll foul it up. And last, to make it cleaner throw savor into it. Savor's the little lavender flower, the one that comes in bunches."

"How will I remember all this?" It seemed impossible to hold that much new knowledge in her head.

"I'll keep goin' till you get it," Tremi reassured her. He held up a drooping mud-colored weed with three equally muddy brown berries hanging from it. "These're bogpips. Try one." He passed her a berry, and she put it in her mouth.

"Ugh!" Alcie spat the berry into the dirt, where it instantly disappeared because of how much it already looked like the ground. "Those are terrible!"

"But safe," Tremi assured her. "If you're lost and desperate, you can eat 'em and they'll keep you alive for a few days."

"If you could stand the taste." She wrinkled her face up and pursed her lips.

"Well, don't get lost, eh? You can eat guara if it's not overripe, but anyone knows that. An' most kinds of nuts, an' field or snow or bundle-berries, but not sunsap berries."

"The yellow ones? I know that. Mother – me ma taught me that."

Tremi seemed to notice her hesitation and reached out to pat her shoulder. "Good. Oh, and one more thing. Halay are important because they're me job. I set 'em into metal an' make charms or necklaces or earbobs or what-all for the city folk."

Suddenly his keen interest in the pieces of steel, iron, and silver in her pack made sense. "Will you teach me?" she asked.

"Tomorrow," he promised. "Now, let's get back to our list. Scallet: do you eat it, wear it, or run fast as your legs can carry you away from it?"

- CHAPTER 9 -
Learning

THE DAYS FELL INTO A comforting routine as the caravan followed the river Trifira on its winding way towards Ianthe. Alcie no longer dreamed, but only because she was too tired from the day's work to bother. Among the traders, everyone had to do their share.

On ordinary days, she scrubbed the cookware after hold-meet, and cared for the arion. Every morning and evening, she fed and watered them, groomed them from top to bottom, picked their manes and tails clear of debris, and checked their hooves for worms or stones.

Tremi kept her company. While creating jewelry out of the halay he collected, he continued her lessons on how to speak and act. Eventually she hardly noticed his accent, or any accents. When Deena and Goso spoke, her mind quickly changed the broad country sounds into words that made sense.

Goso gave her chores too, like scraping mud from the legs of the grimy, long-haired muller, and checking them for injuries, as she knew more about that than he or Deena did. She also took the packages on and off the arion as they sold things to the travelers passing by.

Goso was a strict taskmaster, constantly critiquing her work, but when she did something right there was a grudging word or two of praise that Alcie came to value more than the empty praise the servants back home used to give her just for being around. *He acts like what I do is important,* Alcione marveled. *No one but Stabler ever trusted me with something important before.*

Thoughts of the Stabler hurt less than they had before. Through all that the others said, she was coming to understand that none of her family's friends, the ones who'd shared their feasts and holy days, had survived. She alone was left, and it was clear now that the Stabler had risked his life to save her. *If anyone found out what he did, they'd kill him for treason. I suppose I do owe him a little.*

Each day, Raka insulted her when no one else was around. It was always, "Rich boy, your cheeks are very dirty, aren't they?" or "Rich boy, I did not know that the idea was to take the mud and place it on your own legs. But I am sure that the mullers are very grateful to you."

She would play pranks, like unknotting the tie on a package so it fell off just as they were about to leave, or one night loudly telling her aunt that the new boy had taken more than his share of stew, in front of everyone else.

"I do not think he has, Raka," Huin admonished her, when they had all retired to their small eating group.

"I do!" Raka insisted. She glared at Alcione. Alcie had taken Tremi's lesson to heart, not responding when the other girl made her jibes. But it was very hard, especially since Tremi never seemed to be around or notice when it happened. Since the first night he had defended her, her new friend seemed to have abandoned the role of protector, at least from Raka. When Tremi wasn't teaching her, he and Raka walked the woods together, chatting as they searched for halay.

"Even so, my brother's daughter," Huin had replied that time, "it is not your place to say." Her voice was stern, but she never betrayed a hint of losing her composure.

After supper each evening, Alcie spent time with Romi and the other arion, Sola at her heels as he always was. She could still pretend she knew what they were saying, but she was never entirely sure anymore what she was making up and what she wasn't.

She had begun to see pictures in her head whenever she was around them, jumbled images that she was sure meant something, and equally certain hadn't come from her own mind. She saw the scenery as a strange blur with reds, blacks, and yellows standing out in sharp relief, or close-ups of stones or waving blades of grass.

Sometimes it felt as if the pictures were pushing against her mind, as if someone was insistently trying to speak to her, only she couldn't quite hear them. Once in a while, she heard the voice that she thought was Romi. It made her nervous. Something had changed, and she wasn't sure if it was in the world or within herself.

Romi would comment on Tremi's lessons as they rode. *Feels funny*, he told her as she stumbled over a word. *Again.* In the evening as she groomed him, he pressed close as she stroked his neck, and she felt a warmth in her heart that she wasn't sure was entirely her own.

She didn't dare tell anyone what she heard, knowing they wouldn't understand. She didn't understand it herself. *Have I gone mad?*

For the most part, Alcie stayed close to Romi, Sola, and Tremi and spoke little, even to them. But on the first rainy night, when everyone else had made themselves comfortable in the small spaces unoccupied by baggage and gone to bed, she was still awake. Hearing a sound, she sat up and rubbed her eyes, blinking into the dark.

"Cannot you sleep?" came Huin's voice from the shadows. Alcie sought to catch her eyes in the dark. "It is different from the home you know, yes?"

"Yes," she whispered back. Quickly, she corrected herself. "Aye."

"And how difficult, to keep your secrets here."

"Secrets?" Alcione tried not to let herself sound nervous. She glanced at Raka, who was sleeping so soundly she was snoring, and Tremi, who was sprawled with Sola's tail brushing against his ear. Deena was barely a shape in the darkness and Goso, heedless of the rain and mud, was beneath the wagon. "What secrets do you mean?"

Huin's voice was tinged with sympathy. "For one, you were certainly not born a stable boy."

"Does everyone know?" Alcie muttered bitterly. What was the use of keeping it a secret if everyone was going to guess it anyway? At this rate, she'd never even live to see the gates of Ianthe!

"Only Raka, Tremi, and myself. And it will stay so, if you continue to advance in your lessons. Only they will know that you were not born a poor boy. Or rather, not born poor *or* a boy, true?"

This time, Alcie did gasp. She looked around frantically, afraid the others would hear. "Please, you can't tell anyone!"

Huin's reassuring voice wafted back to her. "I will not. But you should, once we are within the city. You will grow older, and it will be hard for you to hide certain things."

Alcione was glad no one could see her blush. "I don't want to go back to being a girl," she said honestly. "I'd hate it. Besides, how could I tell the others?"

"We would think of something. I am like Tremi; I do not approve of the killing of children, even in war. This Arkos does not yet impress me as a leader. We shall see." She sighed. "Do not you be afraid. I see how hard you try. I will do my best to protect you, whether you are a boy or a girl."

Now accustomed to the blackness after a few moments, Alcie could catch the merest wry twist to Huin's lips. "Even from my niece, if need be. She is still sad, and very, very angry.

"When we stayed at Torwe Tonon last year," Huin continued, naming a neighboring Kayre, "my brother fell ill. He needed care, and the men and women of the town spat in our faces, because we were Grey Folk. The nobles refused to allow anyone to aid us, and he died. His wife and children took ill as well, and soon Raka and I were the only ones left. She has not forgiven."

Alcie thought of the Stabler, and understood. "I know what that's like," she said softly. But it wasn't quite the same. The Stabler could have saved her family and hadn't. She had nothing to do with what had happened to Raka's family! "It's still not fair," she added, scowling.

"What has happened to both of you is not fair," Huin pointed out. "Did you expect the world to work that way?"

With a start, Alcie realized that she had, at least once upon a time. But bit by bit, everything she once had thought was changing. "I did once," she answered. "But I'm learning."

Turning over, she tucked herself in under her cloak and lay her head on a bag of scraps. She said a silent prayer, thanking Tanatos for keeping her alive one more day. Closing her eyes, she drifted off into another dreamless sleep, the names and images of thirteen different inedible kinds of flowers floating through her mind.

- CHAPTER 10 -
Not Running

IT WAS A WARM, SUNNY spring day when the caravan finally left the woods of Karya behind. Alcie rode Romi and tried hard to concentrate on Tremi's lessons, but was drawn to the new world around her. This was farther away from home than she had ever been in her life, and things were so different!

It was warm, much warmer than she was used to in the northern hills, and the crops that were in full bloom here were like none she had ever seen. To her right the river Trifira flowed fast and wide, a ribbon of green and brown instead of the familiar clear blue. Perhaps it reflected the mossy banks where the tall fenwhistle plants clustered.

When they came to a crossroad, they bore away from the river. "Where are we going?" Alcie asked. "Isn't Ianthe on the banks of the Trifira?"

Tremi nodded. "Yes, but we're not staying on the road tonight."

"We're not?" Alcie leaned forward. "Where will we stay?"

"Don't get too excited. It's a little place 'bout four miles from here called Trippleton. Three roads cross there, at the Three Forks Inn – one leads around Ianthe to Turan and the Ampelon woods, the second towards the city itself, and the last winds northeast to Kayre Kymminthë. I suppose you'd know that one."

Belatedly, Alcie remembered Tremi still thought her a noble boy who had trained as a Rider at Kymminthë. "Um, well, I only saw it once. I was too young to train. I don't really remember much."

Tremi shrugged. "No matter. Wouldn't be the same. When the Arkos took power, his followers turned the place to rubble. Folk come up from Ianthe say that's why the arion have lost their wings, now the Talaria have all gone."

Alcione sat back on the pack saddle. "Tremi, can you tell me more about what's going on in the world? There's so much I'll have to pretend I understand, like why the arion don't have their wings, and who the Arkos is, and everything that happened before he became so powerful."

Tremi whistled and shot a sideways glance at her from his seat against the side of the wagon. "That's a lot of questions. Lucky for you, no one in Ianthe knows who you are, so we can say you're a trader like us. I can tell you all I know and that'll be enough. To start, I don't have any real idea what happened to the arion or what caused it. I don't think anyone does."

"But nothing like that has ever happened before, has it?" Alcie looked down at Romi's shoulders, thinking again how strange it was. Moti's pack saddle had been used for the muller, but Romi's (taken from Montelymnë's own stables) had straps that hung loosely at his side, straps that were supposed to wrap around his wings.

Was an arion still an arion without wings? Alcione couldn't imagine them ever being called anything else. But up until a few weeks ago, she couldn't have imagined an arion without them. *But then, is a noble still a noble without her name?* She shook her head, not wanting to think on it.

"Nope," Tremi replied. "An' the Arkos will have a harder time keeping them than he thinks. Lots of people think they're cursed, that they're a sign the gods are angry. Many of them were killed just for being associated with the Talaria."

"But that's horrible!" Alcie exclaimed.

He gave her a sharp glance, reminding her that was something she could no longer say.

"Still…" Alcie thought of the helpless arion, killed only because they were important to the Riders. Before, she had always thought people were mostly good. But the night of the fire had changed everything. There was so much hatred. People who'd lived on her family's land all their lives had killed them and felt *good*. Was the world truly full of so many cruel people?

"As for what's going on in the land," Tremi continued, "I can only tell you what I know. I can only say what I hear from the city and the traders' road, and they don't know much. Listen to what folk say when we get to the inn. They might know more."

"I'll do that," Alcie promised. "But first, tell me what you know?"

"Well—" he paused as a sudden bump in the road caught him off guard. The arion were passing carefully over a large tree branch that had fallen in the path. To their left was a small mud hut with a thatched roof. "We're close," Tremi said. "I'll talk quickly.

"Years ago, things were pretty bad. King Xerxos kept raising taxes to pay for fancy homes for his family and those who did him a service. The new nobility, you know."

"New nobility?"

Tremi raised an eyebrow. "I guess there weren't many of them at Kymminthë, eh? They're families the King rewarded for making him more powerful. He gave 'em land and titles, and paid for it out of the common folks' pockets.

"So folk got poorer and poorer while the nobles got richer and richer. Some of my friends starved, while others died in debtors' prison. Some became thieves and even stole from those they knew. There was no other way to live."

"What about you?" Alcie asked. "How did you survive?"

"Me?" Tremi frowned. "My friend, the one who made my tunic, took care of me."

"What about your parents?"

"Never knew 'em. Me ma died when I was born. I grew up on the streets."

As he spoke, Tremi ground a mortar against flower petals in the small pestle. The bloodthorn powder he was making smelled tangy and sharp, like barra in autumn sauce at the harvest feast.

Alcie stroked Romi's mane, imagining a young boy running wild through a maze of lanes and alleys. She had never been in a city before. She imagined it was like a big castle, with more passages than anyone could ever explore in a lifetime.

"It must have been lonely," she said, "but fun too, right?"

Tremi looked startled. For a moment, he didn't speak. "Yes. Most people think, 'Poor orphan, growin' up with none to call your own.' But actually, though it was hard, I loved the freedom. And even when times were hardest, my friends and I always had each other."

"So if everyone was able to be happy despite the bad times, when did that change? Why did people get so angry?"

"Do you remember that great drought of two years ago?" Alcione nodded. "The loss of water made most of the crops dry up, and even more people went hungry. That's the year I joined the traders. My friend was gone, and no one could afford to share food with me. The halay and trinkets I made weren't enough when no one had coin to spend."

Tremi gestured at the woods with the mortar. "Folk out in the country still had some extra. They could pay more and sometimes they give traders free meals when they enter town.

"But a lot of city folk couldn't leave. When people begged for help, the King ignored 'em. If they tried to fight it, the Riders threw 'em in prison for rebellion. But one man didn't care about all that."

Tremi put down the bloodthorn and placed his hands on his knees, settling in for a story as she'd seen him do around the fire at night. "From what I hear, nobody knows where Arkos Trienes came from, just that he arrived in Ianthe one day and started saying things that got people wonderin'. He said if they could get rid of the Riders, folk could finally make the King listen to their demands. He convinced people that the answer to all their problems was to elect a leader – himself – and let him speak to the King once the Riders were gone."

"But the King is dead now!" Alcie protested. "Everyone said so!" The first time she had heard it, she had been stunned. For her entire life, King Xerxos had ruled over all. But now he, Queen Thenis, and their three young sons were all dead. The royal family was gone.

"He is, and so are the rest of the descendants of the line of Thestrion. By the time the revolution finally took place, no one wanted to talk with the King anymore. They wanted Trienes for their leader. And as no one else had any idea what to do, he had to accept."

"So the people put him in charge, and that's why he has so much power," Alcione said. At first, it had seemed that most people were simply too afraid to stop the Arkos, like Stabler. Some mysterious group of powerful figures must have been behind him.

But over her time with the caravan, Alcie had come to the frightening truth: the people themselves had given the Arkos power over them. They truly believed that what he said would help. That thought was much more terrifying to Alcione than any figures lurking in the shadows.

"Aye, and the traders didn't have much say in it, so we're not for or against him," Tremi responded. "Many in the capital say everything has finally changed for the better, even if they're still starving and poor. There's no real change for the traders yet, so we'll wait and see."

Alcione couldn't think of what to say. She hadn't felt afraid in a long while, but now she realized she had been far more fortunate than she'd thought. If she hadn't befriended the Stabler, if she hadn't gone with the traders, she would likely be dead a hundred times over by now.

INTO THE SKY

As that sank in, the wagons slowly came to a halt. Little Moti stretched his neck to try and see over Romi and Enno to what surrounded them. Alcie looked around curiously. She had never seen any villages except Lymnoi, and this place was very different!

From her vantage point atop Romi, Alcie's head drew level with the top of several mud-thatch huts. These, at least, were familiar. However, these homes were interspersed with several taller buildings made of sturdy wooden planks. The only buildings in Lymnoi not made of straw were the plank-wood tanner and butcher shops, and the old stone citadel.

The wood here was darker, and the houses taller and with square roofs instead of the arches that sturdier northern buildings had to keep snow off in winter.

"Ready to go?" Tremi asked, pouring the powdered bloodthorn into his vial.

Alcie nodded. Tremi held out his hand for the packages she carried so she could jump down from Romi. After she had placed the pack saddle and its contents into the wagon, she lifted Sola out. It took Tremi's help to set the pup on the ground, as he had begun to grow taller and heavier. No one knew what he was, but everyone thought he had to have been someone's pet. He was too friendly to be wild.

With Sola like a shadow at her heels, she brought Moti to the front of the wagon, where Goso usually had the posts set up for the animals to graze. But this time, there were no posts in the ground.

"Come on, boy," Goso told her. "This way."

Alcie and Deena, who was leading Enno, followed him to where a large field had been cordoned off with posts and ropes. "Some of the inn folk will stay with the stock," Goso told her as she inspected the pen, which was already quickly filling with the muller that other wagons had released into it.

"We'll go in and have a pint, see if we can't lighten the load a bit with buyers." He stepped through an opening in the fence and slipped the halters from Inthys and Ocne. They trotted forward into the herd of muller, struggling to get to the large piles of hay scattered all about. Alcie and Deena followed suit with their arion before returning to get the others.

Securing the wagons and animals off the road took the rest of the afternoon. The traders kept up a steady conversation with the townsfolk, catching up with old friends and hearing the latest gossip. Alcie said little, engrossed in the chatter. She caught snippets of sentences and tried to make sense of them.

"...too salty for my taste, my customers would agree..."

"...ten dagats, no less, and that's a bargain, mind!"

"D'you have anything like it in gold? Or green, mayhap? Red is too…"

She learned that Tremi had been exactly right. Whenever the name of Arkos Trienes was mentioned here, it wasn't with the slight fear and disdain that the traders used, but with reverence.

"Aye, the Arkos, gods bless and keep him, has sent men this way many times over the last few weeks to see us. They come with gifts from the palace. Gifts, can you imagine? And all they ask is a room and a place to stable muller. They even pay for their food!" one townsman had crowed jubilantly to Leor, as he looked over the old man's cart of fruits and vegetables.

Alcie shuddered to think of how those people would react if they learned she had never had to pay for food in her life.

At sunset, finished with her chores, she headed off to find Tremi. "Can ye tell me where the halay lad is at?" she asked a trader. She had gotten used to speaking low, and to changing words in her head before speaking. Sometimes, trader cant even came naturally. *If my family could see me now,* she thought, but she didn't know how to finish. *Would they be proud? Or would they turn me away?*

She was directed to the inn. Throwing back her shoulders and making sure her cap was set at a confident angle on her head the way Tremi had taught her, she went inside, Sola close behind her.

The front room of the tavern was dimly lit. Pipe smoke coiled up and clung to the rafters. It was crowded with men in trousers and rag shirts. The women, as Tremi had explained was proper, sat off to one corner near the entrance, the only part of the tavern they were allowed to occupy. Alcione was both nervous and strangely excited walking past the men towards the bar. Tremi sat on a stool there, chatting with the publican of the tavern.

"Here's his pitch, the old dotard. Says 'buy a fine tunic, sir? Ten dagats for as fine a cloth as ever you laid eyes on.' A ratty old rag, it was! So I says, does I," Tremi told the man, fully in his storytelling mode, "that I ain't in the market for a tunic, fine as it may be. Thanks all the same. An' he says, 'well, would you prefer a rotten one? I have those too.' An' he takes out another as could be twins with the first! Nervy fellow!"

Alcie approached the bar and sidled up next to Tremi, squeezing past two large men who argued with loud voices and animated gesturing. "Ah!" said Tremi. "Uger, let me introduce you. This is me pal, Alcion. Alcie, this is Uger, our host."

"Pleasure," said Uger. "Flute for ye, lad?"

"Please," Alcie said, thirsty from the hard work of the afternoon.

Uger turned his back to pour the drink. Tremi studied her, then whispered in her ear, "Not too much. It'll make you silly."

"Silly?"

"Trust me, it's dangerous. Makes you talk."

"Oh."

So when Uger returned with a tarnished steel flute of black liquid, steam rising from its narrow top, Alcie thanked him and made as if to sip, but then stopped. "I'll wait until it's cooler," she said, intending even then to only take small, slow sips.

"As ye like." Uger resumed his conversation with Tremi. Alcie listened to Tremi describe the old man's antics as he continued trying to sell his tattered tunics. As she did, she leaned one elbow on the counter and used her other arm to raise the flute to her lips. Eyeing Tremi as he drained his flute and asked for another, she closed her eyes and gulped.

The vice scorched its way down her throat and Alcie swore she could feel her innards burn. The drink's temperature wasn't too warm, yet something in it felt like fire. Her eyes watered and she choked. "What is *in* that?" she gasped, after Tremi had patted her on the back.

Uger laughed. "Sommat much stronger than yer used to, I gather."

"Aye." Tremi had trained her well. After days of speaking mostly only to him, Sola, and Romi, she had learned to keep her questions and answers brief. And after the close call with Huin, she had worked hard to ensure that even surprise no longer made her loquacious in public.

"He'll have mellonia instead," Tremi told Uger, naming the sweet honey-flavored drink she had told him she used to drink at home.

"Strong lad like yerself?" Uger asked, grinning at Alcione. "Well, each to their liking, I says." He went into the small alcove behind the bar and this time returned with a piping hot mug of mellonia.

"Thanks," Alcie told him, bringing the mug to her lips and blowing on it before taking a small taste. The mellonia was exotically flavored with a spice she couldn't name, and it was wonderful. "Much better," she told him, as he and Tremi watched her reaction.

"Rare to see even a young'un among the traders as can't hold a flute," a man said, coming up to the counter. His face was smooth and handsome. "Yer not from around here, are ye, lad?"

"Up north," Tremi explained.

"Ah. What brings you down this way?"

"Work," Alcie said, repeating the answer she and Tremi had rehearsed. They had prepared for situations such as this one, but Alcie was terrified that she would forget what to say, or be asked a question she hadn't planned on.

"Work's plentiful now," the stranger said. "The Arkos saw to that, when he got rid of the nobles. Now we do our own work and reap the rewards, instead of giving the best of our harvest and makings to those highborn thieves."

"Aye," answered Alcie, looking at her feet.

The stranger continued on, oblivious to her discomfort. "Smart man, our Arkos, bless his soul. You wouldn't know it, lad, bein' from the north, but d'ye know how he got so sure of his power? How he got rid of every last one of those Talaria and their families and made sure none was hiding out, waitin' fer their chance to strike back?"

"The fires?" Alcie guessed.

The stranger laughed heartily. "Some, aye, but that wasn't the plan, lad. No, he told each tenant farmer like me that he wanted proof of our loyalty. Has a copy of the Book of Gold, does he, with the name of every noble in every family alive inscribed in it. An' what does he do? He tells us we're to bring 'em to him, so's he can check 'em off the list himself as he kills 'em!"

Alcione stared the man straight in the eyes, stunned. Quickly, Tremi saw the look in her eyes and told the stranger, "The vice must be gettin' to the lad. Alcie, my boy? Come on, that's a lad." With an arm around her shoulder, he led her away and out of the tavern. Sola, sitting quietly at Alcie's feet, got up to follow.

Alcie took a gulp of mellonia, knowing her face was pale as death. Her fingers clenched around the handle of the mug. "You never told me!" she accused when they were out of earshot of others.

"What, that like as not your family got marched off to die on the scaffold in front of a mob of revelers and gawkers instead of in flames?" he shot back. "They might've, might not. Did you want to know it?"

"They might not have died in the fires," Alcie said, her throat tight. "If I had known, I could have gone after them. I could have saved them before they reached the city."

Tremi raised an eyebrow. "I doubt it. They'd have been killed weeks before the traders came to Montelymnë. And what could you have done? You? Alone, against an army?"

"I could have tried!"

"You'd be dead," he told her flatly. "And who does that help?"

"Why would you care?" she argued. "You would never have met me, and had to go through all this trouble teaching me to take care of myself."

"You're a fool," he told her harshly, "if you think I'd do it and still not care if you live. I'm not going to see you throw away your life for a family that's already dead."

They're not dead! She wanted to scream. *They're only gone for a bit.* But she knew he wouldn't understand and more, she knew he was right. If she died, she would be with her family, but they would never come home again.

She looked up at Tremi, and his gaze was unflinching. "Forget about them," he told her. "You can't spend your life hating the world for what it did to you."

"Why not?" she shot back.

"It'll make you bitter like Raka. And because you're here, you're alive. Whatever you were before, let it go. You're my friend now."

Sometimes, Alcie felt she wanted to do nothing but cry until she melted away. And then there were moments like this, when she was so tired she didn't understand anything at all. "You're my friend, too," she told him. "Although I don't know why."

"You don't need to," Tremi said, putting a hand on her shoulder. "You just are. Now comes the hard part."

Alcie reached down to wrap her fingers in Sola's fur for comfort. "What is it?"

"I want you to come back in with me. I want you to pretend what that man said meant nothing, and prove to me that you're ready for Ianthe."

Alcione shook her head. "Tremi, that's too much. I just...I can't pretend that my family meant nothing to me, that I think those people are right."

"Then don't," he advised. "Just don't say anything. And when someone says something that you hate, block it out. There's nothing else you can do."

"I'll go where you don't have to hear it," Alcie said, starting towards the wagon.

Tremi grabbed her arm. "You can't run away forever," he told her softly. "The whole world isn't big enough for that."

"It is too!" She threw off his grasp. "There's a whole world north of Montelymnë where no one lives."

"And is that a life, being all alone forever?"

"I'd have Romi and Sola."

Tremi gave her a disdainful look and turned to go. "You've got an answer for everything, eh? Suit yourself. I thought you were braver than that."

He began to walk back towards the tavern. Alcione struggled with her thoughts, closing her eyes and wishing it would all just go away. *But it won't. And if I want my family back, I have to be willing to do whatever it takes.*

"...Wait."

Tremi stopped, his back still turned to her. Tugging Sola along at her side, she went to stand by him. "I'm not running away," she said. "Not yet, at least."

"Good." She couldn't see his face, but from his voice she could tell he was pleased with her answer.

When they went back in, Alcione saw some of the men had gathered in a circle to sing medka. Arm in arm, they swayed together like thick tree branches in a strong wind. Others danced to the joyous melody. In their corner, the women laughed and clapped along.

She caught Huin's eye, and the older woman smiled. Alcie nodded to her as she joined Tremi with the men. Determined to put all bad thoughts away, she concentrated only on the song, and on acting like she belonged. *Men are strong, and they don't cry, no matter how bad things get. Hermion wouldn't let that man's words hurt* **him***!*

The lyrics still embarrassed Alcie a little bit, but she couldn't help laughing when they got to the part about the "one hundred warts all wrinkled and brown, on the feet of Old Sela of Kermolly Town." And after a few more verses, Alcie even found herself singing tentatively along with the chorus.

When the singing had died down, the stranger approached again. "Head clear, lad?" he asked. Alcie nodded. "Good. I had Uger save this for you." Bending down to her level, he handed her another flute of vice. He smiled at her. "Take it slow, and ye'll be fine."

Someone called, and the man turned from her. He threw a last glance over his shoulder. "Good luck, lad."

Alcione smiled back at him, forcing the corners of her mouth to turn upwards. When he was gone, Tremi led her over to a small table where Goso was shoveling in supper. He left her, and returned with two plates heaping full of meat, vegetables, and hunks of bread and cheese.

In the manner of trader folk, she spread the brynza cheese onto a slice of bread, and stacked scallet – the tough, roasted part of the meat – with some vegetables, and graze leaves on top. Above that, she placed another slice of bread, and tucked in a sprig of sweetrue for flavor.

As she ate, Alcie sipped at the vice and found that after a few more sputtering swallows, she was able to get it down her throat without wincing too much. Halfway through the flute, the heat of the drink turned to a steady warmth in her belly, and she became pleasantly drowsy.

"It's hot in here," she commented idly. And as she reached for another sip, her gaze went blurry and she nearly knocked the flute to the floor. "And I'm dizzy. Why am I dizzy, Tremi?"

He observed her, blue-green eyes sizing up her condition and coming to some sort of conclusion. "We're going," he said to Goso. "The lad's twizzled. He'll sleep it off in the wagon."

"How't he get so tipsy?" the older man demanded. "Take my eyes off him for one minute, I swear…"

"It was one flute," Tremi explained. "And one too many, it seems."

"I'd say."

Tremi led her to a flight of stairs. Alcie regarded them blearily, wondering why there seemed to be two of each step. As they began to ascend, Tremi's arm around Alcie's back and under one armpit to steady her, they were joined by Huin and Raka. "Rich boy can't hold his drink?" Raka jeered in a whisper, mindful of Tremi's presence. "This does not surprise me."

"Leave off," Alcie snapped. "I'm just fine, I am. Dandy, that's what. Aye." Her voice had thickened as she unconsciously mimicked the accent she'd been hearing all through the evening.

Tremi and Huin exchanged bemused glances. "He's twizzled, only he doesn't know what that means," he told Huin.

"It is probably better that way," she replied equably, unruffled as ever. "Good night, Alcion. If you are well enough in the morning, I would be glad of your assistance at my stall if Goso and Deena can spare you."

"Why'n't I be well enough?" she slurred. *It's so warm in here...I feel so strange.*

Tremi snorted. "You'll have a bit of a headache, lad, if I don't mistake myself. But you'll gain a stomach for the stuff, sooner or late." He spoke softly now. "You've gained a tongue for our cant, and downright quick. You won't let a little flute of vice get the best of you."

"No, indeed," Alcie replied, bobbing her head in agreement. They reached the top of the stairs, and Raka and Huin took the first door on the left. She and Tremi continued down the candlelit corridor until they reached another left-side door, this one on the far end. Tremi took out a key — *where did that come from?* — and opened the door.

By the pale light of the hall candles, Alcie could see a small, cramped room with a slanted ceiling. Four straw pallets were strewn across the floor, just touching each other. She couldn't tell, but she hoped the movement she saw in the straw was only her imagination.

"This is where we sleep?" she asked unhappily.

"Aye. Pick a spot and lie down, that's a lad." He eased her down to sit on a pallet, then unclasped her cloak. Alcie squirmed around in the straw, trying to find a restful spot. Sola padded over from sniffing an interesting corner and lay down beside her. When she had finally found a comfortable position, Tremi covered her with the cloak.

"Don't think about what's underneath," he suggested, "and you'll be fine. Mayhap you're not used to accommodations like this, but t'won't kill you. There now. Just head to sleep."

"G'night, Tremi," she told him, eyes already closing. "I'm glad we're friends."

She barely heard his response as she drifted off to sleep, but she thought he said, "Me too."

She did have a headache the next morning, but it faded quickly, and at the end of the day when Tremi asked if she wanted to try another flute before they left for Ianthe the following morning, she refused.

There were some experiences, she told him, that you didn't need to have twice.

- CHAPTER 11 -
Ianthe

WHEN THE CITY AT last came into view, it looked from afar like a brown forest. Raised, straight spires of what appeared to be enormous trees speared the air from one side. The rest took on the misty image of a distant mirage.

The hazy blur came into focus hours later as a giant wall of grey and brown stones. Tremi said it was twenty feet high and would protect the city, and Kayre Ianthe within it, from attack.

Houses began to cluster by the sides of the road – thatched roof and wooden, and as Alcie drew nearer the gate, some even bore stone walls. Fences surrounded patches of flowers or crops, while other properties had pens of malim, barra, and gent.

Along the main thoroughfare people stayed out of the way of the caravan, treading a fine edge between the wheels and the sewage ditches on either side of the road.

Sola ran behind the wagons, darting off to explore someone's small vegetable garden or investigate an interesting person walking down the road. He never seemed to bother anyone, though, as if he knew precisely who would be kind and who would be mean. And he always came back when he had finished exploring. *He must have been tame before I found him,* Alcie thought. *I wonder why he chose to follow me one day instead of his owner?*

Romi wasn't nearly as at ease with the noise and bustle surrounding him. He hadn't been skittish on the road as a rule, but Alcie had found that loud sounds startled him, and he would spook if something moved too quickly, like a bird flashing out of a tree across his line of vision.

She had fallen off a few times during these scares, but had slowly grown to anticipate them and to use her legs to hold on when her hands were full. Fortunately, they'd sold enough on the road that her lap was no longer full of packages. Tremi, sitting on the backboard working, handed her a few tiny insects and a cord.

"Here," he told her. "I've made the hole already. Just string it through and knot it. Five halay, five knots, all even-spaced. Got me?"

Alcione nodded. Tremi hurried about his own work to finish the last charms, bracelets, carved shell rings, and other trinkets he intended to sell when they arrived.

INTO THE SKY

As they approached the city, Alcie grew nervous. She returned the halay necklace to Tremi and picked up her reins. Romi danced beneath her, hooves hitting the ground more lightly than usual. His neck was stiff, arched tensely as he glared with distrust at the people passing by.

Once, a young boy reached out a hand to pet him and Romi's head darted out, lightning-quick, teeth flashing to bite. The boy cried out and raced back to his mother's waiting arms, where she scolded the child for getting so close. Still, the woman looked darkly at the traders' wagons.

"I know you're afraid, but that wasn't a very nice way to behave," she scolded Romi. Tremi looked up, but didn't say anything. He had long ago accepted that while Alcie would keep silent around strangers, she always talked to the arion.

Romi didn't answer her, but she could feel his heart pounding in time with her own. There was a flash of the boy's wide eyes in her mind as he looked over his shoulder. In that distorted view, his bright yellow hair stood out sharply among the grey of the sky and the pale, golden-white blur of the grass, and the dark wool of his mother's blouse. The image of the boy took on a sinister quality in the stark light.

Alcie wasn't afraid of the city – she didn't think she had any reason to be – yet still she found herself short of breath and slightly lightheaded. There was another flash. For a moment she couldn't see in front of her, only to either side. "Tremi?" she asked. "Can I sit with you?"

Wordlessly, he put aside a three-bug triangle pendant and extended his hands to help her into the wagon. He handed her some cord and side by side they threaded them through beautiful, shining necklaces of halay. Alcie kept her eyes on Romi, trying to will him to be calm with the force of her stare.

Now that she was no longer on his back, that strange thrill of terror no longer tingled up her spine. There was only an ordinary, queasy fear that she was certain was completely her own. *I'd be mad not to be nervous. If I make a mistake, I might be thrown in jail or killed.*

Beneath them, the wagon ceased jouncing and pulled to a stop. "Inspection in two minutes," Goso called, and Alcie sat up straight with a jolt. Romi tilted his head so that his eyes locked on hers. He was motionless, suspended in time. "Easy, boy," she said softly, breaking the moment. She reached out to rub his nose. He didn't try to bite her, but she sensed that the decision was a near thing.

"What's inspection?" she asked Tremi.

Putting away the necklaces, he replied, "When you reach the city gates, you have to speak to the guards and state your reason for being there. Then they inspect you, an' make sure you're telling the truth. Used to be done by soldiers in the King's

Guard, probably still is, only now they work for the Arkos."

"All out!" a voice bellowed from outside.

Alcie looked worriedly at Romi, but didn't dare disobey. Together with Tremi she exited the wagon and walked around to the front to stand with Goso, Deena, Huin, Raka, and Sola. On the ground, Alcione got her first glimpse of the inside of the city.

It was like a giant market, with more people walking around than she had ever seen in one place in her entire life. The streets were wide and paved with what appeared to be a sheet of stones set into the earth.

People rushed by, wearing strange garments – one man's cowl trailed to his ankles and kept his face hidden from view, while a rotund woman wore a headdress that towered so high Alcie couldn't imagine how she could keep her head up, let alone balance the colorful hat to keep it from falling. Another wore a hat atop a wimple! No woman would dare wear something that outrageous back home, common-born or noble. Her gown was cut so low that Alcione was shocked for her. *Back home, women like that would have been turned back at the gates!*

Most of the clothes, though, were so filthy she could barely tell what color they had once been. They were a drab brown faceless crowd. Children tumbled underfoot causing mischief, while merchants stood off to one side. They pitched their wares so quickly she couldn't make out what they said. She thought they sounded similar to Tremi, but they spoke so rapidly she caught little. And then her view was blocked by the sight of a soldier in dented, rusty plate armor.

The soldier had a bristly moustache and dark, stern eyes. "Name?" he demanded.

"Alcion of Lymnoi," she responded steadily, meeting his eyes without fear.

"Purpose of entry?"

"Work."

"Who speaks for the boy?"

"I will." Alcie looked up. Tremi and Huin had responded at the same time. Goso nodded his head, as did Deena, and even sullen Raka did not look inclined to disagree or make trouble. She seemed slightly afraid of the guard, looking away when he glanced in her and Huin's direction.

The guards who inspected the wagon or stood to the side keeping an eye on the arched entryway didn't looked like the sort who found anything particularly funny. Alcie looked at Tremi. He was hunched in a corner, and looked as if he simply wanted the whole thing over. Living with the traders, she thought he must have gone through this many times before.

She stood and waited while the guard searched through her pack, asking where she had gotten the few items remaining within. "From the fires, sir," she answered. "They burned the Kayre near to the village, and me uncle says I can take what I likes. The rest is got off the road on t' way here."

He searched her pouch of items, spilling it on the ground and leaving her to scramble and catch the contents before the wind swept them away. The pebbles were easily gathered, but her unique leaves and scraps of cloth were blown off by a strong breeze. Noting the disapproving glare of the soldier, she decided not to chase after them.

The men searched every nook and cranny of the wagon, checking underneath for caches of hidden merchandise and searching the pack saddles on the arion. Romi barely held still. He tossed his head as the soldiers roughly seized each bundle and opened a corner to check it.

"Clear them and give them gate passes," the lead soldier instructed his men finally.

Just then, there was a shout and a clatter of armor. A huge dark shape flew past her and her mind dimly registered that several of the guards had been knocked to the ground and that there was a broken tether lying in the dirt where an arion had once stood. But the predominant thought in her head was panic – not hers, but Romi's.

Shaking herself free of the fleeing arion's fright, Alcie dashed after him. "Wait!" she heard Tremi call as she dove headlong into the droves of people dodging to let the wild arion through.

"Romi!" she cried, watching him disappear around a corner.

Zigzagging around the bewildered crowds, she tried to follow his path. A pile of spilled fruits and two yelling merchants drew her eye. She stumbled over a stone raised from the path, but gripped the edge of a passing cart to steady herself. Lurching past the ruined merchandise, she turned another corner and kept going.

A feeling of panic pulsed through her, almost forcibly dragging her to the right. Going by instinct, she dodged into an alley. A group of boys skipped pebbles, crouching to eye level to decide which direction to aim. She leaped over the smallest of them, hollering out a, "Sorry!" as she came to the end of the alley and turned left.

Her panic flared, making her heart feel it would burst with fear. The people around her faded to a flurry of colors and bodies rushing past. She turned around, and that same sensation of seeing with another vision invaded her mind.

"Romi!" she called, lost in the sea of foot traffic. Closing her eyes, she was assaulted by a slew of figures nonetheless. Farmers and housewives, children and soldiers, all stood out in relief, the reds and yellows and blacks sharper than reality. Only other arion seemed real, and only once she had been jerked to a stop, a hand on—

Her eyes sprang open, and she knew without a doubt that Romi had stopped. Her vision had returned to normal. There were a few other arion attached to wagons and carts here, mixed in among the muller. But none of them was Romi.

She felt him close, and knew his fear had started to subside, but she couldn't see him. Following her instinct, she began to walk purposefully forward. She turned onto the next street. Standing on tiptoe to look over the crowd, she tried to spot Romi.

"I believe this miscreant is the one you're searching for?" a voice came from behind her. A hand touched her shoulder, and she turned.

There was Romi, breathing deeply from exertion but finally starting to calm. "He's rather canny, finding his way through all these streets to me, hmm?" From around the arion's far side came a young man, holding Romi's rope-reins out to her. She took it and studied him.

He was older than she, almost an adult, and very tall. Thin, with the sort of graceful body and long legs Alcione had always imagined Hermion might have when he grew up. He was clad in a one-piece suit of orange and green patterned diamonds. The long cones at the ends of his hat and his shoes had bells on them. Around his neck was clasped a marvelous multicolored patchwork cloak.

His hair was a beautiful golden-red that shimmered in the sun, more yellow than her own. His laughing eyes were pale, a twinkling celadon green that fit perfectly with an infectious smile. When she took the reins from him, he lifted her other hand with a flourish and bestowed a kiss upon the back of it. "My lady," he said.

With a start, Alcione realized that he had addressed her as a girl. Embarrassed, she noticed that her chest was heaving, her sweaty tunic plastered to her small but at the moment noticeable breasts. Her cap had fallen, too, and her hair had grown back enough that it hung down to her shoulders. You wouldn't have guessed her to be a girl right off – none of the others had when she sweated after a hard day's work – unless you had very sharp eyes. But this young man seemed possessed of those.

"Please don't call me a lady," she begged, clasping her cap in front of her chest in case anyone else had seen. "I haven't told—"

"Alcie!" Tremi came dashing up to her, Sola hard behind him. Romi pranced back, but the mysterious young man laid a hand on the arion's shoulder. Settling, Romi seemed to accept that if his new friend wasn't afraid, he had no reason to be either.

"Thank you for finding him," Alcie said to the man. "I have to go now."

"But wait!" He gestured with one hand and a small, blue flower appeared between his fingers. He seemed to want to place it in her hair, then changed his mind and tucked it behind Romi's ear. "You haven't even told me your name."

"It's Alcion. Goodbye." She reached out for the reins, the makeshift rope contraption miraculously still attached to the halter.

"Rungilivanster!"

Tremi had come up to them. He grinned at the stranger, who smiled back immediately. "Hello, Mat Tremi," the stranger said.

Tremi turned to Alcione. "Alcie, this is Master Rungilivanster, finest magician in all of Ianthe."

Rungilivanster sketched a bow, the conical tendrils of his hat managing to nearly touch his toes without falling off. He lifted his head a bit to look Alcione in the eye. "At your service, young master," he said, and she knew he was laughing inwardly at her. But somehow she also knew, with the same gut-deep instinct she'd had about Tremi, that she could trust him to keep her secret.

"You'll come by and see my show tonight, won't you?" he asked, straightening and looking over at Tremi.

"Of course!" Tremi laughed. "Wouldn't miss it. Didn't know you'd be in town, though. You said you'd be in Cathatiur till midsummer, didn't you? Your visits always surprise folk."

"Sometimes they even surprise me," he replied cheekily. He clapped a hand on Tremi's shoulder. "I was mightily grateful for that buckbell powder you sold me when last we met, my friend. I've used it all up."

"Lucky for you that I've plenty more," Tremi told him with a grin.

"Lucky indeed. Come tonight, at the eighth chime of the bells in the Citadel. I've my usual spot, just the corner—"

"Just the corner of Trifira, border of the Hollows," Tremi interrupted. "Caulburne Alley. I remember. And I'll be there, with the buckbell. I knew I'd be glad of the thought to gather more on the way here."

"Bring your young master Alcion as well, if you please."

"And what about what I please?" Alcione demanded, unhappy at being ignored. She thought she'd rather stay with Romi in the safety of a stable. She wasn't entirely sure she liked the city just yet.

Rungilivanster regarded her seriously. "Would it please you to attend the most magnificent, magical, mystical performance in all of Ianthe? To see wonders of this world that even the Arkos himself could never hope to understand?

"Or perhaps," he said with a glint in his eye, "it would please you best to stay behind, and let everyone else gobble up all of the luckle and toffin that always seems to make its way through my crowd."

That did it. "I'll be there," she mumbled. "But there'd better be a lot of toffin."

Both Tremi and the magician laughed. "For you, my boy, I shall get double. You're a skinny little thing. You too, Tremi. You could both use a solid meal. Perhaps you'd join me for supper?" Alcione spared him a grateful glance, both for the offer of food and for remembering to call her 'boy.'

Tremi shook his head. "We're just in today, and Goso's mad enough to spit about Romi. We're unloading for the rest of the afternoon."

"Ah." Rungilivanster nodded. "So that's why there was an arion here. I'd wondered. Does our esteemed Mat Goso believe he'll be able to offer the Arkos an arion as spooky as this?"

"He's not for sale," Alcie interjected hotly.

"Oh?" One slender, fair brow rose into a crown of golden hair. "And just who does he belong to?"

"To me," Alcie replied, her mutinous expression daring him to disagree.

He didn't. Instead, he laughed again. "Oh, I don't doubt it. You'll have to tell me the whole story behind that at supper tonight. You two!" he called, and whistled to two boys leaning idly against the stone wall of a house. "Take yourselves off to the caravans setting up at Trifira Bridge. Bring this arion along. Tell Mat Goso – he's the big, blond, brawny brute with the animals – that Rungilivanster sent you in place of his two boys here."

Alcie watched as Rungilivanster twirled two silver dagats idly through his fingertips, flipping them with a hypnotic rhythm, over and over. The boys stared as well, then came over to take hold of Romi. "He won't listen to them," Alcie said as Romi started to prance. Her hands tightened on the reins, fearful he might spook again.

"And we've got to go back," Tremi added. "Besides, even you haven't enough spare coin to pay those two louts and still take us for food."

"Don't you be worrying your head about my resources, Little Lord Lack-beard," Rungilivanster admonished lightly, smiling at him. "But if you must go," and here he added a theatrical sigh, "then you must. But you will attend my show and be prompt about it," he insisted. "Even one moment late and I'll know."

Tremi promised, then led the way back towards the caravan. Alcie stole a last glance behind her at Rungilivanster, who tossed her a wink and a friendly wave. "He will know," Tremi shouted above the din of the chaotic streets. "He always does. This way!"

The road back to the caravan was full of twists and turns. Alcie had to keep a firm grip on Romi to stop him from running off. His panic had subsided, but he still looked warily on the crowds pressing in on him as they ducked into narrow alleys. By the time they reached the broad main thoroughfare, the caravan had already found its way to its assigned space on Trifira Bridge.

The bridge was arched and built of solid grey stone. Wide enough for two wagons to pass each other easily side by side, it was also long enough for the entire wagon train to span it and still have a far walk to reach the other end. Seven large stone pillars stemmed from the water for support. Alcie could see that the bridge was well made; the mortar – the sticky mix of sand and lime that held rocks together – could barely be seen.

The caravan wagons were scattered across the bridge. Goso was at the far end, and as Tremi led them over the bridge, Alcione was conscious of several gazes following them. It was clear that many had heard of the caravan's loose arion who'd caused such havoc on the city streets.

"Took yer time, did ye?" Goso muttered when he saw them. He kept his voice low, but his expression was thunderous. "That creature caused a great deal of damage, boy. How will you pay fer it without givin' that monster to me?"

"I'll find a way," Alcie promised. "But you can't have him."

Goso harrumphed. "Well, don't let's stand around talkin'. Round that corner is the stable. T'others are inside. Y'said ye knew how to muck stalls, make hay nets, fill t'water buckets, eh? Well, move!"

Scurrying away as Goso barked more orders at Tremi, Alcie turned the corner and found herself facing yet another wooden building, this one with a long row of windows on the ground, an arion's face poking out from each. Alcie smiled, seeing faces both familiar and strange, and took Romi inside.

The stable was enormous, with two high, upward-sloping ceiling arches that came to a point in the center. There had to be at least twelve stalls on each side, and above the rows of stalls was a hayloft. The borders of the stalls and the doors were painted the deep color of evergreen boughs.

A man came up to her. "That'd be the troublemaker?" he asked, indicating Romi. Alcione nodded. "Just as well the corner's not been filled yet. This way." He led her down the row to the last stall on the right. "Put him in there," the man ordered.

Behind her, Romi tensed. "It's too dark for him," Alcie argued.

The man scowled. "What is this, the royal palace? Aye, fine. I'll move this other one. No matter." Grumbling, he took Welm from the stall across the way. The large arion balked, mainly on principle, Alcie thought. Still, the man simply kept tugging until he came across into the interior stall.

Once it was empty, Alcione took Romi into the stall with the window facing out. A half-eaten pile of hay was illuminated in a shaft of light and Romi charged for it, dragging the reins from her hands.

"Manners!" she exclaimed, then sighed. Arion were smart, but get them near food and they thought only with their bellies. Then again, she thought, reminded of the toffin, so did some people. Wrestling him away from the pile of hay for a moment, she undid the reins but left the halter on just in case. After hugging his neck to show she was glad he was safe, she stepped out of the stall and hauled the huge wooden door shut.

Suddenly, she heard a frantic barking and scratching sound. "Oh, whoops! Sorry, Sola!" Opening the door a fragment, she watched the pup wiggle out.

"Friend of yers?"

Alcie smiled at the other man. "Aye."

The man nodded. "I'd be Buske. I run these stables. Goso's taken near half my stalls till he works things out with the Arkos. He gets 'em fer less if his own staff does the chores for his string. That's you.

"The tools are on the back wall," he gestured, "or near the stalls, or out the back round this corner." He directed her to a turn nearly hidden in the darkness just beyond her. "Any questions?"

Alcione shook her head. "Good," he replied. "Be seein' ye." Whistling, he walked off.

Trying not to think of how much he reminded her of the Stabler, Alcie grabbed a pitchfork and muck pail and got to work. The familiarity of the work relaxed her, clearing her mind. *I'll have to find a way into the palace soon to get that crown! The longer I stay here, the harder it will be.*

She didn't let herself think, *the longer I stay, the more people I'll have to leave behind.* Instead, she cleared dung into a wheelbarrow and made sure Romi had new, clean hay and a full bucket of water, before starting on the others. *Everyone, please wait for me,* she asked silently.

Her family's faces stood out clearly in her memory, Isaura a miniature of their mother,

Hermion's face so like her father's and yet also a mirror of her own. Kanase's gentle expression made her dash away a tear. *I promise I'll find a way to get you back.*

- CHAPTER 12 -

Rungilivanster's Magic Show

At supper, Tremi and Alcione sat together on the backboard of the wagon, a plate of stackers between them. The light meal was so called because you stacked slices of cheese and slabs of scallet between two slices of bread. Sola sat between them, clearly hopeful that bits might fall between the two of them and into his mouth.

"Trifira's the gap between the high and low end of the city," Tremi was saying. "The river curves north and south of it, so the ground about parallel to the bridge is in the middle. Your stable's on Keecy Street, in the high end. Cost is steep, but he'll make up the price by selling the arion to the Arkos." Alcie nodded as he went on. "I don't know what you'll do with Romi after. You still won't sell him?"

"Never."

"I thought as much. Ah, well. It'll work out somehow. Anyway, don't stray far from Keecy and you'll be fine. Just keep out of the bad parts."

Alcie frowned. "How do I know where the bad parts of the city are?"

Tremi shrugged. He pointed up to where the tall turrets she'd once thought were trees rose above everything else. "Kayre Ianthe is atop that hill, lookin' down over the city. Up that way's safe enough, for all the new folk uphill still act as if the high places were for the better-bred."

Tremi reached out a hand to pet Sola and nudge his nose away from the last of the scallet. Taking a bite of the hard, now-cold stacker, he rethought the decision, giving the pup his share. Sola yipped with delight and snatched at the morsel.

"Keep away from the lower districts." He indicated the far end of the bridge. Although it wasn't fully evident from far off, Alcie could see now that the buildings on that end were shabbier. "Unsavory folk live there, and those from places where the King didn't rule. Fenlanders like Huin and Raka, if they'd stayed with their own kind."

Settling back inside the wagon, he looked seriously at her. "Whatever you do, though, keep out of Thieves' Corner. That's the worst part of the city."

Alcie nodded. "I think I can guess why."

Tremi's expression was grim, and distant with remembrance. "Grinning thieves go about their business carefree, while good men and women starve. The old story about honor among thieves? There is none. I hate them."

"Did you…" She wanted to ask how he knew, what made him so angry at the mere mention of thieves. Then she remembered that Tremi's friend had been killed by bandits. "Nothing," she filled in at his inquisitive look. "Go on."

"Well, there's one part across the bridge you can keep to, and that's the Hollows. The largest part of the city, and it's where I grew up. I'll be headin' back on the morrow."

"You mean you're not staying with the wagon?" Alcie frowned. She didn't care for the idea of staying with Deena and Goso, and even less the idea of Huin taking her in. The gentle woman would of course shelter her, but nothing could make her endure Raka's presence more than she absolutely had to.

Tremi laughed. "Forgot to mention that, did I? Naw, I'm for home. Goso and Deena are stayin' with the wagon. Huin has a little spot in Shopkeep Square, just alongside the Hollows. She and Raka will go there."

"And me?" Alcie asked.

"Dunno. We can figure it out come morning. Anyhow—"

Before he could say any more, bells began to chime. "Oh," Tremi said. "And in the west is the Celestial Citadel. They ring out the time every hour on the hour."

Alcie frowned, counting out eight chimes. "Doesn't that mean we should be going?"

It took him a moment to realize what she meant. When recognition hit, he took off running across the bridge, Sola behind him. Alcie followed them, Sola's fur acting as a white beacon in the deepening twilight as he tried to catch up with Tremi.

She turned off the bridge, gasping like a landed fish. *How does he run so fast after eating?* She braced her hands on her knees, winded. *I think I'm going to be sick!*

Heaving in a deep breath, she continued on, following down side streets towards their destination. The shadows lengthened as night settled in. The hanging lanterns along the sides of the streets provided light, but obscured the stars overhead.

A long street lay ahead, with houses that leaned in, glowering over all within their confines. A lone lamp flickered from a small caravan in the center of the street. An audience of children had gathered in front of it. The scent of smoke and candy filled the air, and Alcie started forward.

"You're late," came a rich, booming voice from behind her. Alcione turned to see, but there was no one there. She heard giggles behind her. "This way, if you please," instructed the voice. Alcione turned back around and nearly shrieked. Rungilivanster stood directly in front of her, his face covered by a black mask fringed with tufts of white and colored feathers. The hooked nose of the mask had to be nearly a foot long, and to Alcione staring up at him, it seemed like a sword pointed straight at her head.

"I got lost," Alcie panted, willing her heart to stop racing.

"You got lost?" the magician parroted, twisting around to consider his audience. "I don't believe him," he said in a voice full of laughter. "Do you?"

"No!" chorused some of the younger children.

Taking her by the hand, Rungilivanster led her to the front of the crowd. "I think we should devise a suitable punishment for him," he suggested, his eyes studying her mockingly behind the mask. "Should we make him disappear, then?"

"Yes!" cried the children.

Pulling her close, the magician whispered in her ear, "Play along." And with an outthrust arm, he swept his cloak over her. It didn't feel like she had moved, but she saw instantly that she was no longer out in the street. The walls enclosing her formed a small room. The caravan?

"Where did he go?" she heard Rungilivanster ask from outside. "Oh, friend, are you here? Where have you gone to?"

"He's in your wagon!" Tremi cried out. "I can see him from here!"

"Ah, Master Tremi, you are indeed too clever for me," the magician admitted. "I suppose you think I've stolen him to turn into a puppet for my collection. That is what I do, you know," he told the children in a conspiratorial whisper. "I make puppets of the people who disappear. So don't make your parents angry with you, or they'll come to me and ask me to disappear you!"

"I don't believe it!" cried one.

"Me either!" added another. "You make 'em into dolls or toys! You said so last time!"

Rungilivanster chuckled. "Caught me out, have you? Well, let's just see." Opening the flap of the wagon, he checked the front of it, which was set off from where Alcione was by a small partition. She knew the magician saw her, but from there, no one else would be able to. "Come out the second time." He shaped the words without speaking, and Alcione nodded.

"I don't see him," said Rungilivanster, closing the flap and returning to his audience. Getting into the spirit of things, Alcione decided a little mischief might be in order, in return for his embarrassing her in front of all those people. Finding the back door to the small wooden caravan, she quietly opened it and slid down to the ground. Closing it behind her, she crept to the corner of the wagon and peeked around.

"What?" she heard Rungilivanster cry in surprise. "Why, he was there just a moment ago. I could have sworn it!" But the tone of his voice said he wasn't so much surprised as delighted. "And I've changed him back from a puppet. Where could he possibly have gotten off to?"

"Thought I'd come get some toffin, I did," Alcie said, strolling around from the back of the caravan. "If I'm to be turned into a toy or a puppet forever, I think I'd like to have one last snack first. Don't you think that's fair?"

Eagerly, children offered up pieces of the sticky treat. She selected one and popped it in her mouth. "Mat Rungilivanster, may I sit down now?" she asked politely. She felt a grin tugging at her lips. *This is fun!* She felt at ease in a way she hadn't since she'd entered the city.

The mask and his smile beneath it made the magician look like a plotting imp. He shook his head. "I think not, Mat Alcion. You're a rare one, to get free of my magic so easily. And you've not been punished yet, sitting there eating treats. What say you?" he asked the children. "Is making him my assistant for the night punishment enough?"

"No!" "Make him eat grass!" "Make him disappear into a toy again!"

Swallowing, Alcie said, "I don't think I like grass. And I don't really want to be a whistle or a game-piece." She saw that the children were staring at her now. Even if she said no, they would bother her all evening. If she agreed, maybe they would forget about her faster.

"If you promise it's only for one night, then I'll be your assistant. Agreed?"

Rungilivanster let out a loud peal of laughter. "You drive a hard bargain, boy! But I've my own assistant starting on the morrow, so I'll not lose anything by it. Agreed!"

ERICA CONVERSO

And taking her again by the hand, he led her into the next trick of the show. She had great fun, holding the cage for a piffle that turned into a pluffle, and watching as the large wooden dice she rolled seemed to come up exactly the numbers the magician said, in exactly the order he said them.

At one point, he called up a boy from the back of the audience to join him. The boy's hair caught the lantern's glow, so red it seemed to be on fire. An ysrei of the same coppery color twined around his neck, hanging on like a living scarf. His face was freckled, and his eyes large and dark, though it was impossible to see the color. He didn't speak, but seemed enraptured with the magic tricks they watched together during the rest of the show.

Together, Alcie and the boy held a box from which smaller and smaller boxes magically appeared. They tried to juggle balls that bounced off into the audience, until Rungilivanster showed them how it was properly done. The balls flew through the air in intricate patterns as the boy held Alcie's hand, awestruck. She could see no way of doing the things he did, yet Rungilivanster protested each time that it was not magic, merely a "gift of the eye and hand."

The end of the show came all too soon, and when Rungilivanster disappeared in a shower of glittering dust, the children clapped and cheered. When they saw he wasn't coming back, they soon lost interest and went home, some to the tenements of that street, others darting around corners and vanishing swiftly into the night.

In a few moments they were all gone, save Tremi, Alcie, and the freckled boy with the ysrei. Rungilivanster came out of his caravan, wearing his long dark cloak over an ordinary tunic and close-fitting breeches. The mask was gone, and he raked a hand through his unruly reddish hair as he leaned against the caravan's front door. He smiled at Alcie, tired but exhilarated, looking the way Alcie had felt that first day when she'd gathered up all of the arion that Goso had loosed.

"Did you give him the buckbell?" Alcie asked.

"Gave it to him earlier," Tremi responded easily. "Brilliant show, as always. I'll be off, then."

"When did you...?" But she didn't bother to ask. It wasn't her business. Quietly, Alcie thanked him and made to follow, only to find herself held back by Rungilivanster's strong hand on her shoulder. Beneath his nimble fingers her muscles tensed with nerves. She wasn't afraid he would hurt her, but she wasn't sure what he was going to say.

"Go on ahead, Tremi," she said when he saw that she wasn't following. Sola appeared torn over who to follow, then sat down at Alcie's feet and looked up not at her, but at Rungilivanster.

"Smart pup," the man said, and took a piece of luckle from his pocket. Tossing it into the waiting jaws, he pulled another few pieces of toffin from the same pocket. "For you," he said, handing them to

Alcione. "In gratitude. You'd make a fine assistant, you know, should you ever wish to take it up."

Alcione shook her head. "Much thanks, but no. I've already got a job. Why did you keep me here?" she asked, her anxiety growing. She still wanted to trust him, especially after the fun she'd had tonight, but what did he want with her?

"Easy, lass," he said. "And don't look at me like that," he added, seeing her sharp glance. "You ought to have told Tremi. He doesn't take kindly to liars."

She looked at the boy, standing silently to one side. "Elly, would you mind waiting in the back?" the magician asked.

The boy nodded, and swiftly disappeared around the rear of the wagon. Alcie looked around, making sure no one else was listening. "I know," she replied softly. "But at the time I didn't know him, and I couldn't think of…" She had begun to say, 'a way to escape,' then realized how utterly foolhardy that was. Too many people already knew too many of her secrets.

"Why don't you sit and tell me more about yourself, lass?" he asked, settling his rangy frame on the edge of the wagon's front board.

Alcie eyed him. "Why?"

Rungilivanster shrugged. "Would it help if I told you my secrets before you told me yours?"

"That depends on what they are."

Rungilivanster chuckled. "I knew I was right about you – you do drive a hard bargain. Fine, then.

I'll tell you one secret to start with, one I imagine you've already guessed: I spoke with Tremi earlier in the afternoon, while you were slaving away for our friend Goso." He spoke of the other man lightly, but with an undercurrent of mild disdain. His tone reminded her of someone, but Alcie couldn't recall who.

He went on. "We'd meant only to catch up on old times; Tremi is a dear friend. But that's neither here nor there. The point is, we started out talking about us and wound around to you. Tremi told me a very interesting story that was full of holes."

"It's not!" Alcie replied fiercely. "You said it yourself, he hates liars."

"So he does." Rungilivanster peered at her in the lamplight. "So why would he lie about you, and what could be so dire as to give him cause to do it?"

"Why do you care?" she spat out. His assessing eyes told her that he already had his suspicions on that point. "Please, just leave me alone!"

"No," he said calmly. "Tremi has been my friend for a long time. I wouldn't like to see him hurt."

"He's my friend, too!" Alcie protested. "Please believe that and stop asking me questions I can't answer." Biting her lip, she huffed out a breath. "I was starting to like you, only now you ask too many questions."

Rungilivanster choked back another spurt of laughter as she glared at him. "I've often been told so." Ducking his head a bit so that he met her eyes, he told her seriously, "I find I've come to like you too, lass. Tremi said you were that sort of person, someone people like right off. He's right. Will you tell me how I can help?"

Alcie was troubled by his admission. "I'm not helpless," she said softly. "I've come this far, and I could've done it alone."

"You misunderstand," Rungilivanster objected. "That wasn't an insult but a compliment. I could say you're charming, and it would be true. But you could be ornery and ugly and still be what you are."

"And what is that?" she asked, looking away from him.

"Brave. You can see it in your eyes. After I called him on it, Tremi told me the truth about who you've been running away from."

"Why?"

She could almost feel his gaze upon her back. "Why did he tell me, or why did I ask you? To the former, it's because Tremi and I trust each other, and that ought to speak worlds for whether you can put faith in me, and to the latter, because I wanted to see if you could learn to trust me as well. Apparently it's too soon for that."

"I don't trust anyone," she said. "Not even Tremi. That's why I haven't told him yet. If he found out I lied to him he might turn me in. Huin knows I'm a girl and she and Raka both know I was born well, but they're Fenlanders, and can't tell anyone without getting suspected of mischief themselves. Although Raka hates me," she muttered bitterly. "She'd tell in a minute if she could."

"Oh?" There was a world of meaning in the syllable. "If she'd wanted to, she would have, my dear. There are those who would listen here."

Now Alcie did turn to him, her eyes wide with fear. "That's not true!" she whispered. And then, panic setting in, she tried to hop off the wagon and run. But Rungilivanster's hold on her arms was strong, and he wasn't about to let her leave.

"Listen to me for one bedeviled minute, you little fool!" he told her harshly. And in his words, she finally understood what he'd been trying to tell her. Bedeviled had been one of Hermion's favorite words. A curse without actually cursing, he'd told her. It had also been one of the words Tremi had told her to forget. She stopped struggling and sat back down, sagging against the front board.

"You're like me!" she guessed, praying she wasn't wrong. "You're highborn!"

Rungilivanster slapped a hand to his forehead. "Give the lassie a prize, at last. Aye. Here's another secret if you like: my given name, which very few people – among them your own lucky self – know, is Tion. And you are?"

"Alcione," she whispered.

"Well, Middy Alcione," Tion said, "as one friend to another, I'm asking you what I can do to help. It was bad enough seeing everyone else killed, so I'd like to do what I can to keep you out of trouble."

"Are – are there any more of us?" Her brows lowered suspiciously. "Tremi's not one of us, is he?"

Tion smiled. "Not for a thousand dagats, and never tell him you said so. He'd be absolutely horrified." He loosened his grip on her, relaxing and flipping a coin idly through his fingers.

"I know of two others. One is a dear friend who's left for parts unknown, and the other is Elly." He looked towards the back of the wagon. "I would ask that you don't question them or me as to how we avoided a similar fate."

"And you won't ask me," Alcie stated firmly. "Fine. Did Tremi tell you about Romi?" A sudden thought occurred to her. "You're old enough – were you ever a Rider?"

Tion nodded almost imperceptibly. "One of the Raia, the students, once upon a time. Tremi told me you've rescued all of the arion from your family's stables, and that you mean to keep Romi for your own."

"Yes – I mean, aye, only I don't know how. He caused an awful lot of trouble in the marketplace earlier today, and Goso wants me to pay for it. I've only got a few dagats left, though, and I don't know how to make or sell things."

"And now we come to it," Tion said. "That's why I kept you here tonight, after Tremi had spoken to me. He can't help you, so he asked me if there was aught I could do, being that I'm as clever a fellow as I am. And something came to me, but you'll have to trust me a little for it. Can you?"

"A little," she begrudged him.

"That'll do. I've an arion of my own, Sleepy, stabled here in the Hollows. As far as the barn manager knows, Rungilivanster the Magnificent found him loose during the riots and took a shine to him. I've a fair amount of coin, both from my performances and other..." he hesitated briefly, "odd jobs I do during the daylight hours."

Alcione suspected this was yet another question not to ask him. *It seems like everyone I've met has secrets...or is it just that people with secrets meet each other because they stay away from people who haven't any?*

"There are open stalls in this barn," Tion continued. "One for your arion and one where you, Elly, and the pup can sleep. I'd pay for them. I'd also pay for the damage you caused in your entertaining little frolic this afternoon."

Alcione studied him, trying to gauge his expression in the shadows. "And what would I do to repay you for this?"

Tion angled his head and seemed to consider it. "I don't suppose you'd accept simple charity?" She shook her head. "No? Good for you. How does this sound? You'll help me train Elly, as he's rather shy to be my assistant, and you'll mind Sleepy and see he gets out for a bit each day to take the air, as I can't always do it myself. He won't give you any trouble, as that ruffian of yours did."

"That'll hardly be enough to pay you back for what you're doing, let alone give me a chance to make something to support myself on."

Tion's appraisal of her darkened face yielded an approving nod. "You'll have the rest of the day to yourself, and I encourage you to keep working for Goso over on Keecy Street. He may be a clod, and cheap into the bargain, but he'll not refuse to pay you what you're due."

He took out a coin he'd been flipping and tossed it into the air. Alcie watched it as it came down and disappeared into his hand. "You'll pay me for lodging and stabling, and you'll earn your meals working for me. We'll discuss rates at a reasonable hour of the day. Any spare dagats you earn will be yours to do with as you will."

Alcie nodded, trying to work it out in her head. Sums had never been her strong suit. "You'll still be losing a great deal of money," she concluded.

"Perhaps a bit. And so I will by taking on Elly for an assistant. As I said, it's not for you to worry about that. It's a sorry world indeed when a man can't help his neighbor."

"How can I repay you, though?" she asked, feeling guilty.

Tion patted her shoulder, then nudged her off the wagon onto the ground. "You'll do me a good turn or give a hand to someone else further down the road. That's payment enough for me."

Alcie could swear her head was spinning. "I…thank you," she told him, not knowing what else to say. "I've done nothing to deserve your generosity."

"You didn't deserve what happened to your family, either. And…" His expression turned black for a moment, and she wondered what he was struggling to say. Finally, he simply said, "I have my own sins to atone for. Consider this your way of helping me."

She knew when not to press an issue. "Where do I sleep tonight?" she asked, gathering up Sola in her arms. He had sat silent and alert as a sentry during their conversation.

"Back with Tremi in the wagon. You'll move your arion in the morning, when I come to fetch you. I'll pay Goso whatever he paid others for the damages, and," he gave a wry smile, "likely a great deal more besides. Then I'll explain to him the arrangement we've made. I have only one more condition into the bargain."

Of course, Alcie thought. *It's never that easy.* "What is it?" she questioned guardedly.

Tion's smile was white against the backdrop of the caravan. "You'll work for me as a girl. You'll tell Tremi the truth before I find you tomorrow morn, or I'll tell him myself."

"And what about Goso and Deena and Raka?"

"Leave Goso and his daughter to me. Huin will explain to her niece. Promise me."

"I promise," Alcione said, and grasped his outstretched hand to seal it. Then, she had an unusual thought. "How do you know how all of them are related to each other?"

Tion smiled. "How do you think? I traveled with them last year for a few weeks. I had just become Rungilivanster – simply for my own frivolous amusement, you understand – and I was testing him out in secret. I tried to put on a show and got booed out of town when one of my tricks went very wrong." He winced, remembering.

"If the traders hadn't been leaving the next morning, I'd have been clapped in irons and paraded through the town coated in pitch and feathers. But there's time enough later to tell that tale in full. You need to get to bed."

She reached down to pat Sola, who had curled close to her, and nodded. "Good night, then. And thank you."

Walking towards the bridge, she tried to make sense of her first evening in Ianthe. More nobles, a second job, a place to live with no fear of losing Romi…her thoughts whirled round and round dizzily. What it came down to in the end, though, was Tion's ultimatum. She had made a friend and ally tonight, someone who could help her while she searched for the crown. But would his offer cost her Tremi's respect and friendship?

- CHAPTER 13 -
Truth and Lies

By THE TIME ALCIONE opened her eyes the next morning, the sun was already rising. The air was clear and crisp. Her dreams had been muddled and spooky, the same blend of horrifying imagery and actual past events that she'd accustomed herself to in the weeks after the fire. They didn't come every night anymore, but often enough that she was almost used to their unpleasant nighttime visits.

Last night, she had been caught in a web of spun silverlight, surrounded by the bright lights of the fulgora, whipping around her and biting at her hair. From a distance she could hear Tremi accusing her, shouting, "You lied to me! You're a liar! I should never have helped you!"

Beside her, the real Tremi was still asleep, snoring gently. Goso was asleep under the wagon, with Deena sleeping soundly up front. Raka and Huin had already moved out to their new lodging in Shopkeep Square, and while she would miss the older woman's quiet confidence, she was more than glad to have seen the last of Huin's crabby niece.

Remembering immediately her promise to Tion, she felt her stomach drop. *If he's going to hate me, he'll hate me,* she thought. *Best to find out before anyone else wakes to see this.* So she shook aside the nightmare, scooted across the wagon to Tremi, and tapped him on the shoulder.

His eyes blinked open and focused on her. "It's early yet," he said, no trace of drowsiness in his voice. He had told her, once, of the constant noise of the Hollows at night. The whole quarter was constantly restless, he'd said, never truly asleep even when their eyes closed. Alcie wondered if she would get used to it.

"I have something to tell you," she stated, feeling as if her body were very far apart from her voice. So scared of his response, she almost felt as if she were watching it from someone else's eyes. *Or maybe I just wish I was.*

Her voice came from some other person, while another Alcie stood off to one side, caught in a web of nightmares and fear. She didn't know which Alcione it would be worse to be.

Sensing her sobriety, he sat up and grinned at her. "Whatever it is can't be so bad." But her grave expression didn't alter. "You'd better get on with it, then. What's on your mind?"

"I..." *How to phrase it?* "I haven't told you the whole truth about something, Tremi." *I'm a liar. You'll hate me. I deserve it!*

He didn't look angry, but he was no longer smiling either. "Does that mean you're telling it now?" he asked. His voice had gone cold. "Or telling me you can't tell me?"

"I'm telling it now." Slowly, she reached up and loosed the cap she always slept with from her head. Her hair, now down to her shoulders, swung free. "It used to be longer than this. I cut it before I came to the traders." She faltered, but made herself go on. "I cut it because I didn't want anyone to find out that I'm a girl."

For a moment there was complete silence. Tremi examined her from her hair to her toes. His gaze lingered on her face, her hair, as if he were trying to puzzle out a great mystery. She wanted to flinch from his scrutiny, but forced herself to meet his stare.

"Is that all?" he asked finally.

"Yes," she promised. "There's nothing else. I wouldn't have lied to you, Tremi, only I didn't know you then. And afterwards, I wasn't sure what you'd think, a girl working with arion." The words tumbled out of her.

"I don't like it," he confessed, shaking his head. He looked pointedly at her legs and feet, covered in leggings and boots as opposed to a skirt and slippers. "Not proper, even in these times. But I suppose it's not up to me. Will you be acting like a girl from now on? Is that why you told me?"

"Ti – Rungilivanster," she amended, "knew I was one, right off. He made me swear to tell you, since he wants me to act like a girl if I'm to work for him. I don't know why, but he does. We've made an agreement. I wanted to thank you for that, by the way."

"We all help each other in a pinch," he told her, shrugging it off. "It's what's right. The traders did with me, and I with you, as much as I could. What's your real name?"

"Alcione."

He drummed his fingers against the plank floorboards in thought. Deena gave a great yawn as if she meant to wake, then turned over with a delicate snore. "You were a daughter of the house?" Tremi asked, lowering his voice. "I suppose that's why you looked so silly up on Romi's back. I thought you were just too young to know much riding, but you didn't know any at all, did you?"

"I knew a bit," she confessed. "I *do* love the arion. I spent hours helping the Stabler. And you know that's truth," she added, "because you've seen I know what I'm doing. I may not have ridden much, but I know everything else!"

"Explains a lot," he said curtly. Then he moved to gather his sack and brushed past her to slide out the front of the wagon. "Come on. Let's get breakfast. And later today, if you're not busy, we'll go visit Huin and see if she's got any clothes for you."

Alcione was both shocked and relieved. "You're not angry? Why aren't you mad at me? I thought you hated it when people lied."

Tremi beckoned her to hurry up and hop down. "I do," he agreed, "but I can understand why you did it. Of course, if you lie to me about anything else…" His face spoke volumes. Alcie rushed to reassure him she never would. "All right," he said, after she had sworn it to him by the moon and the stars and every halay-bug under every stone, "I hear you. Now get Sola and let's go. As soon as we're done eating, I'm for the bridge to work."

Between mucking out Adrie's stall and one of the other arion whose name she didn't yet know, Tion caught up to her. "Have you a moment to spare?" he asked.

Alcie walked with him to the far end of the stable, leaving Elly petting Adrie. "I've spoke to Goso and explained everything," Tion told her. "He's a bit befuddled about you being a girl, but I've bewildered him thoroughly enough that he should accept it."

He gave her a cheeky wink. "I wouldn't worry. I came to get your troublemaker and show you where to put him, if you can get away for a bit."

"I just have to finish a few more stalls," she said, "if you can wait."

153

"I can do better," he answered. "Where's another pitchfork?" He lowered his voice, then added, "You don't get to be a rider without knowing ears from tail."

They worked in silence until all the stalls were finished. When Alcie had pulled the clean bedding down from the edges of Romi's stall, she took the lead rope she'd left hanging on a hook beside the door and looped it through his halter. He had been pacing his stall when she came in, stopping every few moments to look out the window at the street. He ignored her, as if to say, *you left me before, so I'm going to pretend you're not here now.*

When she tugged on the lead rope, he gave her an affronted glance. "Yes, I want you to go that way," she said, exasperated. "Don't look so shocked about it."

"He is going to drearier accommodations," Tion remarked. "Do you suppose he knows?"

"He's just angry at me for leaving him alone last night." She rubbed Romi's neck soothingly. "Let's go," she said to Tion. "I told Buske I'd be back to help fill the hay nets."

As they left the stable, they walked on either side of Romi, heading for Trifira Bridge. Alcie was startled by the difference – yesterday the bridge had been empty of all but the shut-up caravan wagons parked for the evening as they settled in.

Now, most of the wagons had been moved off to Shopkeep Square to park along an empty street by the river known as Caravan Way, leaving the bridge open for business. In autumn and winter it was a place for temporary seasonal workers to set up shop. In spring and summer, it was home to the traders.

Trifira Bridge had come alive in the sunlight. The air crackled with the same energy as the market days in Lymnoi that Alcie remembered. Compact stalls were set up along the entire bridge, while wandering merchants milled back and forth, hawking their wares in loud, shrill, and boisterous tones.

A musician was lost in the crowds, sawing away on some sort of string instrument. An artist stood to one side, busily sketching the scene while calling out the virtues of his finished products to the world. A dark-skinned Fenlander crone shook a rattle and offered to tell fortunes for the price of a palm crossed with dagats. Another Fenlander was decked out as a living clothes-stand of merchandise – her widespread arms and neck draped with dozens of beautifully dyed scarves that fluttered in the breeze.

Alcie could see several of the traders from the caravan out as well – those who had merely leased wagon space, like Tremi. She searched, but couldn't find Tremi himself anywhere.

The bridge was a sea of color, with the merchants leading the charge in vivid vests. Many wore colored hats that resembled her rustler cap, presumably to keep them from sunstroke. The carts too were a rainbow: a stand of varied fruits, meat pasties with jam and other fillings oozing out, and a man carrying what looked like several pounds of leather boots. Pitches hawked at dizzying speed filled her ears.

"Boots, made by Mat Cobbler on Hebbery Lane, best boots in all Ianthe! Follow the Bootman if you please, and let him guide your feet to ease!"

"Fine weather for pie, middies! Give joy to your husbands and children! Come, Middy, buy a bushel of quise, do, and have yourself a lovely pie by eventime!"

Alcione heard Tion laugh at her as she craned her head in every direction, trying to absorb it all. Beside her, Elly's mouth was open a little. In the day, his hair was a mop of the brightest carrot-red hair she'd ever seen, and his eyes – huge as saucers – were a dark blue.

"You can blink, you know," Tion suggested to them. "It won't disappear. Even I couldn't do that!"

She smiled up at him, and saw that somehow he had slipped Romi's lead rope from her hand and was now holding the colt steady, keeping a strong hand on his neck and stroking it soothingly. "Thank you," she said, wondering how he'd managed it.

"Magician," he said by way of explanation to her unspoken query. "Or rider, if you like," he added more quietly. "The bridge market will be open until supper every day, you know. And Shopkeep Square is open even later. You should take your meals and breaks there if you want to explore."

"I will," Alcie agreed, already anticipating long walks back and forth across the bridge, a small satchel of toffin in hand. A small part of her thought guiltily, *And when will you do that? Before or after rescuing your family?*

When they had gone halfway across, keeping out of the way of the other passersby, they found Tremi against the side of the bridge, his wares dangling from his neck, arms, and the pockets of a dapper multicolored vest that Alcie had seen Huin working on several days ago. The halay made a stunning display, iridescent and catching the sun like a reflection on a lake. For a moment, it almost seemed like Tremi was wearing a suit of silvery armor.

Alcie ran up and reached out a hand to touch one of the charms she had helped string up before. "Ah, ah," Tremi reprimanded. "It's merchandise now. No grubby paws." He looked down pointedly at her dirt-covered palm and she quickly let it retreat to her side.

"Sorry," she told him, "but everything looks so wonderful. Have you had many sales today?"

"Enough," was his short response. "Market's poor, for all we've got plenty of gawkers takin' up space."

Tion and Romi came up behind her. "Would you like one?" he asked Alcie.

"Oh, no thanks," she said quickly. "You're doing more than enough already."

"I'll have one, then," Tion said, considering. "Mat Tremi, which one do you think would suit me best? Have you one for dancing, or luck in dice, perhaps?"

"You don't play dice," Tremi objected. "Or dance. And if you did, you'd not need my luck to do well at it." He selected one of the four-bug pendants and slipped it over Tion's proffered neck. "For general good luck. Nine dagats, that."

"Nine?" Tion scoffed. "Hardly. No more than five, you blackguard."

"Eight and a half. Took a fair bit of work, finding four that matched just so." Tremi grinned at him.

"Six, and no more. It's bugs and string."

"Eight. Worked hard on that, I did. Pretty bugs, expensive string, and a great deal of my time."

Tion let out an exaggerated sigh. But he and Tremi both seemed pleased, as if this were a dance they did often, and well. "You cut me to the quick, boy, but I suppose I can give you seven for it, if you'll throw in a three-shell pendant and that little bracelet for seven as well."

Tremi's eyebrows raised. "The pendant was six, the bracelet four. How'd you get seven?"

"Eight, and fifteen for the lot, brat."

Tremi grinned at him. "Agreed." Shaking on it, they made the exchanges. Keeping Romi in hand when a young boy darted just behind him, Tion handed the second pendant and the ring to Alcie.

"The pendant is for you," he told her. "No arguments."

Handing the ring to Elly, he smiled. "A pleasure doing business with you, Mat Tremi, as always."

"You as well, Mat Magician, sir," he said, with a bob of his head. "Wear your jewels in health, if not in wealth," he added with a salute.

Rolling his eyes, Tion tugged on the lead rope and led Romi forward.

They exited the bridge for the Hollows, leaving the crowds and color of the bridge. Following Tion as he led her through the lower city, Alcie soaked up the new scenery. At every corner she marveled, not only at the unique architecture and sheer size of the city, but at the simple fact that no one thought the group of them out of place here. Tremi had been right, once again. As long as she kept her mouth shut, she could pretend she was just like everyone else.

If we look so alike that no one can tell noble and commoner apart, then how can we be so different that all these people wanted us dead? She wondered, frowning a bit. *The nobles can't all have been so horrible, could they? I know my family wasn't!*

They settled Romi in a street-facing stall in the Hollows barn. It wasn't as nice as the stall on Keecy Street, but Alcie supposed it couldn't be helped. Tion introduced her to his own arion, Sleepy, a golden palomino with a bleached mane and tail. True to his name, the lazy gelding dozed in a corner when they arrived. He wakened eagerly, however, upon presentation of kert and a new person to slobber over. Alcie knew right away that they would be good friends.

When they were done, Alcie returned to Keecy Street, stopping by Huin's shop for a moment to gather two skirts and a dress Tion had purchased for her. She was to wear them when she helped him with the magic show each night.

However, she and Tion had agreed that since her tunic was already dusty, she ought to keep using it for stable work. It would also make things easier for her, as most folk still weren't used to seeing women anywhere near arion.

That night at supper, with Goso and Tremi sitting in, they worked out her schedule and how much she would be paid. It wasn't as much as Tremi made on most days, and for that she was both grateful and concerned. Tremi had it difficult enough making a living in the city – with less, at least she felt she hadn't fallen into a lucky situation that he deserved far more than she.

She worked in the magic show again that night, and was amazed when Tion went through the entire night without once repeating a trick from his prior show. Tremi mentioned afterwards that he rarely did, and rarely needed to. Rungilivanster the Magnificent was not only a magician, but a court jester, juggler, acrobat, poet, and storyteller.

That night he performed a few tricks first, but then began to tell tales of the olden days. To the magician's delight, Alcie found herself chiming in. Tion told the story of Galamond the Wise, but forgot to tell the children that, "he was a good deal taller than most men and everybody had to look up at him, and that was the *real* reason why they said his head was always in the clouds!" Even Elly had a role, soberly asking if all that had really happened, and if so, where was the proof?

Alcie found her storytelling skills engaged as she made up details, like what might have happened to the bronze saddle Lynceor had sent by messenger to the bride's father. "If it didn't get there, what happened to it?" one of the children had asked. Alcie delighted in spinning the tale of the bronze saddle, and its unusual fate.

Near the end, Tion asked the children for stories about their own lives. She learned that the new harvest wasn't taking well in the southern villages of the Sianna Valley, just north of the city, and the Arkos was displeased. Some of the children's parents were unhappy with the Arkos, and the children themselves didn't know what to make of him.

"Me ma said the Arkos ought to make the magian grow the harvest!" one girl called. "But she said he won't do aught unless he's paid first. That's how they work."

Belatedly, Alcie recalled how the Stabler had told her the Arkos had allied himself with one of the magians – workers of true magic exiled years ago to the islands beyond the sea. *I hope he does go to the Sianna,* she thought unhappily. *If he stays in the city, I'm not sure how I'll manage to get close to that crown!*

Alcie asked Tion later what he intended to use the information for. He simply shrugged and said he might keep it for one of his day jobs as a wandering jester in the higher districts. She wasn't convinced, but didn't try to pressure him into revealing any more.

All in all, her second day in Ianthe was as unusual and interesting as her first, so when she settled into her new home, a stall with fresh straw bedding for a mattress and a soft blanket to cuddle under, she had started to feel as if the city wasn't so frightening after all.

As Tremi had warned, the Hollows were still noisy even late at night, but with Elly and Sola fast asleep beside her and Romi silent in his stall next door, Alcione didn't mind. She tried to think how she might find a way into Kayre Ianthe to find the stones, but inevitably her eyes drifted shut and her thoughts fell away. Perhaps tomorrow she'd find the answer.

"More toffin, please!" Elly murmured in his sleep, and rolled over. Alcie's lips curved up at the thought. She closed her eyes to try to follow him into a candy-filled world of dreams.

- CHAPTER 14 -
The Arkos

IT TOOK HER A FEW days, but the elements of a plan gradually took shape in Alcie's mind. She pieced together the idea as she worked in the stables, only breaking for lunch, where Tremi introduced her to his "crew," a group of trader and city youths who banded together for meals and occasional get-togethers when they weren't working.

She got along well with pudgy Cormy, who ran errands and shared silly jokes, and with solemn Yvo, who carved wooden toys and had lost his father in the riots. She never spoke of her family, but Yvo understood without a word that she shared his reason for sorrow.

Raka fit in well with the other girls in the group, holding court as she shared stories of the road. She giggled with the girls over trivial things, and was at home teasing the boys as well. She seemed perfectly nice – Cormy even had a crush on her, which Raka gently tried to discourage. In fact, she was kind to everyone but Alcione.

Like Tremi, Raka was one of the leaders of the group. Watching from afar, Alcie could see how she might be fun to be around. But now that she'd learned her little "rich boy" was actually a girl, it made her nastier than ever when they were caught alone.

"How filthy our stable girl is today!" She'd remark, pinching at Alcie's worn tunic when no one else was looking. Or, "Is straw in your hair the new fashion, stable girl? I must tell the others at once!" And she'd giggle as she skipped away.

"I'll be glad to be away from her," Alcie mused to Sola as she finished her chores in Keecy Street. "It's time for us to start on our real quest. Orfel didn't open the door to Astraea just by standing around!"

Sola woofed an agreement. No one had been able to tell her what sort of creature he was, but he had become something of a mascot among the crew. At night, Tion used him as a comical part of the act, along with Elly's ysrei, Flip. Everyone loved petting and cosseting him and unlike Romi, who still only gave her an occasional sentence or flash of an image, Sola's expressive face spoke volumes without saying a word.

Now he cocked his head to one side and wagged his tail. "Ready to go?" Alcie asked. Sola trotted up the street and back. "You want me to follow? All right."

Sola started off determinedly up the hill towards Kayre Ianthe. As Sola led her forward, Alcie shook her head with bemused affection. She never considered the illogic of following him. He would lead her where she intended to go. Sola was no ordinary pup. "You are one strange whatever-you-are," she murmured.

The silhouette of Kayre Ianthe towered over the city. Alcie had seen it over the past few days and wondered about how to get in, but then Tion had distracted her with a funny anecdote, or someone had come to buy a charm, or Moti was trying to escape from his stall for the third time that day.

They came into the open square of the Royal Pavilion. As large as any grazing meadow in Montelymnë, it was paved with cobblestone and mostly empty at this time of day. Sola turned to play with Alcione, paws in front and rear end wiggling as he pounced at specks of dust.

She let him have his fun, and joined in by throwing a small stick for him to fetch. But after a few catches he stopped suddenly, head up and ears pricked. Alcie didn't hear anything, but the noise spurred Sola from dead stop into a furious run.

"Wait up, boy!" she called, and dashed after. Fortunately, the streets ahead were empty of passersby, this area having been transformed into barracks for the soldiers who patrolled the city and surrounding countryside.

The homes in the area were now occupied by those who worked directly for the Arkos, but Tremi said many had decided to keep plying their trades in the lower city because it was what they knew. Even in changing times, folk still needed food and clothing.

Alcie barely took notice. Ahead loomed a huge iron-and-silver wrought fence that rose above the highest of the buildings lower on the hill, and traveled the entire perimeter of the Kayre. It crept in and out of her line of sight as Sola went in and out of the main streets and off into unoccupied passages. Finally, he reached a dead end and slowed.

Before Alcione lay a portion of the twenty-foot fence, far to the right of the main gate to the Kayre. It was a thick stone wall against which lay several heavy boxes. Out of breath, Alcie sat down on one. "Well?" she asked the pup. "We're here. Now what?"

Sola lay with his head on his paws and looked up at her. *What? I'm not going to tell you the whole puzzle,* his expression seemed to say. *Can't you figure out anything on your own?*

"Sure I can," Alcie argued. "But this was your plan, not mine, boy."

Getting to his feet with the animal equivalent of a sigh, he planted his front paws on a box. Alcione pulled him up beside her. Sola padded over to stand on a box in the corner. He poked at it with his paw and gave a sharp yet quiet bark.

Looking more closely, Alcie was surprised to find that this one was not properly sealed as the rest were. Tugging hard, she pulled the flaps up and discovered that the box was completely empty. And instead of a fourth side against the stone, where box, wall, and fence ought to have been, there was a hole. A secret passageway directly into the castle grounds!

"Sola, how did you know…?" she breathed. But he had laid down again, and now appeared to be asleep. She smiled, amused and nervous at the same time. "I suppose you've earned a rest." She patted his head and scratched under his chin. He kept his eyes shut, and though she knew he was probably faking it, she let him be.

Accepting that she was on her own, Alcie poked her head into the box and, upside down, tried to make out if there were guards on the other side of the passage. The reassuring sight of underbrush and untrimmed bushes greeted her. Righting herself, she hopped into the box.

The entrance was a brilliant illusion, she thought, worthy of Tion's own flair for trickery. On one side was the wall and boxes, while the other showed an unappealing hedge of wrinkly bundleberries. Hidden in between was a large opening in both fence and wall, and a narrow space behind the bushes where, Alcie hoped, one could get onto the palace grounds.

Heart thudding, she crept to the bushes and peeked around. No one was in sight. She rose slightly to see if her path was truly clear. Praying to Tanatos that the soldiers had gone to the tavern to drink the health of the Arkos, Alcie pushed free of the bushes.

No one was near. Alcie let go the breath she hadn't realized she'd been holding. She could see the Kayre now, and it was a marvel. Gleaming and burnished with gold, it was bigger than any building she'd ever seen.

Even from the outer courtyard, she could see huge windows with light coming from within – glass panes instead of dark tapestries covered them. Countless turrets pierced the sky, with silver, red, and green pennants flapping proudly in the breeze.

Hardly more than specks when seen from far below, it took Alcie a moment to recognize the sentries patrolling the parapets. Forcing herself to look casual, she made her way across the grounds, aiming for what appeared to be a gazebo and a garden beyond. She needed to look as if she belonged here. So what if she was walking the edge of the Kayre? *I'm looking for bundle-berries. Or something like that.*

The gazebo was old and faded, but beautiful in a sad sort of way. Whimsical flowers swirled around the pale yellow structure, with maidens in lovely gowns peeping from between the petals. And there were arion, glorious wings and noble heads raised to the air in salute. Alcie smiled sadly.

The garden was ringed with a badly trimmed hedge, and she wondered if the Arkos considered a gardener too frivolous an expense. She knew from Tremi that it was a reasonable claim, but it didn't stop her from looking with regret at what she imagined once had been.

The plants were shriveled and withered. Left to their own devices, they had twined together so that all got little sunlight and had lapsed into grim tangles. The only splash of life came from the blood-red skurry-weed, curling its tendrils around the garden like outstretched claws. Skurry grew everywhere, and if you didn't cut it, it took so much water from the ground that it killed all else in its path.

Alcie shuddered at the bleak picture the failed garden made. A moment later, the sound of voices had her ducking for cover behind the gazebo, in the shelter of the ruined cluster of plants. Crouched down, she waited as the voices came closer.

"Please, sir, if you'd only let me speak with him!" The first voice was gravelly and low, but female. Alcie glanced from between the bushes and saw a tall, dark-haired girl, urgently tugging at the sleeve of a man clad all in white.

"Let go, you foolish child." The man removed her arm with pinched fingers. He dropped her hand as if it stung. Despite his light touch, the girl flinched.

Alcie took in the man's white robes, the oversized black collar, the five-point white hat. She needed no introduction. This was the magian.

Father said the magians have been in exile since before even he was born. Their hands burn when they touch you, and they can kill you with a word if they're angry. Some said they left to practice their magic in secret, but Father told me he thought the old King banished them before they could rise up against him.

The man was every bit as intimidating as she'd thought. He stared at the girl for a long moment, and she shrank from his gaze. "I only wanted to talk to him," she muttered sullenly. Alcie gave her credit for bravery, and prayed the magian couldn't sense that anyone else was near them.

The magian sniffed disdainfully. "Young Master Warridy has no time for common acquaintances any longer." He stressed the word *common* as he turned up his nose slightly at the girl. "And I have important matters to attend to. You may leave."

His meaning was clear. Squaring her shoulders, the girl made to go. But then she stopped. She stared up at the magian, and Alcie recognized the anger in her eyes. It was the anger she carried around in her heart, the anger that had brought her here to the stronghold of her enemy to find the stones. "I'll find a way to him," the girl said softly. "Not you or anyone will stop me."

She walked quickly away. The magian stayed a moment longer, turning to view the gazebo. Alcie closed in on herself, praying and praying he wouldn't see her. Finally, she heard footsteps moving away. She didn't dare take her head from her chest. Minutes passed before she finally had the nerve to look up and see that the magian was gone.

It took her a shaky moment to look around, and ascertain that the way was clear. When she could stand, she began to walk to the edge of the garden nearest the castle walls. Approaching the hedge wall from one side to keep out of sight, she saw that the entire field beyond it was filled with soldiers and servants. What in the world was going on? And how would she ever manage to get through?

She was about to return the way she'd come when she heard the murmur of various conversations drop to an awed hush. Moving closer, she anchored herself to a bare branch among the hedge and leaned out to get a better look.

The spectators gazed up along the gold-embossed walls of the Kayre's inner courtyard to see a slender figure standing upon a marble balcony. From her vantage, Alcie could see that he wore simple clothes: a brown robe and a brocaded ivory over-cloak. Pale skin stretched over a small, unlined face, and he wore his hair in short, pale blond ringlets. Upon his head was a plain circlet of gold that glinted in the sun.

The Arkos.

He held up a hand and let it rest upon the stones surrounding the balcony. "My friends," he addressed them, his voice not resonant nor loud, yet compelling all the same. "Welcome. I appreciate you taking the time to hear my words."

As one, the audience raised their right hands in the salute Alcione knew had become traditional for soldiers of the Arch-master's regiment as they passed on routine inspections of the city. It was a gesture the Arkos himself had devised, folk said, to show respect without the groveling degradation of kneeling or scraping the ground in deep bows and curtseys.

The only one who did not make the salute was the magian, standing opposite a man Alcie assumed to be the captain of the guard. The message was obvious: if any dared to harm the Arkos, they would have to get past his protectors first.

"As many of you are aware," the Arkos began, "it is now the two-month anniversary of our rise to power, and thus to freedom." With a start, Alcie pressed her hand against her mouth. Two months today since her family…and she hadn't even known! A sob tore at her throat, but she forced it back down.

The Arkos continued. "We have done exceedingly well in this time, having rid ourselves of the contaminating influences of our past and replaced them with new dreams for the future. We are committed to raising enough food so that no man, woman, or child will ever starve again, and while the crops yielded this spring are not as plentiful as we would have liked, we must do the best with what nature offers us. And we must then make further improvements."

He spread his arm from one side of his body to the other, indicating everyone in the audience, and presumably everyone in the city as well. "Every person among us is responsible for each other's success. Every man and woman among us can be held accountable for failure. And so I come among you first, my most loyal brethren, to ask your suggestions at this critical juncture between our present and the glorious future which lies before us."

No one spoke at first. Then, timidly, a hand raised in the middle of the crowd. "Speak your name," the Arkos invited, "and your thoughts, my friend."

"I be Gilmey, Arkos, sir. I'd be one o' the militia ye sent t' examine the situation in the Sianna Valley. I'm born there, an' folk need help wi' the plantin' if ye want enough fer the fall crops t' feed all the city an' beyond. So I, uh…I propose draftin' some city folk as ain't got as much money to help out. On'y the farmer's can't afford t' pay 'em."

The Arkos seemed to be digesting the information, as he remained quiet for a moment. "That's all, sir," said Gilmey, struggling to fill the silence.

The Arkos looked down at his audience. "Mat Gilmey makes several good points. I shall be happy to dip into the city's treasury to pay extra laborers in the valley basin for the rest of the planting season.

Yes?" he pointed to another raised hand in the crowd.

"Pardon me, sir Arkos, but what'll the city's pockets be worth if ye bankrupt us payin' folk for every job as needs be done in the whole of the land? Oh, and me name is Tup Miller."

"You too are wise, Mat Miller. I am indeed humbled to be charged with the leadership of such a wise populace. I will look into this. Perhaps some workers will consent to volunteer, as the work will be beneficial to them come the onset of winter. Or perhaps we could encourage a trade – workers in the field could receive a larger ration of food come winter."

Alcione was spellbound. As the conference continued, she found herself listening intently to each of the suggestions the crowd made, and the rational, courteous manner in which the Arkos answered each of their queries.

When a quarrel broke out, instead of ordering the disturbance removed, he called for the two men to be brought to the front. The captain stepped forward with a few of his men, ready to drag them away. But the Arkos simply held up a hand.

"Not yet, Captain," he said, his voice oddly gentle. "They will state their grievances respectfully, and then I will help them to a fair outcome. Gentlemen?"

Like a parent teaching feuding boys to mind their manners, the Arkos conducted the men to explain the problem. After, he made a judgment and the men went back to their places, having shaken hands and agreed to abide by the decision.

It was impossible. How could this man, who treated equally each and every one of his subjects, from his counselors on the balcony to a young chambermaid too small to be seen above the crowd, be the same one who had sent her family to their deaths?

Queasy, Alcione sank to her knees behind the hedge. No wonder so many people had been willing to follow him to revolution! He was charismatic and intelligent. He spoke with the way of one who had been book-learned, as a priest or even a noble.

Instead of treating peasants as if they were kings, he treated them like themselves. And more, he treated them as he allowed them to treat him. He was doing his best to care for them, and although Alcie knew from living in the Hollows that his promises weren't always carried through, she knew now why hearing them had incited people to riot for him. To kill for him.

With ice in her heart, Alcione found a dark thought forming in her mind. *If I had been living as I do now, scraping by with only help from kind people like Tion and Tremi to survive, watching rich nobles wasting food while others starved, I might have followed him too.*

- CHAPTER 15 -
The Crooked Man

IT WAS A DIFFERENT Alcione who ran from the ruined garden back to the wide field of the outer grounds of Kayre Ianthe. She felt numb, her fingers icy as they tightened into fists at her sides. Trembling, she made her way towards the hedge of bundle-berries, too shaken to notice her surroundings.

"Hey, you!"

Skidding to a halt, Alcie's eyes wheeled to find the source of the voice. A guardsman stood behind her, looking grim. "What are you doing out here?" he asked. His face made it clear he would brook no nonsense.

Alcione was racking her mind for a good explanation when Sola bounded out of the bushes with a happy-go-lucky bark. In his jaws he clutched a branch of berries like a peace offering. The guard laughed.

"What is that thing?" he queried. "He looks like an o'ergrown ysrei!"

"Not exactly sure," she told him, and exhaled before she could feel faint from nerves and relief. "But he's mine. I was chasing him when he ran down here all of a sudden. Strange little fellow, he is," she said, lapsing into city cant.

"That's so," the guard agreed. "Well, young master," he said, and Alcie realized she still had her stable gear and cap on to cover her hair, "it'll be dark soon, and you'd best take your young friend and get on home. Captain Trafford wants everyone out by sunset. Are you done visitin' yer family?"

Alcie realized he thought she must have come in earlier. She barely missed a beat as she answered. "Aye. I was on my way out when he ran off." She scratched behind Sola's ears and removed the branch from his mouth. "Good even to you, sir."

"And to you." With a respectful tip of his head, he walked away.

Alcione regarded Sola as they walked towards the front gate. "You sure know just when to show up," she told him. "I wonder how?"

Sola yipped, and offered her the branch for her to throw to him. "You'll look awfully silly chasing a flying bunch of berries," she informed him. "But it's your choice."

When they got to the gate, Alcione simply nodded to the guard on duty. Not having been there earlier in the day, he had no reason to suspect her, and besides, he seemed distracted by Sola. The pup allowed the man to pet him and even gave him several eager licks on the hand.

Alcie watched with fascination. Sola was rarely so friendly with anyone upon first meeting them. *You're bamboozling him!* Tremi's term for tricking someone was apt, Alcie was certain. *Not that a Talaria would have been so lax at a gate. Still, it's no chance you're so nice all of a sudden. What are you, Sola?*

The guard opened the gate immediately, and after letting him bid a final farewell to Sola, Alcie took her pup and left the Kayre behind, starting downhill towards Caulburne Alley.

She had only reached the far end of the Royal Pavilion when the Citadel bells began to chime, but she was too tired to bother running. Walking at a pace she could manage, Alcie made her way across the city towards the Hollows.

When she arrived in the alley, Tion's show was in full swing, with Elly holding Flip in his hands as the ysrei tried to catch bubbles that seemed to appear from nowhere. They floated past his snout, popping as he got close to them. The children laughed uproariously as Elly teased the little ysrei. "Can't you go faster, Flip? You didn't get them all!"

At first, Alcione couldn't put her finger on just what was different about the show this time. After scolding her for being late, Tion brought her to the front and they held court for the children with the tale of Glissaudio, Singer of Waves, an old favorite of hers because of the funny scrapes he managed to get into.

She lost herself in the magician's embellishments, attempts to make her laugh and cheer her up. Somehow he knew how upset she was. Already, it seemed he could read her emotions just by looking at her. And yet something was off tonight. This time, the tension seemed not only to belong to her, but to Tion as well.

Just before the end of the show, she realized what it was. A silhouette detached from one wall of the alley. It was the figure of a man, lean and bent into a crooked shape against the stone building. Shifting his position a bit, he retreated from the glow of the lantern and disappeared.

After the show Alcie looked for him, but he was already gone. "Who was he?" she asked Tion.

"A friend," he replied. His voice was gentle, but his eyes told her not to ask more.

They packed up the props from the show in a companionable silence. Elly wasn't very strong, almost sickly compared to the energetic street children, but he never asked for help or took a break. She found she admired his determination. In a way, he reminded her of Hermion.

Tion offered to walk them back that night, and he and Elly laughingly filled Alcione in on what she had missed earlier in the show. By the time they reached the barn the three were all giggling together, as Elly put Flip on Sola's back, showing the trick he had intended to do before.

Sola treated the ysrei with care, but when Flip accidentally dug his claws into Sola's side, he yelped and tossed Flip back towards Elly's waiting arms. But Elly overbalanced, and boy and ysrei went crashing backwards straight into Tion.

Alcie watched them and stifled back a laugh. Then, she saw something move out of the corner of her eye. It was the shadow man from before. In the darkness of the unlit barn, all she could make out was a crooked form, angular and gaunt. He walked towards them with a noticeable limp in his left leg.

"If that is the best trick you can manage, magician, it seems well I did not twine my fate with yours."

His voice was oddly hushed in the noisy streets of the Hollows, yet distinctly clear. He spoke insultingly, but the acerbic words were tempered with what Alcie thought might have been a hint of indulgent amusement in someone less grim-looking.

Tion's face brightened as he steadied Elly and walked forward to embrace the man in the shadows. "Dar!" he said happily. "I felt almost certain that was you before, but I didn't dare stop to see."

"You would have lost your concentration."

"I would have alerted the entire crowd to your presence," Tion corrected mildly. "Be thankful I didn't."

"You'd never be so clumsy." The man called Dar eyed Alcie from over Tion's shoulder. "And who are your little minions?"

Tion turned back to them and chuckled. "Street urchins I picked to be my helpers. As you can see, they're rather clever, aren't they? The girl is Alcione, the boy Elistair."

"Unusual name for a girl."

"She's from the north. I'm told it's quite common there."

"Ah."

Well, Alcie thought. Whoever he was, this Dar made even Tremi at his most reluctant seem chatty.

"How long have you been back?" Tion asked. "And how long will you stay? Is there anything I can do to aid you in your work?"

Dar held up a hand to stop the barrage of polite but adamant questions. "I have been in the city for two hours. I intend to stay until my lord Arkos has need of my services elsewhere. As such, a place to sleep would be advantageous."

What? Alcie mentally revised her opinion. No noble would work directly for the Arkos! Tion himself kept a low profile, and spoke of the Arkos only if someone else brought him up first.

Perhaps the shadowy man was simply a soldier Tion had befriended. The magician did seem to be friends with everyone else who crossed his path.

"You can sleep in the caravan with me. I'll make room. That is, if you two don't mind staying on in the stall?" He shot a glance at Alcie and Elly, who shook their heads. "Is Storm with you?"

"Yes. I took the liberty of stabling him next to Sleepy."

"That's fine."

"Could you spare the time to him? I've other work to attend to and…" He trailed off, grimacing at his lame leg.

"I'll take care of it," Tion assured him. "Come with me and get some rest. You must be exhausted. Alcie, can I trust you to see to Stormweaver's comfort before you go to bed?"

Alcione nodded. She assumed from their talk that Stormweaver must be an arion, but did he belong to this man? The stranger called Dar couldn't be a noble, and he clearly wasn't a commoner if he could ride. Who was he?

Walking inside the barn, she heard the two men leave, talking in low murmurs. Elly took Flip and Sola and went into their shared stall.

It was dark, and Elly shivered a bit before Alcie tucked one of the cloaks they used for blankets around his shoulders. He nestled wordlessly into the pillow made of fresh hay. Flip lay at his head, tail curved around his coppery curls. "Alcie?" he asked softly. "What do you dream about?"

She debated how best to answer him. She knew Elly was aware of her nightmares, and she'd woken to see him shuddering in his sleep as well, fighting a host of private terrors. He looked so much younger than his ten years sometimes, and yet on nights like this his eyes were old with horror no child should have to carry.

"I dream of my family," she said softly. "I miss them very much."

Elly nodded tearfully. "Sometimes I wish…sometimes I wish I was with them."

Alcie took a sharp breath. "I know," Elly said, holding up a hand to forestall her comments. "I'm here, and I'm lucky. But…" He sighed. "It's just so hard sometimes. I hate lying. I don't want this to be forever."

"I know," Alcie whispered. *It won't be,* she promised. *Once I find the stones, I'll start searching for the gate to Astraea so we can both get our families back.*

She sat quietly beside Elly until he finally fell asleep, her thoughts turning back to that afternoon, and the Arkos's speech. She had calmed down, but the unanticipated sight of the man who had changed her world so much still unnerved her. Arkos Trienes was not at all what she had expected, and what he was frightened her. She turned the day over and over in her mind, but it gave no answers. So after a while, she stood and slipped out of the stall to check on the rest of the barn.

She saw that Sleepy, like Romi and all the rest of the arion, was resting in a cozy corner of his stall. But next door, on the end of the row, she could hear signs of agitation. There was a scuffling that marked a hoof scraping the ground, and then the shuffle-

shuffle of an arion pacing his confines in the darkness.

Alcione went to the door of the stall and peeked over the top. A large arion loomed in the dim light. When he saw her, he ambled over and popped his head over the stall door.

Up close, the arion called Stormweaver was enormous! Looking up at his massive yet well-shaped head, Alcie felt a surge of awe for the man who could ride and tame so great and dignified a beast. His muzzle seemed a paler shade than the rest of him, which even in the dark seemed more grey than black.

He lipped gently at a strand of her hair, then huffed out a sigh and rested his chin contentedly against her shoulder. Looking down over the top of the stall door, she could see that his hooves were as big as soup bowls, and his girth was impressively round, but not so much rotund as powerful.

"You do look like you could call a storm down, boy," she whispered. "I'll take good care of you, I promise." *Even if your master does work for the Arkos.*

Making sure he had water and food if he needed it, she returned to her stall, where Sola opened one eye to see her come in. Groggy, he stumbled over and settled in next to her as she lay down.

"I don't know what to make of today," she confessed to him. "The Arkos can't be a good person. He killed my family! And yet, if I hadn't known what he'd done, I would have thought him wise and strong and everything good in a man. Oh, Sola, why does everything have to be so confusing? Is he a bad man or not?"

Sola licked her cheek sympathetically. "The Stabler, Raka, the Arkos…all of them do good things and horrible things. But a person can't be nice and cruel all in one. If you're mean to someone, even if you're not mean to another, that makes you a bad kind of person, doesn't it?"

She nestled into the bedding and pulled her cloak tightly around her. Closing her eyes, she said a silent prayer to Tanatos. *If you're listening, please help me. There's so much I don't understand. I don't know what you want me to do…*

- CHAPTER 16 -
A Test of Courage

THIS TIME, ALCIONE'S dreams led her to a room with no windows and no doors. There were no lanterns – in fact, no furnishings of any kind – and yet the room was bathed in an eerie blue-green glow. Alcie stood in the middle of the room with her feet on a floor that felt like feathers.

"What is this place?" she wondered aloud.

An impression in her mind gave her the word, *trial*. It was the same kind of feeling as when an arion pressed an image into her mind. A room of trials. "I'm to be tested? What kind of test?"

Courage. The room seemed to reverberate with the word, but she didn't know whether that was the point of the trial or an encouragement to her in facing whatever was to come. Abruptly, the room and its echoes fell away.

Now she floated high above the world, coasting along lines of stars as if swimming through a lake. Flipping onto her back, she experimented with twists and somersaults. Seeing no limits to what she could do, she swam higher and encountered even more stars, sparkling like fulgora. No...they *were* fulgora.

The sparkling bugs swirled in a silvery cloud, winking tails lighting up every color of the rainbow. She began to swim away from them, remembering their presence in previous nightmares. As she scooped her arms through the weightless expanse, she felt a pressure grip her ankles. Slowly, inexorably, it drew her back down.

There was wind. Bright lights flashed. Lightning streaked through the center as she was dragged round and round. Thunder rang in her ears, and when she screamed, the sound caught in the whirlpool and circled with her. She struggled, flailing wildly, but could not break free.

Between the flashes of lightning she caught snatches of faces – the faces of her family and new friends. She tried to reach them, but they were torn away. She cried out, and the sound was no more than a whisper in the immense storm. She could hear them pleading with her, but the jagged crack of the lightning swallowed their words.

She could see no escape. Closing her eyes and covering her ears, she tried desperately to shut it all out. *Leave me alone! I can't help you!*

Tossed end over end in the maelstrom, Alcione had no sense of time passing. No matter what she did, no matter what she tried, she could find no way to break free. She knew now that she was in a dream, yet she could not seem to wake up. She would have to find another way out of this trap.

Looking up, she saw that the spiraling whirlwind closed in on itself. She struggled towards it, only to see the storm bounded by a giant wall.

Or was it a wall? She watched five turrets thunder by, with five dark mirrors beneath them. As she looked closer, the wall appeared to slow, and she began to make out the shape of a giant crown. The five dark ovals she had taken for mirrors were in truth stones. Behind each was a figure, pounding on the glass.

Her parents occupied two of the stones. Anguished, she tried to go to them, but try though she might, she could not get close. Her sisters, parted equally cruelly, beat on the walls of two more stones. "I'm coming!" Alcie called raggedly. "Please! Wait for me!"

The last figure was Hermion. He did not call out, nor try to break free. The expression on his face, a mirror of her own features, was bleak. Empty. The figure he made nearly destroyed Alcie. This was a Hermion she had never seen before. She had seen him angry, afraid, hurt.

She had never seen him broken.

In that moment, Alcie closed her eyes. *I can't do it,* she thought. *If Hermion has given up, what chance do I have? I'll never be as brave as him!*

Courage.

INTO THE SKY

It was what the room had demanded of her, and right now it seemed impossible. Alcie ached inside, a wordless pain that she couldn't push away. She wallowed in the sorrow, letting it wash over her and beat her down.

It seemed a lifetime, or no more than seconds, when something in her finally snapped. She wasn't going to give up. She was going to find those stones! *If my brother truly has lost hope, I have to bring it back to him! If our places had been reversed, he would never have given up on me! Not even if the seas rose and the stars fell. Never!*

Opening her eyes, she squinted through the mist and forced away the image of the crown. Concentrating only on the whirlwind, she looked down this time. Below her was a vast black pit. Her exit, she hoped. *But how can I reach it?*

There were no objects to grab onto, and nothing to stop her spinning. She looked and looked, avoiding the faces, and still could find nothing. "What do you want?" she whispered, Hermion's vacant eyes boring into hers. And that's when she finally saw.

Feathers.

The image in the stone rippled, and in her brother's place was a feather, more real and substantial than anything else in this nightmare world. She gathered her strength and, she prayed, her courage.

Waiting until the stone came around again, she stretched out her arm as far as it would go. The first time around she missed the feather, and a shock like lightning rippled up her arm, warning her. A second try would hurt much worse.

"I don't care!" she called to the room. "I'm going to do this, no matter what you throw against me!"

Reaching out a second time, she braced for the pain. But this time, she caught hold of the feather and was suddenly anchored in the storm winds.

Looking down, she saw the feather was connected to other feathers, and the feathers to a wing. Romi's wing, black and whole as it had not been in weeks! There stood Romi, fierce eyes looking down into the pit and reflecting the unending dark within. He looked up, those eyes seeming bottomless – yet not empty – and she knew what she had to do.

Pulling herself together, she used both hands to tug her way down his wings until she could wrap her legs around his middle. Romi stood patiently, ears pricked forward. He looked like the pictures she'd seen in her books, of arion ready for combat.

She anchored her knees underneath the wings where they sprouted from Romi's shoulders. Her hands were buried in his mane, holding on for dear life. His head turned to acknowledge her. When their eyes met, she nodded to him and slowly the arion began to move through the winds.

Lightning broke. She shut her eyes briefly, then opened them again. Romi had come to a halt. He was waiting for her to tell him where to go. They would never reach the vortex if she allowed the lightning to blind and distract her from her purpose.

Closing her hands around tufts of mane and her mind to outside distractions, she focused with steely resolve on the pit. Ever so slowly, Romi began to move once more towards the dream's exit.

Gripping tightly to the only steady thing in her world, Alcione forced the arion onwards. They inched closer and closer to the pit. *But what if it's not the exit?* The thought crept insidiously into her mind. *What if it's nothing but a big, black hole and I never get out again?*

Romi stopped. "No!" she protested. "I can't believe that. We have to keep going!" The arion didn't move. He didn't trust her. "You have to believe me!"

Why? You don't believe in yourself. The accusation was harsh, bitter, and true. But it came in a different voice – not Romi's, but the room's elusive embodiment. "I'm scared," she told it. "And I'm not sure if this is the right way. But I have to try."

Go out? Which way, leader? A pulse in her mind shrieked with fear.

This was Romi. Alcione had never heard his voice so clearly before, nor found herself so certain it was him. "Don't be afraid," she soothed.

Suddenly, she found her terror gone. Somehow, because he doubted, she found that she was now sure. "I've made up my mind. All I'm asking is that you trust me, Romi. Please!"

The arion's will battled against hers, his panic threatening to overwhelm her concentration and send them both back where they had started. Even as the ghostly mirages flashed before her eyes, she was bombarded by distorted versions of them in her mind – herself and Romi floating up, cascading down, ricocheting over and over like ripples on a pond. She was certain now that this was what Romi saw. But she refused to give in. "I'm not scared of that pit, boy! We're not going to be scared of it!"

Romi ducked his head away and drew parallel with the pit as they came close. Clutching the arion with her knees and calves alone, she stretched both hands out to touch the pit's edge. Pushing one hand through, she pulled it back out whole. "See? Now go!" Nudging him forward with a skill and assurance that she didn't possess in waking life, she found she could encourage the arion with her body as well as her mind.

With a sound like the snapping of chains, Alcie broke free of Romi's arguments and the arion dove into the dark.

In an instant she was back inside the blue-green lit room. This time, Romi stood beside her, his eyes a turbulent mix of anger at being overruled, admiration at the strength of his rider, and a challenge that the next time, besting him would not be so easy. In a way, she knew it was both Romi and not-Romi – Romi and the spirit of the room. *That's fine*, she thought, and knew when he inclined his neck in her direction that they had heard her. *I'll be ready.*

The room flooded with an iridescent rainbow of silvered colors.

Triumph.

She had succeeded at the trial, with Romi's help. She didn't know what it meant, but when a wide door opened at one end of the room, she wasn't the least bit afraid to walk over and open it. Light, pure and golden, flooded the room.

With one hand on his shoulder, Alcione walked with Romi to the edge of the light. Side by side, they left the trial of courage and awoke.

- CHAPTER 17 -
Something Wild

"ALCIE!" ELLY PEERED over her, blue eyes concerned. "Sola and I tried to wake you, but nothing worked. Romi wouldn't wake up either. Was it another bad dream?"

She rubbed her eyes. "Yes," she said, sitting up slowly. "But it's over now. I'm fine, Elly." She thought about it, surprised. "I'm really fine."

Sitting back, hands on crossed legs, he regarded her gravely. "I was worried," he confessed.

She laid a reassuring hand on his thin shoulder. "It's all right," she told him. She stood, then pushed the wooden boards to open their stall window. "How late is it?"

The sun high in the sky gave her answer. "I've got to get going!" she said. "Buske will have me carting muck till next year if I don't get down there!"

Shooing Elly out, she changed into her stable clothes. "Elly, have you seen my other boot?" she called, hastily stuffing last night's skirt and blouse into her pack.

She sped through the morning, working double-time to get through the chores at the Keecy Street barn. Her thoughts skittered every which way, wanting to dwell on her time in the Kayre and the trial in her dreams, but constantly drawn back to the mundane. She broke for lunch with Tremi and the others down by the bridge, but nearly missed them.

"Late start?" Tremi guessed as she dashed to sit beside them.

She nodded breathlessly. Raka took her leave, bidding a friendly farewell to the other boys before shooting a dark glance at Alcie. Cormy and Yvo followed, on their way back to work, but Tremi stayed a few extra moments as she devoured a stacker and a half.

"You settling in all right?" he asked when she paused for breath and a drink of water. "I mean, it's not as if Rungilivanster isn't good folk – he is – but I wanted to check on you all the same."

She smiled, grateful. She was lucky to have him and Elly looking out for her. "I'm fine," she said, wondering that it should be true when her whole world felt turned upside down. "Thanks, Tremi. Really, thank you."

He looked oddly suspicious. "For what?"

She grinned. "For being a good friend."

There was a moment of embarrassed silence, and Tremi cleared his throat. "You'll like this one,"

Tremi said. "This morn, an old hag comes up to me and says…"

They spoke of lighter topics. Alcie listened as he spun a tale of his customers' recent antics, and she told him how mischievous Moti had taken her disarray as a signal to try for an escape. If she hadn't caught him nudging the bolt of his stall back with his teeth, he might have gotten free.

"I'd better get going," she said when they stopped laughing. "I've got to head back to the Hollows." She'd almost stumbled and said 'to look after Tion's arion,' before realizing Tremi would only know him as Rungilivanster. *So many secrets,* she mused as she trotted across the bridge to the other barn.

Elly met her at the door to the barn. "Tion says he's got a surprise for us," he told her. He was practically bouncing, an excited wriggle that reminded Alcie of her brother when he had a secret he was just about to share with her.

The young boy led her inside, his curls bouncing as he flickered in and out of the light coming through slits in the roof rafters and from the windows of the outer stalls. A figure waited by Romi's stall in a pool of sunshine. Coming closer, she recognized Dar.

In daylight, he looked vastly different from the forbidding figure who seemed hewn from shadows. She could see now that he was tall, even slouching against the stall door to ease the weight on his injured leg.

His hair was a wavy tree-trunk brown, nearly black. Tied behind his neck, it cascaded to just above his shoulders. His skin was pale, unblemished, and covered a face that made Alcie's heart jump a bit. He didn't look feminine, she supposed, but he was rather beautiful for a man. And his eyes…

Alcie had never seen eyes quite like his. Large and intense, they were blue – but not Elly's dark blue or Sola's indigo, not sky blue nor her own blue-grey. Dar's eyes were a warm, luminous shade of azure blue that looked almost violet in the sunlight. Crinkles at the edges of his eyelids gave him a slightly worn and exhausted look, while long lashes veiled his expression when they shuttered down. From beneath them, he peered at her intently.

"Where is Rungilivanster?" she asked finally.

"In the Pavilion, I believe," Dar responded. "Playing the buffoon, as usual."

Alcie almost giggled at his dry tone, but thought he might not react well. One of Dar's brows lifted cynically. "Well?" he prompted.

"It's just that…" She ducked her head, avoiding his eyes. "The way you say it, so gloomy. But he's so good at it, how could you be?"

She thought he might stand there forever, his face stuck in that contemptuously aloof glare. But then his lips creased upward in the barest hint of a smile. "That he is."

"I'd better get to work on the arion here, then," she said, pulling open the stable door and motioning him to move elsewhere.

He stood, but put a hand on the door, close to hers. Although they weren't touching, she could swear she felt heat radiating from his palm. "I've done all that," he told her. "Tion wanted you to do something different this afternoon."

"What was it? Did he have an errand for me to run?"

Dar considered. "Not so much an errand as an assignment. He wishes you both to learn to tack up an arion. Elly has proven quite capable, so now it is your turn." He slanted her a look as he let go of the door. "Try not to embarrass me, child."

"I'm not much younger than you!" she protested. Seeing him in daylight, she was sure of it. He couldn't be much older than Tion's eighteen years. Suddenly, she realized something. "You called him Tion!" she said. *I thought the only ones who didn't know him as Rungilivanster were Elly and me.* "How did you know his name?"

Dar shrugged. "We have been friends a long time. I had been a stable boy in his family's employ since I was a young child. We were practically raised together."

Alcione smiled. Now it made sense – Dar's education and knowledge of arion, his choice to follow the Arkos, and his knowing Tion's name but not turning him in. If they had been friends since childhood, Dar certainly would have tried to protect Tion. But that didn't necessarily mean he didn't agree with the Arch-master's policies and ideals. It would also explain why, if he knew they were nobles, he hadn't seemed at all surprised.

"I see," she said. "All right. I can tack up an arion too."

"Come along, then."

They gathered the necessary supplies, leaving out the wing-straps that hung on a wall, gathering dust. The saddle and pads looked incredibly large. "That's too big for Romi."

"But not for Storm," Dar replied.

Storm was even taller up close. His hooves were bigger than Alcie's feet, and his knees higher up than her own. But he immediately recognized Alcione and came to sniff at her belt for snacks. Finding none, he lifted his nose to hers, and licked her chin. "Thanks," Alcie muttered. But it made her smile, and she gave the giant arion a hug around what little of his neck she could reach. Dar watched the encounter with his usual reserve.

"Are you finished?" he queried when she had let go. Suddenly shy under his penetrating gaze, she nodded. "Good. Now, let's begin."

She began to reach for a saddle bag, and stopped as Dar snorted with disgust. "I thought Tion said you worked in a stable before."

"I did! For years!" Alcie bristled at the implication that she was lying about her experience.

About her real name and past, fine, but never her love for arion! But Dar didn't seem to care that she felt insulted. Carefully centering the saddle over the door and draping the rest of the tack over and around it, he opened the door to the stall.

"Wait, don't leave!" Alcie pleaded.

He didn't. He simply opened the door wide and stood behind it, leaving a free path for Storm to walk out. *What in the world is he doing? Without a halter to grab onto, if Storm decided to take off, no one would be able to catch—*

"The halter!" she gasped, racing to get it. As she scrambled back and tried to stand on tiptoes to reach over Storm's ears, Dar returned and closed the door behind him. Taking pity on her, he pulled the halter over Storm's ears and looped it under his chin.

"Yes, the halter," Dar muttered, looking thoroughly annoyed. "How did you manage to survive this long being so thickheaded?"

Before she could question what he meant by 'survive,' he went on. "If you don't halter your arion before you tack him up, you may as well not bother. If you've an arion with a knack for trouble, as I'm told you do, he'll be off and running the moment you put a pad to his back."

Alcione nodded. "I should have known that. But then, don't arion almost always have their halters on? If there's a fire in the barn, you need something to hold onto to get them out quickly." Fire. *No, don't think about it!* "That's what the Stabler back home used to tell me."

"Very good. You've redeemed yourself slightly. Now, let's get on with it."

She reached up and tried to sling the pads over Storm's tall back. "I begin to think perhaps we ought to have started with a pony," Dar said, using the term for a small arion and looking torn between vexation and enjoyment.

"It's fine," Alcie assured him. He made no comment as she struggled with the pads, and then with hefting the huge saddle up and over Storm's back. She hooked the girths in place, and then crossed behind Storm to stand on his other side. Dar met her there, looking furious.

"You really *don't* know anything, do you?" he accused. "You never go behind an arion! You could have been kicked!"

"Storm wouldn't hurt a fly!" she told him. "He's a big old sweetie, right boy?" she said, patting his nose as he turned to look at the commotion.

"Any arion can kick if given the motivation," Dar said loftily. "And if it does, you won't want to be the target of its hooves. Arion are not people. When they get frightened, they do not care if you get in their way."

"Fine, fine," Alcie grumbled.

"Not fine," he disagreed. "Promise me you won't do it again."

"Why?" Alcie asked. "What do you care if I get kicked?"

"I oughtn't," he said. "It probably wouldn't hurt you anyway, as you've a head hard as rock. Do as you wish, then."

Alcie looked at the ground, feeling ashamed and thoroughly vexed. He wasn't so old! And even if he did know so much about arion, that didn't mean he had to be such a snotty stick in the mud! Even Tremi wasn't so bad when he was acting superior. "I promise," she said, "if you promise to treat me like I'm an adult."

"You're a child." It was a statement without malice, but also without room for debate.

"I made it here on my own. I have a job. And I'm not about to be bullied. I can do this myself." Pushing past him, she buckled the girths, yanked the stirrups from his hands, and attached them, walking deliberately in front of Storm to get to the other side. "I'll do things how I see fit," she told him as she came back around for the bridle. "And if I do them your way, it'll be because I decided it sounds like a good idea, not because you said to."

Dar regarded her eyes as they spat sparks at him. "Quite finished, little one?" he asked patiently. "You've a hot temper. Be warned: you're not the only one. I don't like being shoved."

Alcie straightened to her tallest height and made to push him again. Quickly, he caught her hands. "Once is enough, thank you," he said, twisting her wrists just enough to make her cry out, but not enough to really hurt her. "Mind your manners, *child*."

Sick to death of his calm demeanor and poise, she reverted to the only thing she could think of. She stuck her tongue out at him.

"I see you two are getting along marvelously," Tion said from the corridor. Storm stood with his saddle askew, muzzle-deep in the dregs of his bucket of mash.

The two sprang guiltily apart, equally mortified and furious.

"He started it," Alcie accused. "I was doing just fine until he started ordering me around."

"She went around Storm from the back and expected me not to say anything. She fights me on every issue, and yet she thinks she ought to be treated like an adult."

"All he does is talk about how much he knows, and not a kind word for anything I know, anything I get right!"

Tion held up his hands. "Peace, you two!" Shaking his head, he let himself into the stall. "I must admit I'm surprised. I had thought you two would rub along quite well together, arion-mad as you both are. And you, my friend," he addressed Dar. "I can count the number of times you've lost your temper on one hand. Middy Alcione," he turned to her, "I am impressed."

"She's a brat, and not worthy of your time, Tion."

Tion clapped Dar on the shoulder and propelled him away from Alcione. "That may be, but I think I'll judge that for myself. Elly's watching Romi and Sleepy. Will you keep him company? We'll only be a moment."

"Aye. I still think you're a fool, though."

"Who doesn't?"

Dar stalked away, stiffly proud gait marred by the dragging sound of lame leg against the dirt. "He's the most arrogant person I've ever met!" Alcie exclaimed. "How do you stand him?"

Tion smiled. "One gets used to him. Dar can be a bit...abrasive...but he's also one of the most caring people I know. I'm sure he only meant to keep you safe when he warned you not to walk behind an arion."

"He didn't have to be so rude about it!"

"Perhaps not, but it's his way, saying things directly." He tugged Storm away from the mash, ignoring the arion's nicker of protest. "Will you help me with the bridle? Can you reach?"

Alcione took the bridle from him and let him lift the reins over Storm's head. Tion slid the halter off the arion and watched as Alcie inserted the bit and poked at the corner of Storm's mouth to get him to open it. Sliding the bit into place, she pulled the halter up as far as she could reach and let Tion pull the top of it over Storm's ears. "I meant to ask: why are we doing this?"

Tion stepped away to let her adjust the throatlatch and noseband. "Because I need to be sure you know how to tack an arion before I teach you to ride."

Alcione abandoned the bridle and turned to him, wonder suffusing her features. "Tion, you mean I…you mean you're going to…" He nodded. "Oh!" And she dove at him, throwing her arms around his waist. "Thank you!"

He patted her back. "You are more than welcome, but we'll have to do it now before it gets dark, and you'll have to keep quiet about it. If anyone knew Dar and I taught you this, it would raise some uncomfortable questions."

"He'll be teaching too?" Alcione stepped away and finished adjusting the noseband.

Tion nodded. "He's a better rider than even I am, and that's not a compliment I give lightly."

"But he's only a groomsman!"

Tion regarded her, his face incomprehensible. "Did he tell you that, then? Well, he is a remarkably talented groomsman as well, but a better rider by far. And his current position–"

"You give me too much credit," Dar interrupted. He had returned with a tacked-up Sleepy and Romi in hand. Elly balanced precariously on his shoulders. Flip balanced on Elly's own shoulders, claws digging in for purchase. Together, they looked like a strange, misshapen statue. Elly's grin was infectious.

Suddenly, Alcione was too happy to be mad at anyone. "Let's go!" she told them.

They made their way to the northern gate of the city. A guard stepped up to inspect their passes and ask their purpose. "My siblings and I," Tion indicated Alcie and Elly, "are accompanying our friend to Trippleton. We're paying a surprise birthday visit to our aunt."

"And you?" the guard asked Dar.

"Business for my lord Arkos," Dar replied, handing over a sheet of vellum, "with regard to these arion." The guard couldn't read, Alcie knew, but she glimpsed the seal of the Arkos and knew that it meant the same thing to her as it did to him. There was only one copy of that seal in the entire city, and it was kept in the hands of only one man.

"Let pass!" the guard ordered the men above. With a great clanking, the portcullis that protected the city was raised. "Be back before eventime bells ring, or come in the next morning after the sun rises," he advised.

"Aye." Dar led the arion forward, and Alcie, Tion, Storm, and Sola followed. They walked until they were out of sight of the walls. Alcie looked up at the clouds and breathed deeply of the country air. She hadn't realized how suffocating the city's smells and crowds were. Tion let her have a turn at walking Storm, but the big arion moved so fast that she could only keep up at a jog. She handed him back after Storm had taken her for a short run.

Finally, they came to a stop on a secluded part of the road. Alcie looked around. The river was nowhere in sight, and the walls of Ianthe were a far dark line on the horizon. They were surrounded by a field of yellow-brown stalks growing as tall as her waist. A few trees broke up the monotony of the landscape, and she could hear a distant brook burbling, but she couldn't see it. The arion strained, trying to get loose to graze.

"Where are we?" Alcie asked Tion.

"This," he gestured to the endless waves of golden stalks, "is the windlestrae. It stretches the entire northern plain from here to Kymminthë, and into the high corners of the world."

"It's a plant that has no worth save as a poor man's grass in a pinch," Dar said with a scowl. "Flowers won't even grow in it. It's useless, but good for riding. If you fall, you won't crack your head on dirt or cobblestone."

Switching arion with Dar, Tion took Elly over to Sleepy. He fiddled with the stirrups, and brought out a length of rope from the saddlebag. He tied this to the bridle, then lifted Elly into the saddle. Delighted, Elly sat up straight and tall in the saddle. Alcie could see that he had ridden before, and felt keenly how much he'd missed it.

Flip scrambled around to cling to the saddlebags. Pulling Sleepy behind him, Tion came to take Storm's reins from Dar.

"Your turn," Dar said, coming to Alcie with Romi. Shooing Sola to the side, he grabbed her and swung her up. Romi danced sideways, but Dar had a good grip. A sharp tug pulled Romi back as Alcie found the stirrups with her feet.

"Are you sure this is wise?" Dar asked of Tion.

"She can handle it," Tion replied breezily. "Right, Alcie?"

Despising the idea that she couldn't handle her own arion, Alcie sneered at Dar. "Of course, Tion," she said, glaring down. "I can handle anything."

Dar scowled, then abruptly let go of Romi's reins. The arion stood still, giving Dar a distrusting look. "Be it on your own head," he said, and used his good leg to spring into Storm's saddle. He only winced a little when his lame leg banged the left stirrup. Alcione felt a stab of sympathy, but squashed it. Holding Romi's reins the way she'd been shown and trying to keep him from fidgeting, she waited for Tion's instructions.

The lesson began simply enough, with Tion explaining to Alcie and Elly how to keep a proper position at the walk, and Dar demonstrating. Alcione had to admit that his posture in the saddle was lovely, as fine as her father's had been when he went out to patrol the Kayre every few days and see that the workers did as they ought.

INTO THE SKY

Her own posture wasn't nearly as good. After all those weeks in the pack saddle, the reins felt too thin in her hands, and her legs had less to grip. It didn't help that Romi made trouble at every opportunity. He seemed determined to take a bite out of Sleepy's tail, and while Alcie tried to follow Tion's directions to keep the arion apart, she had the sense that she wasn't doing a very good job.

What's the matter with you? She tried to project her thoughts into his mind, the way he did to her, scowling down at his ears. She pictured herself sitting tall and graceful in the saddle, with Romi's head up and him walking proudly on at a steady pace. An image returned to her: Sleepy's tail waving in the breeze. The picture was accompanied by a feeling of annoyance.

To make matters worse, Elly was doing perfectly well. His posture was enviable, and he didn't seem the least bit unsure, even when Tion untied the lead rope to go help Alcie.

"He's just high-spirited, that's all," Tion told her, patting Romi to soothe him. "If you stop being nervous, he'll stop prancing about. He's only picking up on your tension."

"But how can he tell?" Alcie asked.

Tion raised an eyebrow. "You talk to them. Can't you tell what they're saying from the way they move, the way they act?"

At first she thought he was speaking of the strange connection she and Romi had. But then she realized he meant how she always spoke to the arion, like how he chatted amiably at Sleepy and Storm on their walk out. She nodded, confused. "Well," Tion said reasonably, "what makes you think they're any less able to tell what you're thinking from the way you move?"

Or what you think in your head, she added ruefully.

"Feel how bunched your lower leg muscles are, as if you think you'll fall the moment you ease up on the pressure," Tion said. He tugged her thigh forward along the saddle leather. "And how tightly you hold the reins." He slid them out of her hands and made her gasp as she nearly toppled onto Romi's neck.

"Romi notices when you tense up, and he thinks it means you're scared. So he thinks there's something to fear when it's simply a case of you two being afraid of each other!"

Alcione looked down at his twinkling green eyes. "I'm right here," Tion said. "Nothing will happen to you."

"But what if he runs away with me?" she questioned, looking at the miles of windlestrae that seemed to go on forever.

"Then Dar will fetch you," Tion assured her. He shot a glance at his friend, who nodded reluctantly.

I don't trust Dar, she wanted to say, but she knew it would hurt Tion's feelings. Dar, however, seemed to know exactly what she meant to say, and he turned away from her, watching Elly to make sure the small boy kept his balance.

Alcie watched as Sola walked alongside Sleepy. Elly smiled, talking animatedly with him and Flip. His reins were loosely held and with no hint of fear. Behind him, Flip crouched low, as if trying to dig his way to a more solid perch.

Sleepy, lazy as always, meandered along the windlestrae at his own pace, poking his head down occasionally to snatch a bite. Elly, who had no problem with letting the golden arion eat his fill, was startled when Tion called out, "Pull his head up! You're teaching him bad habits!"

Still smiling, Elly tugged hard on the reins. Sleepy ignored him. "Pull harder," Tion told him. "You've got muscles, lad, use them!"

"It's tough," Elly replied, but pulled again. Sighing, Tion walked back to him and knelt to look Sleepy in the eye. Left on his own, Romi began to try to imitate Sleepy. Trying to prove she could be better than Elly in at least one small thing, Alcie pulled him up hard, making him yank at the reins in protest. He jerked his head, but she held on as best she could and tightened the reins again while he settled.

Meanwhile, Tion had bent over to tap Sleepy on the nose. "That's right, it's me," he said to the arion. "You're setting a poor example." Straightening with a maneuver that had Alcie blinking at its speed, Tion gave a hard tug on the reins that had Sleepy tossing up his head in comical astonishment.

"Try it again, and there'll be consequences," Tion warned. "And you," he added, looking to Elly, "don't let him do it again."

"Okay," Elly promised.

They practiced until Alcie's legs grew sore and Elly was huffing and puffing for breath. Tion allowed them to stop for a few moments and when they did, Sleepy put his head down again. This time it caught the boy unexpectedly, and he fell forward onto the arion's neck. Tilting forward and then back to steady himself, he sat down directly on Flip's tail.

The ysrei barked out a shrill protest, then made a leap towards the closest new perch to escape. Pouncing from Sleepy's rear, he aimed for Tion's shoulder. Romi, behind Tion and thinking the ysrei meant to land on his face, spooked.

Alcie was still holding the reins in her hand when Romi half-reared onto his hind legs and pushed Tion aside. Flip, without Tion's shoulder to land on, tried to catch onto Romi's foreleg and ended up scratching him.

"Help!" Alcie cried. With a sharp whinny, Romi burst into a gallop.

Clinging for dear life, Alcione tried to remember how to keep her posture, but when Romi leaped into the air, seemingly trying to jump his own shadow, she lost control and grabbed tight to his mane, the scattered reins well out of reach. "Help!" she cried.

Out of the corner of her eye, she saw Tion holding Sleepy back from following her. The ground was a golden haze beneath her. Her stomach lurched and she floundered, trying to sink her feet into the stirrups and regain her balance.

Romi zigged and zagged through the tall grass, darting this way and that as if to dodge a horde of invisible pursuers. Alcie thought she saw the large grey form of Stormweaver thundering by as they turned. Hazarding a glimpse behind her, she saw Dar in hot pursuit. "Hold on," he commanded, and she couldn't think of a good reason to argue with him.

Like the windstorm in her dream, everything seemed to move impossibly slowly. With crystal clarity she saw a tree nearing, and watched with horror as Romi advanced towards it. He skidded around the trunk at the last second, and time seemed to snap back into place as he accelerated once again.

The windlestrae broke off as the drumming of hooves was joined by the nearing gurgle of the stream. Romi flew along its banks, coming dangerously close. The water wasn't deep, and Alcie could see large stones jutting out as it lapped by. They wouldn't drown if Romi went in, but one bad step could kill them both. She remembered seeing it happen once to one of the Montelymnë arion. He'd gone down with a hoof in an animal den, the crack sickening. His leg had hung limp, the bone sundered. No choice but to put him out of his suffering.

She closed her eyes. *Romi, stop!* She begged, reaching out her mind to him. Behind her eyes she saw the river to her right as a colorless gleam, catching the sun and dappling. The rocks didn't stand out in his vision.

Swallowing her fear, Alcie opened her eyes and made a reckless grab for the left rein, using only her stirrups to balance as she reached down to snatch at it. Suddenly, Dar was there beside her. She could hardly see his movements, but somehow he had Romi's reins in hand, and was dragging them away from the stream, Storm leading.

As they slowed, Alcie saw that Dar's own reins were tucked in the saddle pads so they wouldn't fly away. He was controlling Storm by leg movements alone. Eventually they drew back to a trot, then a brisk walk, and finally a full halt. Romi was trembling and wide-eyed.

Dar yanked Alcie up to a sitting position and barked, "Are you injured?" in the same tone one might ask, "Are you out of your mind?" She thought he might have meant both.

"I'm... I'm all right," Alcie assured him weakly.

"That arion is far too advanced for you," Dar raged. "I told Tion he should have put you on Storm but no, a rider has to learn on their own arion and no one else's – idiot! Hang on to the saddle."

With barely a flicker of movement, Dar nudged Storm into a trot. Romi, disliking being left behind, followed. When he tried to reach out and bite Storm's neck, Dar used part of his reins to flick the unruly arion on the nose. Alcie didn't think the reins had even made contact, but Romi looked stunned, and didn't try it again.

"I think you may need to revise your plan," Dar informed Tion sharply when they returned to the others.

Where Alcie stiffened at the reprimanding tone, Tion merely nodded. "Alcie, I think you ought to ride Storm from now on, at least until Dar and I have had a chance to teach Romi a bit more about being ridden."

"But I was doing a good job!" she protested. "It wasn't Romi's fault Flip scared him! And I held on when he ran away with me – I could have stopped him!"

"He would have stopped eventually," Dar agreed evenly, "with or without you."

Dismounting, Dar looked at Alcie. "Off," he ordered, and she hopped down. Storm shifted, and Dar's injured leg twisted as he staggered to rebalance. He leaned on Storm to remain upright, left leg trembling with the strain.

"Does it hurt?" Alcie queried, suddenly unaccountably curious.

Dar's face was pale, and he threw her a furious look. Without answering, he boosted her onto Storm, then moved to take hold of Romi. Swinging easily into the shorter arion's saddle, he yanked Romi's head up from a mouthful of windlestrae and turned him to face Tion. Romi chafed at the sudden change in riders, but didn't try to break loose again.

The rest of the lesson was a haze. Tion kept calling out instructions, so Alcie didn't have time to reflect on the terror of a few moments earlier. Storm was calm and easy to ride, although it was hard to wrap her legs around his middle because he was so large. Still, he made no move to take advantage of her lack of control. Much as she hated to admit it, Dar had trained his arion well. If he wasn't so irritating, she might have admired him.

The sun was sinking towards the horizon when Tion bade them halt, to end things on a good note. They walked the arion in a circle for a few moments before Tion helped her and Elly down to the ground.

Dar stayed on Romi longer, doing the same sorts of exercises she used to see her father practicing and teaching to her brother. The Stabler had explained to her that an ordinary morning on an arion would include exercises that stretched an arion's legs, made them practice each pace to hold the tempo steady, and made them practice stopping and starting when asked.

Romi fought the entire way, tossing his head when Dar asked him to stop, trying to run away with him at the three-beat canter stride that was just slower than a gallop. But whatever the feisty arion tried, Dar was perfectly balanced and kept the reins loose and steady.

"Has no one ever ridden this creature?" Dar asked angrily when he finally brought Romi, sweating and mouth green with foam, to a halt.

"Well," Alcie confessed, "not really. He was worked with a bit over the past year, but before that he was completely wild."

Dar looked fit to burst. "Do you mean to say no one has trained him in anything, and you thought you, a mere beginner, would come to no harm at all on his back?"

"He was fine all the way to Ianthe! And Romi would never hurt me!" Alcie replied, tightening her grip on Storm's reins. "He's my friend!"

Dar's eyes flashed with something painful as he looked at Storm. "Don't ever assume that," he told her flatly. "Arion aren't like us. There's something wild in them. Don't forget it."

Alcie looked at Storm. "I don't believe it. Storm couldn't hurt anyone."

Tion came over to them, leading Sleepy. "Alcione, even the gentlest rain can cause a mudslide if the circumstances are right. The dearest friend can betray you without meaning to. Romi doesn't know his strength, nor what's expected of him. He doesn't know you're only a beginner. He could hurt you very easily without any intent to."

Alcie looked at them. They were all friends, even Dar – maybe. They hadn't betrayed her yet, but that didn't mean they couldn't. It was a sobering thought.

A friend of mine fell the other day, she remembered the words of a letter Hermion had written from Kymminthë. She had read them over and over in the months he was gone. *His arion wasn't wild or anything –*

just spooked by some birds. They tell me his leg will take the whole summer to heal, maybe longer. None of us ever forgot to check the skies after that.

"I think I see what you mean," she said after a moment. "May I keep riding Storm in the lessons, Dar?"

Dar nodded. "You're welcome to. And I'll continue to work with this brat of yours until I'm satisfied he's learned some manners. You'll work with Romi, too. Tion was not entirely wrong." At this he flashed a cheeky grin at the magician, who rolled his eyes. "A rider does need to learn his – or in this case, her – own arion. Romi must trust you above all others for him to truly be yours. It will take a great deal of work."

"I can do it!" Alcie replied quickly. "Work doesn't scare me. And no arion will, either!"

Dar laughed suddenly. "I can see we'll have to work on teaching you some humility. It doesn't do to be too brave."

Alcione said nothing, only turned to stare at a patch of sweat on Storm's neck as she wheeled him around to return to Ianthe. Though she was tired, she walked quickly to keep up with Storm's huge stride. "When will we do this again?" she heard Elly ask over her shoulder.

"When we can," Tion assured him. "You've both done well today."

Alcie kept going. *I didn't do well at all!* It seemed she couldn't even be humble or brave properly, let alone ride an arion well!

After a bit, Dar came up beside her with Romi. "Would you like to walk him back?" he offered, lifting the reins towards her.

"Aren't you afraid he'll run off with me?" Alcie shot back.

"He's too tired," Dar replied frankly. And then he added, "Oh, don't be cross. I might have saved your life, you know."

"Keep mentioning it, why don't you?"

"Children," Tion chided. "Do try to behave."

Without looking at Dar, Alcie switched arion with him. She sensed Romi calming even more as she drew close. A throb she hadn't even realized was there had begun to ease.

"You know," Dar remarked casually, "you might try to smile a little. You just rode an arion and didn't manage to muck it up too badly. When I first rode Storm, no one was there to catch me."

Alcie looked at him. "You mean *you* fell?" she asked wonderingly.

Dar smiled. "I most certainly did not. I simply took a moment to practice an unscheduled dismount."

Slowly, Alcie began to smile as well. A giggle escaped her. And then she was suddenly helpless with laughter. Elly and Tion were laughing too, and her heart thumped with joy. *I did it! I really rode Romi!*

Alcione let the cool air and the warmth of the setting sun play along her face and back, and her smile grew broader. For a moment, she met Dar's gaze, and something passed between them, an understanding that she thought only arion people could share. *We've made it through*, it seemed to say. *And wasn't it wondrous?*

- CHAPTER 18 -
Summer

O VER THE NEXT FEW weeks, summer began to ripen. Flowers bloomed in the window boxes of houses in the Hollows, new fruits and vegetables came into season, and once it rained for six days straight. "If I never see a storm cloud again," Alcie swore on the sixth day as she trudged through mud and muck to get to Keecy Street, "I won't miss it!"

Working at both stables and then doing the magic show at night took its toll on her strength and she found herself once again mercifully unable to dream. She was up before dawn every day for the Keecy Street barn, then back to the Hollows over dinner to take Romi and Sleepy for daily walks, back to Keecy Street, to the Hollows for supper, and then to Tion's wagon at evening bells.

She made mistakes often, once forgetting to latch the door properly on Moti's stall (she found him later eating from Welm's huge pile of hay, the larger arion cowering in a corner from his small neighbor's bullying), and there wasn't a day that went by when Buske didn't holler at her or threaten to kick her out on the streets.

Since his tirade was often more exasperated than angry she didn't worry much, but every day she tried her hardest to do better. The tiring work gave her strong muscles and calluses on her palms. Each night, she fell asleep satisfied with her own improvement, but preoccupied with plans. She would get to the crown. She just had to figure out where it was, how she would get there, and how she would get back out again. Simple.

She thought about it daily as she wandered the winding alleys of the Hollows. One afternoon she found a group of children playing games, and joined in. Alcie was clumsy and got bruised all over from catch-me-if-you-can or here-to-there, but it thrilled her that the children of Ianthe accepted her just as she was. She wasn't too unladylike, nor yet too much of a girl to play with the boys.

On days when she finished her work early, she wove braids out of the discarded mane and tail hair the arion shed. They were threaded with chestnut and black, blond and silvery grey, and she tied them with scraps of ribbon taken from Huin's shop.

Tremi came by to see her every so often and when he saw the first of her braids, he told her he might be able to sell them for her. From then on she spent any of her extra time making the braids, and even joined Tremi to sell them herself whenever she had extra time.

Trifira Bridge was wonderful fun. She soon picked up the patter of the traders and, after much work and improvisation, invented her own pitch. "Arion braids to band in your hair!" she sang out. "With ribbons and bows and garlands to wear! Come, Middy, come, and buy a charmed braid! T'will gladden my pocket and brighten your days!"

As the days passed and she found herself no closer to a plan, the dreams returned, different this time. She and Romi floated along the sky, dancing with twinkling stars and shimmering in and out of sight between the clouds. Her brother rode ahead, but no matter how she hurried, she couldn't catch a glimpse of his face, nor even of which arion it was he rode.

Dar was often gone, away on "business" for the Arkos, but when he was around Tion let them have lessons. Alcie learned to walk and trot with confidence, that the rising in the saddle was called "posting," and that it was even harder at the faster, two-beat trotting pace.

The phrases "Heels down!" and "Shoulders back!" echoed through her mind after each lesson, and she squirmed under Dar's disapproving glare if she so much as put a foot towards walking around Romi's back end.

She practiced how to fall properly (although Storm was very gentle and never spooked), and how to keep her balance when the arion's huge hooves tripped their way through the windlestrae. She and Elly challenged each other constantly to be better; he was the more natural rider, but she was taller, and had an advantage in control.

She practiced grooming and tacking with Storm and Romi. She thought maybe she had grown a bit taller. She felt the slightest bit closer to meeting the arion's liquid black eyes. She continued to hear his keen voice in her head, bolder and more talkative by the day. Sometimes they even had short conversations.

"Why do you like guara better than other fruits?" she asked him one day, idly combing her fingers through his mane.

Sweet. Different – taste not like others.

"Did you have other fruits when you lived in the wild?"

He nickered and bumped her shoulder with his. Images flashed into her head of sun-berries and harshak, and a strange yellow, rough-skinned oval that was like no food she had ever seen.

She was growing accustomed to how Romi talked not only with words but with images, and feelings. When he was sad, she knew it if she stood close enough. Her stomach rumbled with his hunger. When he was content, she could slip into his warmth, close her eyes, and pretend that they were one. When she listened to his feelings, sometimes she could forget her own.

INTO THE SKY

She could forget Dar's business, and Tion's work when he wasn't a magician. She could forget how her brother would have loved to ride through the endless fields beyond the capital city. Could forget his flyaway hair, the same golden-red color as her own, waving in the breeze as he galloped Romi, chasing the wind in her memories.

Most of all, she could forget the crown, even for just a few moments, and forget how badly she was failing. She had gone by the entrance to the Kayre nearly every day at first, but the proximity put her no closer to an answer. How could she sneak in to the enormous grounds to search for the stones, when she hadn't the first idea where to look?

She heard the voices of the people in town. "What a grand summer it is," they exclaimed, "now there are no nobles to bully us about!"

The crops were starting to flourish after all, and they talked of a grand harvest festival when autumn finally came. Tion took her and Elly out of the city to the south. In the swells of the Sianna Valley they gathered handfuls of sun-berries from a local farm. A friendly girl near her own age gave Alcie pungent bouquets of strena fresh from the ground. Cutting into it made her eyes water, but it was a delicious treat atop the stackers, sitting side by side with Elly and Tremi against the wall of Trifira Bridge.

The days were burnished with sun, the city alive with color and cheer. A girl wearing Alcie's face joined the crowds, living a life that was not her own, becoming a person who was not herself. And if one fishwife's voice reminded her of her mother, or a street dancer's steps flashed through her mind with her sister's form and face instead, she pressed the thoughts down deep. The dark-haired girl selling flowers in the square didn't look a bit like Kanase.

She locked away thoughts of the Arkos, caging them behind the gates of the castle she still didn't dare venture through. She told herself only a great rider could breach the walls of the Kayre to find the crown she sought. She was only a poor, foolish girl, with a half-wild arion and a life woven from a tangle of lies. But she was drawn to the top of the hill, to the verge of the gates time and again, to stand helplessly among a sea of people, chills running down her spine.

The sun grew so hot that people stopped working during the hours it was highest overhead, using the time to do tasks indoors or nap. Markets stayed open later at night, and Alcione let herself be carried along in the hazy heat of the days like a leaf drifting down a river. No thoughts, no worries, and – if she pushed it down deep enough, guarded her heart fiercely enough – no guilt.

The girl she'd known for thirteen years slipped farther from reach as each day passed. The dreams brought her close to her family each night, and when she woke in the morning, she forced herself to smile. To greet Elly and the day with a confidence that belonged to someone else.

INTO THE SKY

When she thought of her family, she closed her heart off, like shutting a window against the sun. It burned for a moment, but then there was only the dark and the cold. She repeated a mantra to herself as she willed the mask to return: *Wherever they are, surely summer can reach them, too.*

- Chapter 19 -
A Change in the Air

A ND THEN, THERE WAS a change in the air. It was still hot, but Alcie could feel the barest bite of autumn wind nip into the stall. Shivering, she changed quickly into her clothes, careful not to trip over the sprawl of Elly and Flip.

She checked first on Romi, Sleepy, and Storm. She filled hay nets and refilled water buckets. Pumping water from the well outside the stable, she dragged it back. Her hands no longer blistered and bled as they had at first. Over the months they had become rough and calloused, strong enough to do whatever was asked of them.

Just like I am, she thought. With summer's end nearing, the Arkos had his mind on preparing for harvest time, as did everyone else. *There won't be a better time to sneak back into the palace,* Alcie thought. She had come no closer to discovering the whereabouts of the crown and the legendary stones, but a need to try enveloped her, trembling inside like a match catching at a wick, just before the flame.

The harvest would begin in a week's time. No one would suspect a thief of being so brazen as to sneak into the palace when the Arkos was out rallying the workers in the city and the fields. And his best guards would follow him, protecting the leader and not the residence.

The fateful day dawned like any other. She finished with the Hollows arion early and headed to Keecy Street. The market on Trifira had begun to stir.

"Good morn!" Tremi called out as she passed by.

"And good hunt!" she called back, returning the greeting common to the traders, who "hunted" their customers rather than waiting to be discovered.

Buske was wide awake when she arrived, having started without her. "Here," he said, holding out a pitchfork.

Her chores took most of the morning. By dinner, she had worked up an appetite. With new braids in hand, she went to the bridge to eat with Tremi. As usual, he had stackers to spare.

"Did you hear?" he asked as he handed her one. "T'Arkos is makin' a speech today in the Market Square, right before sunset. Most everyone is takin' the afternoon off to hear it. I reckon he's trying to stir up more volunteers to help with the harvest.

Wouldn't catch me doin' that. I'm a salesman, through and through!"

"Everyone will be there?" Alcie asked, intrigued. She hadn't bargained on that; if the Arkos had been in the countryside, crowds would still be all over the upper city. She would be more conspicuous if he remained in the city. "Will his guards follow him?" she asked lightly.

Tremi raised an eyebrow. "And where else would they be? There's nothing of value in the palace, not anymore. Where the Arkos goes, the guards go."

Then today is the day! It'll have to be today, or never. Alcie swallowed a large bite and choked a bit on it.

Thumping her on the back, Tremi stared at her. "You're not thinking some odd thought, are you?"

'Odd' was a keyword, so they could speak about her past in public. Alcie shook her head. "Why would I be?"

Tremi waved a warning finger in her direction. "If you are, get it out of your head. Like as not they'll catch you at the gate and toss you in the dunge. You don't earn enough dagats selling these," he poked a braid, "to get you out of that kind of mess."

Alcione shrugged. "I suppose it's good I'm not thinking anything, then," she told him. "But I don't want to listen to him talk for hours. I'll be in the barn with Romi. Maybe I'll polish a few saddles." *Tremi,* she thought, *you taught me how to change my speech so I don't make anyone suspicious. But did you teach me well enough to hide my thoughts from even you?*

It seemed she had. Tremi took her at her word, and she departed after learning a few more details about the speech. It would take place at the fifth chime of the bells, in the square in front of the palace gates. Tion had asked Tremi to relay the message that his show would start an hour late, as he was taking Elly along.

Strange today, Romi thought to her during their afternoon walk. *Thump-thump beat faster, air come in/go out quick.* An image flashed through her head of diving from the clouds straight at the ground. It made her heart beat even more quickly. *Do that?*

Alcie thought an image of the palace, and then of the secret entrance. She tried to project the feeling of intense fear – it was close enough to the surface that it seemed easier to show it to Romi than explain. But afterwards, it wasn't easy to put that fear away, so as she finished the last of her chores in Keecy Street, she was still nervous.

Just before the appointed time, Alcie ducked into a secluded part of Shopkeep Square that she'd never been to before. Trying to look casual despite the pounding of her heart, she approached a vendor whose cart looked as if it might fall over at a strong breeze and bought a meat pasty that looked like someone had stepped on it.

"Careful what you eat," Tremi had warned her once. "Make sure folk aren't avoiding the place. That's a bad sign."

She had seen enough people go to this man to believe his food was safe, but that didn't make it sit any easier in her stomach. All the same, it was good to have the pasty to carry – she'd look like any of the poor girls about town, eating supper on her way to another job.

With Sola following, she made her way up the hill towards the palace. When she got in range, she let him take the lead. Casting a glance around to make sure the crowds were otherwise occupied, she ducked into the dusty back-ways of the upper city.

Soon, they were in front of the stack of boxes. With relief, she saw that not only were the boxes still there, they seemed virtually untouched. No one had discovered their secret…yet. Sola sat down on top of a box and regarded her. "Wish me luck, boy," she told him, and heard a quick, soft yip in reply.

Wasting no time, she opened the empty box and wiggled down into it. She heard the bells chime the fifth hour, just as she'd hoped. Now, she had to wait. As she did, she took Hermion's dagger to her hair once more, chopping it short. If she was caught, it would be the worse for her if they saw a girl in stable-boy clothes. She couldn't count on her cap staying atop her head if she had to run for it.

The time passed torturously slowly. After dusting hair from her tunic and sorting out the last jagged edges of her new cut, Alcione sneaked glances from behind the bushes to see what was going on, and to plan a course of action.

She would go through the gazebo and gardens again, and up towards the main entrance to the palace. As she went, she would have to look for side entrances and exits that the servants – no, they were called "aides" now – used. If she could, she would slip in that way.

If not, she would have to try and enter through the main gate, and think of some excuse to be going in the opposite direction as everyone else. Most of the guards would be at the speech, but they'd never leave the palace fully defenseless. Alcione took a deep breath. *This is it.*

Checking to make sure no one else was about, she emerged from her hiding spot and began to walk quickly across the grounds. She was much faster than she had been the first time – a result of hard work and riding practice – and reached the gazebo in moments.

Once in the gardens, she broke into a run. She tried to peer over the hedges to see the people whose footsteps she heard crossing towards the castle gates, but she wasn't tall enough. By the time she reached the edge of the gardens, the bells had stopped.

I think they've all gone! Alcie thought miserably. *Drat! Now what will I do?*

Just then, a sound drew her eyes to a portion of the palace wall to her left. A young woman came flying down the path towards the gates, cursing and muttering uncomplimentary things about a stew that refused to boil.

Watching her disappear around the corner, Alcione made her way determinedly forward. There was a heavy wooden door built into the wall where the woman had appeared. The scents coming from within indicated that it led to the kitchen.

Taking a chance, Alcie tugged at the door. As she'd suspected, the careless young woman had forgotten to bolt it in her hurry. Closing it behind her, Alcie tiptoed inside.

The kitchen was entirely empty, save for one well-fed orange cat who dozed contentedly on the floor. Going past it with care, she reached the other end of the large room and looked out onto the inner ward of the palace.

Kayre Ianthe was ensconced behind four walls and their protective towers, but the main building itself was placed in the center. Remembering the layout of Montelymnë, she knew that important objects, such as jewels, would likely be kept in this central building.

But she knew something an outsider would not: in Kayre Montelymnë, the most precious treasures had been located not in the audience chamber, nor in the lord's rooms, but in a simple study off the side for the lord's scribe, beneath a hidden trapdoor, in a tunnel that gave on to the cellar. This tunnel, which also connected to a secret door in the audience chamber, was meant as an escape for the family of the Kayre in case of intruders.

The inner ward was frightfully silent as Alcie made her way around the tower that was the heart of Kayre Ianthe. A rustling in the bushes sent her ducking for cover, darting behind the shadow of a stone bench along the outer wall. She held her breath, hoping no one could hear her frantic heartbeat as it threatened to thump right out of her chest.

She crouched behind the bench for what felt like forever before another cat sauntered out from its napping place. She let out the breath she had been holding as it pinned her with its slitted stare.

Thank goodness! Cats have better ears than humans, but I'd better be quieter just in case. Alcie reached to pet the grey cat as it twined between her legs and purred. She moved towards the inner tower. Peering around the corner yielded a view of open space, but no people.

Holding her breath, she turned and made her way up to the heavy wooden door, thanking Tanatos that it was in the same place as the one in Kayre Montelymnë. It was open just a crack. She paused for a moment, falling to her knees and listening for movement.

There was silence within, so Alcie gathered her courage and squeezed her way in. *I suppose Tremi was right,* she thought. *No one **does** care about thieves getting into the Kayre, or else they'd remember to bolt their doors.*

Or mayhap the Arkos has got everyone so addle-brained that they really think their neighbors are all good people now that all the evil nobles are gone, she added sourly. The city had been peaceful that summer, she knew, but it wasn't all flowers and happy thoughts. People were still people, after all, and she had come to know that meant they weren't all good, even if they'd gotten what they wanted.

Putting away that thought, Alcione looked around and knew a momentary wonder at the beauty in front of her. The tapestries that would cover the windows at night were hung by pegs on the walls. She could see the depictions of ancient myths in the colorful weave and was awed at the level of detail in the images.

Now isn't the time! Alcie scolded herself. She gave the room a cursory look, noting the sparse furniture and scattered writing instruments and stacks of paper bound by ribbon. Getting on her knees, she crawled under the table to feel for the lines of a trapdoor. If there was any, it had been covered up long ago.

She searched the rest of the floor quickly, but concluded that there could have been no trapdoor anywhere on the floor. Or at least if there had been, it was underneath several layers of dirt by now. *If there's no door, then perhaps at the top of the stairs...*

At the top of the stairs in the back of the room, she heard a quiet whistling. Not the kind to call someone to you, but a quiet melody that seemed somehow familiar. She made her way to the window and poked her head up just over the sill, crushing her hat in her hands.

A girl made her way across the courtyard, nose buried in a book. Alcie couldn't see her features, but a fall of long dark hair cascaded down her back, unbound by wimple or cap. Troubled by some sound she looked up, and Alcie's heart thudded as the girl scanned the tower up and down.

Finally, she seemed to accept that no one was there. Shrugging, she turned back to her book, the whistle taking up the merry tune where it had left off. Alcie's pulse banged in her ears as she tried to calm herself. She had just turned to study the second floor of the room when she heard a great commotion outside, a roaring sound that filled her ears. *That must be the end of the speech!*

Scrambling down the stairs and out of the room, she tripped. Instinctively, she aimed for a pile of paperwork stacked beside the table for a softer landing. It broke her fall, but the papers scattered everywhere, leaving her sprawled in a pile of crumpled sheets.

With horror, she looked at the giant rip in her leggings, and her scraped knee. Blood seeped slowly onto the work below her. Frozen, she knew she there was no evading the evidence she was leaving everywhere. *I'll hang for this,* she thought. *Or they'll burn me, just like they burned...*

It was the thought of her family that got her back to her feet. *I can't die here! I...I have to get out of here!*

With dust all over her, the torn part of her legging flopping uselessly against her boot, and blood dripping down her leg, she ran. Her knee stung with sharp pain at every step, but she put it aside as she sprinted back across the inner ward towards the kitchen.

She burst into a room and saw with despair that she had reached the pantry instead. Shelves of stored food stretched as far and high as the eye could see. Her mind reeled. *There's no way out!*

And when she turned around, there stood a round old woman, hands at her hips.

"Stealin' from the Arkos, eh?" she snarled. "Come with me, lad."

- CHAPTER 20 -
Caught

THE OLD WOMAN MARCHED Alcione out of the pantry with a vise-like grip around her wrist. Alcie only barely had the presence of mind not to scream. Again, it seemed that she was separate from her body, watching with dispassionate eyes as the woman raved.

"The Book of Tanatos says: 'If a thief should come unto ye, ye shall cut from him his thieving hand.' I says we ought to chop both yer hands!" she screeched. Others who had returned from the speech averted their eyes as she passed.

Finally, they arrived at a small door beside the main gate. "Fetch the captain!" the hag howled up to a man standing atop the wall above the door. "We 'as us a thief!"

A moment passed, and the door opened. A man walked out, sword sheathed at his side. His moustache was impeccably groomed and looked, to Alcie's mind, like a dark wall atop which a large, once-broken nose loomed. His mouth, thin and unpleasant, curved downwards so forbiddingly that it might have been stuck that way.

"So, you think you can steal from the Arkos?" he asked, his deep voice booming.

Outside of herself, Alcione saw what the man was looking at: a grubby street urchin with torn, dusty clothes and hacked-at hair. Tremi's words echoed in her ears: *I thought you were braver than that.*

"N-no, sir," she stammered out. "I be from Gaoler's Row. M-me sister's dying from 'unger. Me da been in the bottle again, me ma's dead. Wot else could I do?" She took the accent from Vlas, gatekeeper of one of the prisons in the lower quarters, who sometimes visited Tremi's stall for trinkets for his wife and daughters.

"J-just wanted bread, a-and somethin' to take to her, somethin' special. She ought to has that, if'n she'll die soon, eh?" Alcie stuck up her chin defiantly.

The captain of the guards nodded, his face looking even harsher. "Aye, lad. Well, then." He looked at the old woman. "Fetch the boy some bread, Cookey, for wasting my time with such nonsense. Go!" he thundered when she refused to move.

"As for you," he glowered at her. "I'll give you something special for trying to steal from the Arkos."

He dragged her inside, where a ladder led up to the parapets of the palace. With the door closed behind him, the only light was from above. "Climb," he told her. She didn't dare disobey.

There were still a few people milling about in the courtyard below and beyond the gates. Atop the walls of the palace, two more guards stood at attention, looking very much afraid. "Captain Trafford, sir," they said as one. And then, "What can we do for you, captain, sir?"

The man called Captain Trafford smiled, a nasty smile that unfurled queasily across his face under the bar moustache. The guards stiffened in response.

"Five lashes for the scofflaw," said the captain. Alcie saw him brandish a length of rope.

"A warning to others who break the law!" called the captain as the two guards each took a firm grip on one of her arms. Alcione braced herself, and repeated to herself over and over, *I am braver than this. I am braver than this.*

The first strike of the lash was the worst pain she had ever endured. She screamed so loud that there was no room for thought in her mind. The second came like a clap of thunder in her ears. By the third, she slumped in the arms of the guards. At the fourth, she thought she might die. At the fifth strike, she hoped she would.

They tossed her out of the palace gates so that she lay on the ground, motionless, like a broken rag doll. Two filthy crusts of bread landed beside her. She stared unthinking at them as time blinked by. It might have been hours or mere minutes before she felt a wet nose pressed against her forehead. Sola.

With her eyes closed, she reached out for a familiar mind. Romi. She could barely feel him, but as the pain washed over her like a crimson tide she gripped to the lifeline of his thoughts. She stared at the hay through his eyes, at the stall, at the setting sun. They did not speak, but she sensed his awareness of her. He was there, and it was enough.

Dimly, she was aware of the bells. She counted. It was the tenth hour. Tion's show would be over now. *Will they miss me?* She tried to rouse herself to her feet, but found it impossible. No one touched or spoke to her. They walked by as if she didn't exist. Soon, it was late enough that no one walked by.

It was just past eleven when she heard a familiar voice. "Rungilivanster, hurry! I think I see her!"

Tremi knelt by her side. "I never thought you were *this* foolish!" he exclaimed harshly, and he was the angriest she'd ever seen him. "What have you done to yourself?"

Tion and Elly came into her field of vision as well. "Lass, what in the world is this?"

"She's bleeding!" Elly said, leaning over to look at her back. "Who did this to her?" He looked back at her, the first anger she'd ever seen from him tightening his features. "Does it hurt much?"

After considering the situation, Tion lifted her into his arms. She moaned, but he hushed her. "Unless you think you can walk?" he asked.

"Have...to try," she whispered, her throat parched.

Carefully, Tion placed her feet onto the ground. She stood gingerly, and shut her eyes as a wave of pain washed through her. But when it had calmed to a dull throb, she saw that she was still standing, and forced herself to put one foot in front of the other.

They walked downhill in silence. Alcie gave no explanation of what she had done, nor what had been done to her. When Tremi tried to press her, Tion told him it could wait until the morrow.

At Keecy Street, Tremi turned for home. "Glad you're not dead or in the dunge," he told her. But he looked upset, and Alcie knew that in the morning she would pay for having lied to him. If he ever spoke to her again.

"Come along, Elly," Tion said. "We'll all be sleeping in the caravan tonight. Dar won't be back until the end of the week, anyway. Alcic, we'll have to peel you out of those clothes and clean the wound, or you'll get an infection. Do you want Huin?"

"I don't mind," she whispered. "Don't bother Huin for this, please. It's nothing. I trust you."

Tion didn't reply. When they reached the caravan, he had Elly fetch some stingwort. "It's in the green bottle, the one next to the feather-fan. This will hurt," he told Alcione.

He stripped off her ruined tunic first, and balled up a piece of it. "Bite down hard," he told her, as he placed it in her mouth. "It's late, and we don't need anyone coming round asking questions."

Tion took the bottle from Elly and removed the stopper. The liquid sloshed as he moved behind her. "Hold on to something," he suggested.

I'm braver than this... was her last thought as she slipped into darkness, running from the river of fire as it coursed down her back, scalding her skin and turning her vision from black to shimmering silver and finally, endless white.

The white rolled away like fog to reveal the blue-green room once more. This time, Alcione stood with both Sola and Romi at her side. She was wearing her favorite shift, the one her mother had made specially for her – not a hand-me-down. Kanase's beautiful flowers decorated the hem and neckline. Beneath her feet, the feather-floor squished between her toes.

The room smelled like flowers. "What's the trial this time?" she asked, sitting down and making herself comfortable. The room seemed to want her to feel safe. It took its time answering, and she fluffed the feathers, running her hands over them gently.

Are you clever? The room's voice was like wind, like a light-voiced lady trying to whisper with a sore throat.

"I'll try to be," Alcie promised.

Riddle, said the room. And it changed.

INTO THE SKY

The room she now stood in was familiar. It was the bottom floor of the tower in Kayre Ianthe. But something had changed. As Alcione studied the tapestries, the mounds of paper, she tried to make out what it was. There.

A huge box sat on the table. Pulling open the flaps, Alcie looked inside. It was empty. She leaned forward to search the deepest corners, confused. She had been certain this was the item out of place. But as she leaned, she lost her balance and fell.

"Help!" she cried, hearing Romi's frightened whinny and Sola's yip from behind her.

Inside the box was yet another room. This was one she had never seen before. It was a circular room, and bore resemblance to her room atop the north tower at home. Her bed was there, and beside it her nightstand and the box of trinkets and stones she'd collected, but not as she recalled. The light was wrong.

Instead of the tapestries that had once covered her windows, there was a strange material that felt smooth, like metal, but was clear and colored. She looked around to find five windows, each a different shade. Above the windows the ceiling jutted into peaks like towers – or like the points of a crown.

The first window was a sage green with mesmerizing swirls of white and silver and darker green mixed in. She came to stand beside it. Beyond the window, she heard the twitter of songbirds, the chittering of ysrei and ketcha. A whispering like wind chimes caught her, and she thought she could make out the words "riddle" and "puzzle." She strained, but could understand no more.

Another window was like a vivid sunset. It started gold at the bottom and worked its way through shades of pink to violet. Pressing her ear close, she heard the chanting of deep voices, speaking a tongue she had never heard. Perhaps hooves beat on stone punctuating the sharp words, but she couldn't be sure.

A third window was variegated shades of pale blue and green. When she touched it, it felt wet. *Is this what the sea looks like?* She traced the patches of darker blue within and watched as they shifted and whorled under her fingertips. A gentle rushing filled her ears, and she heard the distant squawk of sea-mews, the birds that nested by the Trifira River. A girl's laughter, brassy and unrepentant, floated to her. "Follow me!" the girl cried, and the sounds receded.

The fourth window was blue-purple, and light reflected past it in triangles and squares. It looked like her mother's diamond pendant, glittering and cool. In its light, she heard the bustle of Trifira Bridge. "Look!" she thought she heard Tremi call to her. She tried to press closer, but the voices splintered as they passed through the prism window.

She took a moment to move towards the last window. The colors were…indescribable. Perhaps it had once been orange, but that hardly explained the bits of it shot through with cerulean and green and indigo and white. It was as if someone had taken a rainbow, broken it to bits and pieces, dusted it with light, and sprinkled it down onto the glass.

There were no voices here, but music. An instrument she couldn't name played a song that made her heart soar, and brought tears to her eyes. Closing her eyes, she saw her family as they once had been. Her father danced with her mother, while Kanase sighed romantically over them. Isaura danced lightly with Hermion, her eyes merry.

The song spun around her, wrapping her in memory. Isaura flounced away, singing as she twirled around the floor with an imaginary prince. Hermion turned to Alcie. "Dance with me, sister?" he asked, holding out a hand.

She took it, and laughed as he whirled her in a circle. Isaura had caught Kanase by the arms, and the two of them giggled as Isaura mimicked her brother's movements, bowing to Kanase as he'd bowed to Alcione, and taking the lead as the melody swelled. Alcie lost herself in it, skipping and prancing, too elated with the rising notes of the song to dance properly.

When the music faded, so did the figures, leaving her by herself in the tower. It was as if she'd lost her family all over again. Sinking to the floor, she pressed a hand to her mouth to stifle the sobs. "Please," she whispered. "Please take me with you. Please don't leave me here all alone again!"

Riddle, thundered the room, and it echoed from every wall, lined every corner and danced in every mote of dust caught in the colored light. *Where are they?* And then, in Hermion's voice: *Where am I?*

"But I don't even know where I am!" Alcie protested. "I don't even know who I am anymore! Please, give me a sign! Please!"

Her voice broke on the last word. But there was no answer. "Please!" she shouted over and over. Still, there was no answer. "I'm here! I won't move, I promise! Please come! Don't leave me here alone!"

Not enough, the room admonished. *Thought you were braver. Cleverer.*

The room dissolved. She stood in the center of the ruined papers by the table, blood staining them. Sola's head was bowed in sorrow. Romi looked confused. She saw in his eyes that he didn't understand the room either, and he wasn't happy at being confined. She tried to reach into his mind, to see if he knew more, and she found herself rudely shoved out. He didn't want her in his mind.

"Please," Alcione whispered one last time. But even the room's voice had abandoned her now. She closed her eyes, understanding that for the first time in her life, she was truly, completely, and deservedly alone.

- CHAPTER 21 -
Alone

S HE AWOKE ALONE.
Tion and Elly had gone, and even Sola was no longer by her side. When she tried to sit up, the pain of the night before came rushing back to her. Her back was stiff and she had trouble stretching. She was barely able to reach her tunic and sighed to see that the back of it was in tatters.

Struggling, she dragged it over her head, wincing every time she moved farther than her aching muscles would allow. Her tender skin flinched at any contact, but she made herself continue. When that was done, she saw that her legs were bare, and that her knee had been cleaned as well. There was no grit around the wound, and the scab over it was free of dirt.

She was used to scraped knees, so pulling her torn leggings over her underclothes – which Tion hadn't touched – wouldn't have been hard, if she hadn't had to stretch down to her toes to do it. She didn't bother with her boots – it was warm enough outside – and only felt a twinge of remorse in taking the blanket Tion had left over her for a makeshift cloak.

The sky was pale grey and overcast, signaling rain in the next few days. A woman hanging laundry outside gave her a strange look, but Alcie paid her no mind. Limping a bit on her injured knee, she hobbled towards the barn in the Hollows.

Walking inside, she saw Elly and Tion by Sleepy's stall. The young boy started to go to her, but stopped when Tion laid a hand on his shoulder. "Elly, I think Sleepy and the others could do with some kert." He put a few coins into the boy's hand and sent him off. As Elly passed her, he looked up, wide-eyed and nervous.

Tion beckoned her over. "Don't say anything yet," he said, when she began to apologize. "Just…sit over there." He gestured at a trunk full of supplies. He looked upset. Tion never looked nervous or out of sorts. *Please,* Alcie thought, but didn't know what she was pleading for.

Leaning back against Sleepy's stall, Tion tipped his head back to look at her. "What you did last night was very foolish," he said.

"I know, and I'm sorry! It's just…"

"Save the explanations for another time, Alcione," Tion interrupted when she looked hesitant. "I don't imagine they'll be the truth anyway. I really thought I could trust you." He ran a hand through his hair. Alcie stared pointedly at the ground, unable to meet his eyes.

"Alcie, do you have any idea of the possible repercussions of what you did? Look at me," he commanded. "Do you?"

"I-I…Tremi said I could have died."

Tion nodded. "That's right. But it might not have been just you. If they'd decided to bring you before the Arkos, if they'd beaten you until you confessed who you really were, gods…there are so many ways it could have gone wrong. And then it wouldn't have been just you, Alcie. They'd have looked at the people around you, too."

Fresh terror bloomed in her mind. "You…you mean you and Elly."

"That's right. And perhaps even Tremi and Dar. If what you had done had gotten us found out, we'd all be dead." He paused, and drew in a heavy breath. "I can't protect you if you take these foolish risks, Alcione. It was dangerous enough letting you work as a stable girl."

"A-are you going to make me stop?" The idea that she would never get to work with the arion again scared her almost as much as getting caught had.

Tion shook his head. "You have obligations now, and you'll have to fulfill them. I'll finish up here, but you're to go straight to Middy Huin and purchase yourself a new tunic and leggings, and then to Mat Buske for the rest of your chores. This afternoon, when I take Elly out, you'll go back to

Middy Huin and aid her in her work. You will get no compensation."

When I take Elly out. Alcie realized that he meant to go riding, and she wasn't allowed. Instead, she would have to spend the afternoon with Huin…and Raka. "From now on," Tion continued, "you will spend all your spare time at Huin's shop. Clearly, I've let you run too wild. You need to act like a young woman, not a ruffian."

"No more riding?"

Tion raised an eyebrow, but it didn't seem lighthearted as it had when he'd done it before. Now, he looked as if she'd simply asked a very stupid question. "No riding. Don't ask me about that again, Alcie."

Miserable, she nodded. She wanted to tell Tion why she had done it, but under the dull silver morning sky, it no longer seemed possible to believe in legends, let alone make others believe. She had failed the test in her dreams, and her family seemed farther away than ever. She couldn't explain it to him now. She barely still believed it herself.

With regret, she turned over her old tunic and leggings to Huin, who promised to mend them for an additional ten dagats. That, plus the cost of the new clothing – which lacked dye of any color and was an ugly mud brown – nearly cost her entire savings.

Tion explained the situation to her, and Huin nodded, her face paling as she saw the wounds on

Alcie's back. Raka said nothing, her face dark and accusing.

Alcie tried to speak to Tremi during dinner, to apologize, but he would have none of it. "I'll call the guard myself if you don't get away from here," he hissed under his breath. The fury in his voice stunned her into leaving.

When she limped into Buske's barn he gave her an apprising glance, but said nothing. She forced herself to get through her chores, determined not to mess up more than she already had. This was the only time she would have with the arion during the day. She couldn't afford to lose it by being a bad worker.

The rest of the afternoon was an exercise in stubbornness. "Made a fool of yourself, rich girl?" Raka snickered when Huin went to the back to get materials. But then she turned serious. "You could have hurt Tremi. I told him not to look for you last night." She brushed past to take a seat, deliberately elbowing Alcie's back.

Whenever she got up, she found an excuse to pass Alcione, and to get in a snide comment and a poke to Alcie's back. By supper, it was all she could do not to shove the other girl to the floor.

The next day was no better. Somehow, everything seemed to hurt worse. Tion told her that it was because it was starting to heal, but she didn't believe it. She had spent the night back in the tower room in her dreams, her ear pressed to each window.

This time, they stayed silent. She tried to leave, but the room had no door. So she sat upon the bed, awake within and tormented by a riddle she couldn't solve, until dawn.

"Rich girl," Raka commanded when she arrived the next morning. Huin was nowhere in sight. "My shoes are dirty. Clean them."

Alcione stood still. Raka stepped over and did something. Alcie's back exploded in fresh agony and she bit her lip to keep from screaming. "Get on your knees," Raka told her, "and clean my shoes. Huin is at market until the bells chime next."

This time, Alcie bent down. If she cried for help, Raka would hurt her worse the next time. Or right now, if no one heard her or cared to come. She began to polish the pointed toe of Raka's boot with the edge of her tunic. "No," said Raka softly, and there was a menacing quality to her voice this time.

Looking up, Alcie saw a hungry smile on Raka's face. "Lick them clean. With your tongue."

She could have picked no worse insult, Alcie thought dismally. To kneel in front of another was considered surrender by a noble, and would result in a loss of lands and title. But to kiss their foot was to become their servant, to give up all right to property or name for all of time.

"No," Alcie said.

Raka snarled. "This is *my* world, rich girl. Once, I was on my knees, begging from people like you to save my parents, my sister, my baby brother!" Her voice rose, almost hysterical. "They made me lick the floor – every inch. And then they threw me out, to watch everyone I loved die!"

Dashing the tears away from her eyes, Raka clenched her teeth. "Lick. My. Boots."

At last, Alcie understood. At their core, she and Raka really were no different. And finally, aching and miserable, Alcie could see the other girl without anger. *If our places had been reversed, would I be like this too?* She shook her head. *I would never do this to another. No matter what happened! But I can be stronger than her,* Alcie thought, feeling a stab of pity.

She bent her head and licked Raka's boot. "Again," the girl commanded, and this time the knitting needle gently touched her back from above to emphasize the point. Alcie licked her boots a total of ten times, the taste of the malim leather like dust in her mouth. On the last time, she bit down, but Raka merely laughed. Her toes were much farther back in the shoe.

"Get up, and fetch me a pail of water," Raka said. This Alcie could do with ease. As she did, the bells began to ring. Huin met her at the door, and Alcie gratefully set down to the work she was given, letting the tasks fill her mind until there was no room for the turbulent mix of emotions inside. She had no gift for sewing like her sisters, but she knew enough to mend a pile of clothes.

After supper, she made her way to the Hollows stables. Elly was staying with Tion for a few nights, until Dar came back, and he was the magician's only assistant until Alcie stopped limping. Tion wanted no questions asked.

Ignoring the empty stall that had been her bedroom for months, she stepped into Romi's stall. He was the only one who hadn't abandoned her. Sola still hadn't come back, and for all her asking, no one had seen him.

Not-feel-good? Romi asked her. An image of an arion kicking his hooves at his stomach popped into her head. That was the sign that an arion was colicking, his insides twisted up so he couldn't relieve himself. Alcie checked Romi for a moment, looking for the signs, before she realized that Romi was actually projecting the thought because he was worried that *she* had colic.

Not like that, she told him. *Sad.* She wondered if arion understood the thought. An image came to her of flight, of what Romi saw from the sky. Then an image of the stall as he saw it. *My life isn't the only one that's changed since we left home,* she realized. *Romi is as much a prisoner here as I am.*

"I'll find a way to get your wings back," she promised him. "I don't know how, but when I get to Astraea, I'll figure it out. We'll go together."

As they stood together in the stall, Alcie closed her eyes and reached out with her thoughts, searching for Romi's mind. She felt him come closer, and lay his muzzle on top of her head. With the pressure on her head, she had something to focus on as she pressed upwards towards him.

He seemed to understand what she was trying to do. She could feel his intent to lay down, and she stepped away to let him, seeing herself dizzily through his eyes and her own at once. Laying down with her arms around Romi's neck, her head on his shoulder, Alcie shut her eyes. Through Romi, she saw herself relax, pale hair meshing with the golden straw in his vision. More images assaulted her mind, and then stopped.

Alcie felt Romi close his eyes as if she had closed her own again. Now came a barrage of sounds and smells, far stronger than those her own ears and nose could produce. The warm, sweet scent of hay, the foul reek of manure, and even the smell of the barn wood and the paint coating it tingled in her nostrils.

She heard other arion snorting and rustling. She identified a restless pacing of hooves as Sleepy, who always became more active at night since he spent most mornings dozing in his stall. A scrabbling above was birds and perhaps a nest of ketcha in the loft.

Tentatively, she pushed a thought at him. *What was it like to fly? When you were free? Show me?*

She was still unsure of how much speech he understood, so she added an image of him with wings out beyond the woods of Karya.

Slowly, a vision blossomed within her mind. Unlike the images he often sent, this moved, and she was mesmerized as she saw herself – Romi – go from a walk into a trot. Aiming for the edge of a hillside she had never seen, he stretched his wings and moved into a canter. His wings caught the wind.

He soared.

That night, Alcie had no nightmares. Her mind was tangled together with Romi's. Unchained from the lies and pain, they flew over the woods beneath a curtain of glittering stars, free as the wind whistling through feathers.

- CHAPTER 22 -
Secret-Keeping

THE CRISP AUTUMN CHILL was creeping closer one morning when Dar returned. He arrived without fanfare, and without any greeting to Alcione. She didn't see him, only saw that Storm had returned to his stall.

She fed him, Romi, and Sleepy, and hurried off to Buske, shivering a bit under her cloak at the driving rain. There was a commotion in the barn when she arrived. People were everywhere. Some boys she didn't recognize were busily cleaning and clearing and hauling things away. "What's going on?" she asked Buske.

"The Arkos has decided to take a look at the arion. What he plans on using them for, no one knows. But he'll be here any moment. Get to Welm and clean his hooves. None of the boys will go near him."

Alcie almost laughed – Welm was ridiculously gentle for his size – but she had the sense to refrain.

Buske didn't look in the mood for a joke. She hurried to Welm's stall, stopping to snatch a pick from the supply pail.

Welm seemed more agitated than normal, afraid of the commotion outside. But Alcie knew how to handle him; Stabler had shown her what to do with an anxious arion. Shushing him and behaving as if nothing out of the ordinary was happening, she stooped and ran a hand down his leg, squeezing just above the hoof to get him to raise it.

She proceeded with the rest of his cleaning as if it were a normal day, letting her confidence convince Welm there was nothing to fear. And in soothing Welm, she found her own mind beginning to calm.

She'd stay out of the Arkos's way and slip out the back whenever she got a chance. Never mind what Buske would say – he'd probably be too busy to notice her. *Thank goodness Romi's not here,* she thought. And then, *oh, no! I'd better ask Tion what's going on. I have to make sure the Arkos isn't planning to visit the barn in the Hollows as well.*

There was a scuffling, and then all conversation in the row halted. She heard a familiar voice, the same level tone she had heard one afternoon in a sunny pavilion.

"I thank you, Mat Buske, for allowing me to disrupt your morning."

"'Tis an honor, Arkos, sir. I've twenty-six arion here, and I've been keeping 'em in top shape."

INTO THE SKY

Alcie peered over the door. The Arkos stood there, surrounded by guards. Thankfully, it appeared the captain and his henchmen from the other day had remained at the Kayre.

Up close, he seemed younger than she had thought, perhaps no older than Huin. His face was wet with the rain, his golden curls damp. His cloak was black unrelieved by brocade or patterns of any kind, and the hood lay slightly wrinkled behind him as he turned to study Adrie.

"That one will do nicely," he said, "and that one," he said of Helar, in the stall one to the left. "I will recompense you for their care, of course."

"Thank yer kindly, sir. As I said, 'tis an honor."

The Arkos went on down the stalls, looking at each in turn. Alcie held her breath as he agreed to most of her family's arion, sparing only Moti for his size, but agreeing to care for him and the others in case he should want them later.

"Do you know from whose stables these arion hail, Mat Buske?" the Arkos asked.

Alcic's stomach sank. "I don't, sir, but I have a young'un as does. Alcie!"

She debated running. But if she did, the guards would simply stop her and bring her back. Then she'd be in worse trouble.

"Yes, sir," she said, tugging her cap down as far as it would go as she shuffled out of the stall. She kept her head down, gaze fixed on her feet. "Eight of the arion are from Kayre Montelymnë, Arkos, sir."

"And how do you know such a thing, boy?" queried the Arkos. "Don't be afraid to look at me. I'm no noble, that you must fear my face."

Alcie looked up tentatively. His face was so earnest. *It's all a game,* she told herself, pretending hard. *I'm just a peasant. I don't really hate you for what you did to my family. I don't!* "Nephew to the Stabler there, sir," she said, thanking Tanatos that Buske didn't dare correct her gender. "I took care of the arion with him. Don't know the others."

"That's all right," the Arkos assured her. He looked into the stall at Welm. "That one, there. Has he been ridden?"

"Aye, sir. By the master of the house, but not oft. He's gentled, but slow."

The Arkos considered it. "A good beginner's mount, you'd say?"

Alcie nodded. She'd often thought so herself. "He'll not spook easy, and his trot's fair smooth for his size. He'd be fine – if the beginner's tall, sir."

The Arkos let himself into the stall. He ran a hand along Welm's back, then reached down to take one of his hooves and inspect it. He ran a hand along the soft center of the hoof, checking for soundness. "He'll do as well. I thank you, Mat Buske. And you," he turned to Alcione. "That was a good assessment. I could use someone of your skill, boy, if you like."

Alcie shook her head furiously. "N-no, sir. No thank you, sir. I-I like my life as it is."

INTO THE SKY

From Buske's glare she could see that she had been rude, and that he would be furious with her later, but she couldn't help it. Fortunately, the Arkos laughed, dispelling the tense atmosphere that had flooded the room at her words. "I like people who speak their minds. If you ever change yours, let me know."

He walked out of the barn, taking Buske by the arm and propelling him into a discussion of how best to transport the arion to their destination, and when they might bring new arion in from certain places he had in mind.

As soon as they were outside, Alcie ducked out the back. She ran to the Hollows and was comforted to see that all was as she had left it. She didn't know where to find Tion this early in the day, and Elly was already awake and gone too. She gave Romi a brief hug and listened with relief as the dinner bells rang.

She bought stackers from Igren, Tremi's favorite vendor. He was in line ahead of her, and didn't spare her a glance. She looked down, knowing that she deserved his coldness. He had asked her never to lie to him, and she had broken her promise. Her father had always said an oath-breaker was one of the worst things a person could be. *Your name is only as good as your word,* he often said.

"Tremi, I—" She tried to apologize, but he shook his head.

"No," he told her. "Not now." She was left behind as he took his meal and went to join Raka and the others.

Alcie ate her stackers in silence, inside an empty building that was being made into a pub by some of the locals. It often served as a spot for street vendors to huddle on a rainy day, as the owners were currently street folk themselves trying to move indoors. She sat atop the half-finished bar, her feet kicking idly against its side.

She sneaked an occasional look at Tremi, who sat with Cormy, Raka, and Yvo. The other girl would stare brazenly back at her sometimes, a slight smile curving her lips. Tremi looked at her once too, with sadness and some other, indefinable emotion in his eyes. She tried to whisper that she was sorry, but the words caught in her throat. She was sorry she had lied to him, but not about what she had done.

That afternoon, she went to take Romi for a walk down the barn aisle before going to Huin. Ever since she had started sleeping in his stall, they had grown closer, and she felt herself instinctively seeking to find images to supplement the words she used when speaking with him. She no longer questioned whether the voice she heard was simply in her imagination.

She asked if he had seen anything out of the ordinary, projecting the words with an image of the men she had seen this morning. Romi replied in the negative. She thought he understood some words, the ones that were said most often to him, like *yes, no,* or *ride.* Others, like *Arkos,* were beyond his understanding.

A moment after she and Romi returned to the stall, she heard a voice across the way, in Sleepy's stall. "What's going on?" Tion was asking someone.

Quiet, Alcie thought to Romi, showing him a picture of himself walking, hooves making no sound.

"It's better if you don't know," a voice replied. Dar. "Just trust me, for old time's sake. This isn't something that should concern you."

"And why not? I thought we had no secrets from each other."

"You haven't told me the identity of the boy."

All was quiet. *He means Elly,* Alcie thought. *So Tion told Dar where I was from, but not Elly?* For that matter, she realized, neither Elly nor Tion had ever mentioned what house the young boy came from. She had pressed him gently about it at first, but when Elly seemed reluctant to say, she hadn't given it another thought.

"It's not my secret to tell," Tion said finally. "And if you want to say the same, I'll understand. But just tell me this: do I have cause to worry for him, or for Alcie?"

Something sounding like a sigh came from the other stall. Dar said, "No, nor for Sleepy or that rascal Romi. I've arranged it so you won't be troubled. That said, if you could find a place for those children to go that wasn't here, it'd be better."

"They're too young to be out on their own. Where else would be safe?" Tion argued. "There's barely a civilized world left beyond here. Cathatiur is no place for children alone, and hurricane season is coming, so Turan is out of the question. I told them I'd care for them, Dar. I'm not going to leave them out in the cold because it's easier for me."

"I know," Dar said heavily. "I know. I'll make some inquiries and see if I can find others to foster them. Rungilivanster will leave before winter. The Arkos will be moving ahead with his new project, and you shouldn't be there. I had your word."

"You have it still," Tion replied. "Despite all your mysteries. As it stands, I expect the Arkos intends to send me south, anyway. But I'll not go before the children are settled."

They exited the stall, and Alcie barely breathed as they made their way out of the barn. *Leave Ianthe?* Impossible. She had come here to get that crown, and she wasn't going anywhere without it. *And what about Tremi? And Tion, and Elly? Am I never to see them again? What will I do?*

The question still weighed on her mind as she sewed quietly under Huin's mindful eye later that day. When Huin turned away, Alcie glared as Raka's foot streaked out to kick her in the ankle. *There are some people I won't miss!*

That night, she lay awake into the small hours of the morning, unable to sleep. Elly dozed beside her, snoring softly. *He looks so innocent,* she thought, his face barely visible in the light of the lone lantern hanging from the barn wall. *Too young for such secrets.*

But then, she reminded herself, *so am I.*

He thrashed in his sleep. "Papa!" he wailed. "Don't leave!"

Quietly, she shook him awake. He blinked into the darkness, and slowly focused on her face. She knew how it felt to wake from a nightmare alone, and tried to spare him that when she could.

"It's all right," she whispered. Crumpling against her, she could feel him shake as he wept. The moment stretched on as the darkness enveloped them.

"Tell me about your family, Elly," she said when he'd calmed a bit. "Something good – before…before all this."

He nodded. Several times, he tried to begin but shook his head, overcome. She was going to let it go when he said, "I was going to be a rider."

He paused, and she took his hand. "Father used to take me into the sky with him on clear days. We'd go up beyond the clouds, my brothers on either side with their arion. Up there, we didn't have to be who we were on the ground. We'd laugh, and my brothers teased me for being so small. But up there, everything was small, so I didn't feel it. Everything was just a grand game with tiny little pieces. Sometimes…"

Blinking away more tears, Elly pulled his hand back, shrinking in on himself. "I used to wish I could live up there. If I was a rider, I didn't have to be anyone else. No world with nobles and kings and…"

He didn't say any more. He didn't have to. It was a shared remembrance – that their families had been people, imperfect and wonderful and much more than just their titles. Alcie lost herself in thoughts of her own parents and siblings.

"Alcie," Elly's voice broke into her musing. "You said once that you always wanted to be a rider. Why?"

She smiled at him. "I wanted to make my family proud. I wanted to be a hero who protects the land, who people look up to. Whenever I saw my father coming home, that dark point on the horizon, I'd think to myself, there is nothing better in the world than that." She remembered the dream of flying she'd had the night before. "And I've always loved the arion. I think, even if the rest never came true, I'd never stop wanting to ride."

The words echoed in her mind long after Elly had gone back to sleep. *What do I have left?* She wondered. *The Talaria are gone. The arion's wings are lost. And no matter how I try, I can't find the stones. Is this life all there is for me? Maybe I was a fool to think one girl on her own could be a hero.*

When sleep claimed her at last, she dreamed again of the room in the tower. In her dream, the city beyond the purple window was filled with weeping.

- CHAPTER 23 -
Broken Bond

T HE SUN BEGAN TO show its face the following
afternoon as Alcie returned to the Hollows to
check on Romi. She found Tion there, with Sleepy.
She saw Dar's dark hair behind Storm, and heard
him telling Elly about the different parts of the
saddle. "You're going riding," Alcie said, her heart
sinking.

Tion nodded. "Yes. But I've spoken to Huin;
you can have the afternoon off if you want to come
along. You won't be riding, but–"

"Of course I'll come!" she replied quickly.
"Whatever you want me to do." *Anything to get away
from Raka, even for just a little while.*

Tion gave her a brief, tight smile. "Good. Dar
and I are going to work on Romi's manners a little.
Meanwhile, you'll need to keep an eye on Elly. He'll
be riding Storm today. Sleepy's a bit feisty after being
inside during the rain."

They went out through the gate, Alcie riding double with Elly on Storm. Once they were out of sight of the guards, however, Tion made Alcie dismount and walk alongside the arion. "It will help strengthen your muscles," he told her, but she knew that he meant it as punishment.

It's not fair, she thought unhappily. *He doesn't understand! And I can't tell him. I thought he trusted me.*

But then, she realized he had thought the same of her, and thought she had betrayed that trust. And she had. So she kept silent as she jogged to keep up with Storm. Romi struggled under Dar's hold, but the dark-haired rider kept the rebellious arion under perfect control.

Romi sent an image of her riding him, and another of bucking Dar to the ground. *Don't you dare,* she warned him. *No.* She sent back a vision of Dar dragging him back to his stall with strong ropes. *He looks like someone you wouldn't win against in a fight.*

He didn't stop fidgeting, but he didn't send Dar flying to earth either. She felt a wave of disdain pressing against her. *I can't help,* she told him. *They don't like me either right now.*

The windlestrae was drier than ever despite the rains, and here and there a patch of it had simply given up the ghost and fallen over. Sunbeams escaped the clouds in a few places, giving the land a dappled look. Alcie stood and watched as Tion took Elly through his paces – walk, trot, and rising trot.

Elly was still too inexperienced to canter, especially on an arion he'd never ridden before.

Storm behaved perfectly, obeying every command so quickly that it seemed he understood the words Tion was saying. Dar held Romi still, backing the arion up a few steps when he got too antsy, and occasionally turning him in a small circle. Romi became more and more agitated, but Dar's face remained emotionless.

"I…I think he wants to move around more," she told him hesitantly.

Dar looked startled, as if he had forgotten she was there. "We don't always get everything we want though, do we?" he mused with a half-smile. "One could even say that not getting what you want teaches patience. He'll have his turn."

After a few more minutes, Tion and Elly came over to where Alcie stood. Tion took out a lead rope and clipped it to Storm's halter. "I don't expect any problems," he said as he handed the rope to Alcie, "but you never know. Keep a firm grip, just in case."

He nodded to Dar, who nudged Romi forward. As if by some tacit agreement, the two broke into a trot, following the circle Elly had flattened into the windlestrae. When Sleepy drew even with Romi, the bay arion's ears drew back against his head and he pulled forward to nip.

In a motion that Alcione barely saw, Dar had the arion's head swung to the outside and had pushed him into another of the tight circles. When they came close to Sleepy once more, Dar held Romi's reins short, so that the arion's head came up and his neck arched. He looked uncomfortable, but the line his bowed body made as it curved around the circle was beautiful.

"I want to ride like that someday," she whispered.

Elly nodded, intent on watching Romi. "Me too."

They continued for a few more circles at the trot, each of the riders rising in the saddle as their arion's outside leg moved forward. At Tion's nod, they broke into a canter, lovely and careful as dancers on a stage.

Sleepy, for all that he stood like a haystack in his stall, had a fluid canter that made him look like a golden star, streaking through the bleached-dry fields. Romi, with a shorter stride, was not nearly as beautiful, but there was such joy in every movement, even as Dar held him back. He tossed his head in the air and whinnied.

But then it all went wrong. Romi skidded to a sudden halt, wrested the reins from Dar's hands, and began to buck. He twisted and writhed as the talented rider struggled to regain balance and control. Alcie wanted to run to them, but she held fast to the lead rope. She tried to reach into Romi's mind, but the arion was too panicked to let her in. Elly looked down at her from Storm's back, worried.

INTO THE SKY

She watched as Tion swung around and tried to catch Romi's reins. But Sleepy grew nervous around the thrashing arion, and side-stepped away when Tion tried to reach out. Finally, Dar took his feet out of the stirrups and pushed himself off to one side. Romi, sensing he was free at last, took off at a mad gallop.

Tion dismounted and came over to his fallen friend. After an agonizing few seconds, Dar lifted himself up and stood, leaning heavily on Tion. Together, they walked back towards Alcie and Elly. Dar's limp was even more pronounced now, and his face was creased with pain.

When they got close, Dar reached out and took the lead rope. "If you want to see your arion again, go after him. He'll not listen to me, not today." He shook his head, disappointed, and lay an arm over Storm's neck, breathing deeply.

Tion nodded to Alcie, and she began to walk determinedly in the direction of her wayward friend. After the first headlong dash, he had stopped in a patch of windlestrae that was slightly more green than brown. As the reins lay over his head, he munched contentedly.

She didn't speak to him; she was too angry. Instead, she looked behind her to make certain the others were occupied with Dar, and then slapped her back with her hand as hard as she could. The fresh wave of agony that erupted she then sent speeding into Romi's mind. *That's how I feel when you do that,* she told him.

She showed him picture after picture: of him staying with Goso, of the Arkos sending him to pull a cart, of a barn on fire, of arion dying in battle. *I'm doing my best to save you from this,* she told him. *But you have to help me!*

Romi backed nervously away from her. His nostrils flared, and his ears began to tip back. The sight of her own arion afraid of her made her feel even worse. "Stop it, you great brat!" she cried. "I'm doing everything I can to keep you safe, but you won't listen to me!" She ran forward, intending to grab his reins and drag him back to Ianthe.

Sensing her intention, Romi didn't run, but instead moved lightning-quick to bite her. He came away with a snatch of her tunic and grazed her shoulder so that it bled a bit. Ignoring it, she took the reins and marched back to the others.

Dar looked at her, from her toes on up to her eyes. She knew she looked a sight, and ruining yet another piece of clothing hadn't been the thanks she wanted to give Tion for letting her come along. No one said anything as they resignedly set out for the city, Dar riding pillion with Elly on Storm.

I didn't think I could feel worse than I did when Tion told me I couldn't ride anymore. But after this, he'll see Romi goes to the Arkos for certain. And Dar will make sure Romi ends up in the worst place possible.

When the walls loomed up before them, Romi tensed up again. But Alcie was in no mood to argue with him. She simply yanked the reins, hard enough that his head popped up as he tried to fight back. She yanked again, and he dropped it, beaten. She sensed his resentment, but he knew that if he didn't go inside the city, there would be no supper, no warm place to sleep. And it was getting cold out.

Once she put him back in the stall, with a full bucket of water to make certain he didn't overheat, Alcione went out to face Tion and Dar. "That arion isn't fit for advanced riding, let alone a beginner," Dar was saying. "He's barely broken!"

"And what would you have me do? It's not his fault he's caught up in this mess. He doesn't deserve to be put down, and that's what would happen if you gave him to the Arkos," Tion responded. "I don't know what his plans are, but I've been watching the arion he chooses. I doubt Romi would suit his purpose."

Dar said nothing to that. Tion turned to face her. "Let's get some salve on that gash and get you to Huin so she can patch the rest of you up."

"I'll do what I can," Dar said as they headed out towards Tion's caravan. "But I make no promises."

"Just…" Tion didn't finish. Sighing, he led Alcie away.

- CHAPTER 24 -
Treasures

WHEN TION DEPOSITED Alcie in front of the tailor's business in Shopkeep Square, Huin was nowhere to be seen. Alcie watched Tion disappear around the corner before she stepped inside to face the inevitable.

"Your trinket," Raka said without preamble when Alcione entered. "Give it to me." The other girl had a predatory smile on her face, as if she had been waiting for this moment.

Alcie looked down at her pouch, where she still carried her special stones. Raka snorted. "Not those, foolish rich girl." She reached towards Alcie's neck and yanked underneath her collar, her hand gripping the chain of Alcie's locket as she drew it out from underneath the tunic. "I want this."

"No," Alcie said, grabbing it back. "You can't have it." She stepped away from the other girl. She'd taken much from Raka, still feeling that trace of pity for her loss. But pity had gone far enough. "If you touch it again, I'll hurt you."

Raka laughed harshly. "Really? How will that look to the guards I call? I will tell them you stole it, and that I was trying to return it. Who do you think they will believe?"

Enough. "Me, that's who," she replied hotly. "You're one of the Grey Folk. If I say you're the thief, they'll believe me, not you."

The slap rang in her ears. As Alcie was reeling from the blow, Raka gave a good yank and the silver chain around her neck broke. "Speak so to me again, rich girl, and I will tell them who you truly are. I will tell them you are a daughter of Montelymnë, and this trinket will prove it."

Alcione's eyes widened. "You wouldn't! Huin would never—"

"My aunt will never say anything. If she said I was a liar, I would be killed. She will never defend you before me."

With a sinking sensation, Alcie knew her words to be true. No one would defend her if it meant sending Raka to her death. Not even Tion, because it would jeopardize his protection of Elly. If she didn't give up her locket, Raka would call the guards, and one of them would die.

Alcione handed her locket to Raka. The other girl looked unsure for a moment, but then pocketed it and quickly sat down to her work. She began to hum a tune under her breath that Alcie recognized as one of the medka Tremi sometimes sang. "You can sit down now, rich girl," Raka said after the chorus. "I have what I want."

"I have a name," Alcie told her hotly.

"And I do not care," came Raka's response. "Set to your sewing."

Huin came in a moment later, and saw only the two girls tending to their work. Alcie focused on a pattern of a rose in black thread. She willed herself to stop her hands from trembling. When she accidentally pricked her finger on the needle, the drop of blood that welled up there matched the deep scarlet of the cloth.

That evening, she pled a headache and left Huin and Raka selling the work of that week, mainly skirts and leggings for the coming autumn weather. The weaver plied her trade mainly among other merchants, and so used the hours that they were free after the markets closed to sell her wares.

Alcie passed Cormy on her way out. He held a bedraggled bunch of flowers that she suspected was for Raka. He gave her a funny little smile. She thought he could have been her friend had it not been for Raka hating her so much. What lies had Raka told the others, to keep them from coming too close to her? Or had it been Tremi who warned them away of late?

When she got out, she wandered the city. She bought a quise pie and used one of the scraps she had brought with her from Huin's shop to hold it away from her tunic. The sweet taste of the pulpy purple fruit inside the flaky crust soothed her nerves a bit, but not much. When she finished the pie, her stomach hurt so much that she wished she hadn't eaten it after all.

She tried to walk the feeling off, and ducked into an alley on the southern border between the square and Gaoler's Row, where the dyers plied their trade. The stench was near unbearable, making her lose her supper in a sidewalk trench where the excess dye drained away.

Gaoler's Row was as harsh a part of town as Tremi had warned her, she saw. There were fewer torches lit, and she heard a man's exaggerated whisper suggest something that shocked her ears. A woman's sultry laughter followed.

Determinedly, she walked forward as if she belonged. She walked along avenues until she came to a street where the imposing stone edifices of the Row ended.

The Unsavory Quarter was hardly what she had pictured. The blocks of tall, looming buildings with leering faces from her imagination were replaced with the reality of squat, mud-colored tents, where men and women clustered around tiny fires. The smell of smoke and slightly rotten meat wafted to her.

A young girl met Alcione's glance, then ran to hide behind her mother. The woman looked up. Alcie could see that her face and hair were dark like

Huin's, but her eyes were old and her face pinched with worry lines.

"We have nothing for you, *bikutha*," she said tiredly, using a word Huin had scolded Raka over. It meant "outsider."

Alcie nodded. Seeing the young girl, her eyes so full of fear, Alcie dug into her pouch and found one of the stones she'd taken from the areas in the shadow of the bridge, by the quay. It was a favorite, with chinks of shiny green interspersed within the ordinary grey.

Carefully and slowly, she advanced, cupping the stone in her hands. "I don't need anything," Alcie said to the woman, looking at her and her daughter. Their shabby rag-dresses fluttered like leaves in the night wind. She offered the stone to the girl. "Here. Please take it."

The woman tipped her head to one side. "What do you want?" she asked. "Did someone tell you old Wazi would give you a fortune for a piece of stone?"

Alcie shook her head. "I have heard nothing of you, Middy Wazi. It is only a gift, from one scared child to another. It helped me when I was frightened. I thought your daughter might like it. Please…"

There were no words for why she had done it. She had never before had to justify wanting to do something kind. *All I want is to feel like I'm not all bad, like I haven't done wrong to everyone I still care about. And maybe it wouldn't feel as if no one ever wanted to be kind to each other again.*

INTO THE SKY

She knew it wasn't true – that Elly and Tion cared for each other, and Cormy and Tremi cared for Raka, and even Raka cared about Huin. But Alcie sensed Tion's attachment to Elly went beyond mere protection. In a way, it seemed almost like an obligation. And Raka wouldn't hesitate to use anyone to get her own way, whether she loved them or not.

There's so much cruelty in the world, she thought, hand outstretched. *I never knew. Will anything ever be like it was again?*

Wazi stretched out a small, crooked hand. She whispered something in her own language, the hissing tongue of the Fens, and Alcie could not tell whether it was a curse or a blessing. But when she handed the stone to her daughter, Alcie saw the young girl smile with wonder over the cracks of color in the stone.

"Thank you," Alcie whispered, eyes watering. The woman nodded, and left with her daughter.

In the darkness of Gaoler's Row, she heard voices. Silhouettes tucked together in alleys and in doorways seemed unnaturally tall and dark. She began to walk more quickly.

A man came close to her, a strange and frightening look on his face. "Ye lookin' fer trouble, lassie?" he asked her, looking down the front of the drab gown she had worn away from Huin's while the tailor patched up her tunic.

"No," Alcie said, but the man had a hand on her wrist.

"Are ye sure? Fer ye've found it if ye have. But I can be a lovely sort of trouble if ye've a mind to enjoy yerself." He backed her up against a wall.

Tremi had taught her to fend for herself, but she had never had cause to fear that she would need this part of his training until now. *I guess there really isn't much good left in the world after all,* she thought miserably. She lifted her leg and thrust her knee towards the spot that Tremi had told her.

The man howled and as he let go of her wrist, she shoved him as hard as she could to the ground. "You haven't got strength on your side," Tremi had warned, "only speed and surprise." She took the second part of his advice and ran away, as fast as her legs could take her.

- CHAPTER 25 -
In Their Hearts Always

S HE RAN UNTIL SHE had no more breath. She didn't know where she was going, only that she had to get away. The bells from the temples in the Celestial Citadel rang softly in the evenings so people could sleep, but they seemed louder now. One chime, two, until eleven chimes had passed.

When the echoes finally died away and she found that the ground beneath her feet had turned from cobblestone to a smooth, paved way, she looked up.

She had never been to the Celestial Citadel before, even though it was close by Trifira Bridge. The old stone temples gleamed softly in the torchlight. The statues atop the granite pillars were made from iaspis. The rare mineral glowed faintly even in darkness. Statues lined the tops of the pillars: heroes with swords unsheathed, ready for battle. Arion, wings poised as if ready to break free of the stone and take flight.

"Do you seek shelter?" a guard asked. Numbly, she nodded, and let him lead her inside. He wore deep blue robes over light armor, with gauntlets of fine leather. Unlike the guards at the Arkos's gate, his helm looked too shiny to have seen battle.

He led her into the nave, and from there to the altar, lit by a few lonely candles. She looked around and saw dimly that the windows at the top were done in stained glass. They were so like those of the temple at Kayre Montelymnë...

Standing beside the candles, she remembered mornings when her entire family had gathered together; she remembered sunlight streaming through the windows, bathing her hands in fragments of quavering color. Suddenly, something came alive inside Alcione that she had thought dead forever.

It felt like coming home.

The altar was not empty, as she had thought. The Citadel guard deposited her in front of an old, balding man in a sage green robe. The Caliarkos, Speaker for the Gods. At home, Brother Diskai had never attained the robe, and only wore the shawl of his office. This man was a true pursuer of the faith, a man of intimidating power. But his eyes were kind, and the smell of him, wood incense and soap, nearly brought tears to her eyes.

She knelt before him, as she had been taught, and made the sign of her faith: a hand touched to her heart, her head, and finally from her mouth to the air above her. It was a promise, that you would never keep what was in your mind and heart from the gods, and that those thoughts would be pure and good.

"My daughter," said the Caliarkos, and she looked up at him. "Tell me what grieves you so late at night."

It was that epithet, and how seriously he spoke, that finally burst the dam of tears she had been holding back throughout the day. She let them stream down her face, rubbing them away with her sleeve, but mostly just letting them fall. The Caliarkos sat with her, saying nothing, waiting.

She hiccupped, and scrubbed at her cheeks. The tears began to dry. "Father," she said, and faltered. "Sir, my father is dead. All of my family is dead."

The Caliarkos did not move to comfort her. His eyes said enough. "That is a heavy burden for one young as yourself to bear. But you need not bear it alone. Tanatos cares for all, and Samandiricl takes under her wing all who are friendless and lost. And here I am, and my brothers as well. Is there aught we can do to aid you?"

What was said to the brothers was said in confidence, with the certainty that no one, not even the King himself, could demand words from them. "Father, do you recall the story of Orfel?"

The Caliarkos nodded to himself, his head barely seeming to move with the jowls obscuring his neck. "The man who defied death, for love of another. A tragic accident, a long and brave journey, and five stones scattered to the far corners of the land. The legend goes that he who wore the Crown of Geyende would be blessed with a long, fruitful life."

"Whatever happened to that crown?"

He tapped a finger against his knee. "I am not sure. When the line of Orfel was supplanted by Heriot, the crown was kept in the armory, and then retired to the tower in the ayrlea, with the rest of the Orfelian regalia. I do not know what has happened to it since the death of the King."

"Could the Arkos have found it?" Alcie asked.

"The Arkos had his men search the tower from top to bottom in the days after the fire," the Caliarkos told her. "He found much treasure at the top of the tower, but no mention was made of that particular crown when he announced his findings."

Alcie noticed he made no mention of the Arkos, nor did his face flicker once at speaking of the dead King. "What is an ayrlea, Father?" she asked.

He took a moment to formulate an answer. She thought he seemed confused by the line of questions. "It was the meadow from which the arion used to take flight, on the far side of the Kayre, looking out towards Cathatiur. The winds were favorable from there, and the city's Talaria lived in the stone tower at the foot of the Kayre walls. It was heavily guarded, and from thence could the Talaria protect the King within and without."

INTO THE SKY

He studied her. "You came here so late to ask me such things, child?"

Alcie shook her head. "It is nice to hear old tales, Father. I...a friend used to tell me them, back home in the north. I miss my family so much, sometimes, that I wish I could take the stones and go find them."

She looked at him. If anyone would know, a Caliarkos would, and he was bound never to lie. "Father, do you think it is true? That if one took the five stones to the Mirror of Astraea, one could pass through and bring people back?"

This got the old man's attention, and he considered the matter, tapping his fingers on his robe with one hand, and his chin with the other. It seemed his fingers moved double as the rest of him stayed still.

Finally, he said, "This I do not know. But the story of Orfel was handed down in the Book of Truths, and it is same book from which we hear of the great deeds and wonders done by Tanatos. It is true that historical records say that Geyende died and was restored. But to the stones themselves, and the truth of that tale, I cannot say. Orfel was supposed to have said the stones were only to be used in greatest need. No one since has ever tested it."

"But isn't it true," Alcie asked, phrasing her question carefully, "that if there is an Astraea, that there must be a way to it from here? If Tanatos is

287

real, mustn't the rest be as well? Otherwise, how could we know what the real truths were?"

The Caliarkos smiled. "A good argument. Nevertheless, one that I suspect none will ever have the chance to prove. Even if one had the crown, one would have to find the mirror. It is said to be in Skyreach, well beyond the farthest borders of the land."

"But what if it is there?" she pressed.

Her vehemence seemed to startle him. "It may be, my daughter. But that is not for us to dwell upon."

"Why not?" Alcie questioned. "If I can't believe that's true, how can I believe in all the rest? How can I know that my family is in Astraea? How can I even know if it's a good place for them to be? If the gods are real, there has to be proof somewhere. Because right now," she caught the sob and forced it back, "right now it seems like they're just a silly dream. The gods didn't stop my family from dying."

"'Theirs is not to force our will, nor keep us from harm, nor do us ill.'" The Caliarkos quoted a passage from the Book of Truths. "The gods could not stop your family from dying. They brought us here, and we wished of them our independence. They granted it, but for that there is a price. We are responsible for ourselves now, and for each other.

"But," he added, "do not forget the words of the philosopher Gammet: the gods may not guide our actions, but we are in their hearts always.

Tanatos is with your spirit, and you may take of his strength to overcome your trials. Samandiriel sees you, and she will bless your efforts if they are pure. The gods do not forget their children, even when those children stumble and lose their way."

"The gods do not forget," Alcie echoed. "But they forgot my family."

"They did not," the Caliarkos corrected firmly. "Your family was part of a larger plan, as are you. But you must have the courage to find out what it is. You must live for them, or their deaths – whatever the reason – will be in vain."

What is my reason? Alcie thought. "I don't know what the gods want of me. How will I know?"

"You will feel it," he assured her. "But for now, you should rest. This is my post until the dawn, so my bed will be empty. Take the second door on the right. Do not protest, my daughter," he said, when she began to. "This helps me fulfill my promise to the gods. When my mother passed on, I too struggled to find my path. I am still finding it, in every person I aid."

The bed was simple. A wooden frame was covered by a hay mattress over which a coarse blanket lay. To Alcione, used to sleeping on the ground, it felt wonderful and strange. She thought of Romi, and of Sola, and of all the people whose trust she had betrayed. Her heart ached at the thought of parting with them forever.

But her path was not with them, not yet. For her entire life, her family had been her world, the only people she truly knew and cared for. They were the people who would have died for her, who would have sheltered her through anything and who loved her despite all their differences and disagreements. She would not let them die in vain.

If I stop trying, if I move on, it will mean that the Arkos won. It will mean that I allowed the world to replace a King with a man who wiped out fathers and mothers and children without a second thought. Whatever the nobles did, a man who kills children because of their names is a monster.

She pulled the blanket tight around her. *I have to keep going. Otherwise, when I die, history will speak of my family and those like them as the monsters instead. That will be the Book of Truths that the Arkos writes. I can't let that happen!*

My family wasn't perfect, she thought, *but neither are the people here. For Tion, for Elly, and for all those who died, I have to make sure that people understand that what the Arkos did was wrong. And for that to happen, I need my family back. I can't do this without them.*

- CHAPTER 26 -
The Choice

ALCIONE AWAKENED IN the church bed, in the room with the blue-green glow. The scratchy blanket now looked like a silk sheet, and the hay had turned to fluffy cloudspun, the soft material light as the feathery floor. She was more awake than she ever had been in the room of trials, feeling even the light brush of the wind as it drifted past her. It felt as if she had woken in another world.

"Whatever you throw at me, I'm going to figure it out," she told the room as she got up from the bed. Her voice echoed eerily from walls she could not see. "I won't stop until I do."

The room began to vibrate gently. *Who do you love?* asked the room.

Alcie smiled. "That one's easy. I love my family."

Really? The room lurched, and abruptly Alcie found herself standing in the middle of Caulburne Alley, watching Tion perform a trick with Elly. The audience was filled not with children, but with all the people Alcie had come to know during her journey.

Goso and Deena sat in front, with Huin, Raka, Cormy, and Yvo behind them. To the right, instead of houses, there was an aisle of stalls, with arion whose heads popped out over the half-doors. Buske stood with Sleepy, Moti, Welm, and the rest of the arion from Montelymnë. On the end stood Storm, with his owner beside him.

Dar regarded her with his serious blue eyes. She knew it wasn't really him, knew that the room of trials was behind the sudden appearance of this unlikely crowd. But it didn't stop her from feeling as if the strange, crooked-leaning man was judging her, and finding her lacking.

She turned away, looking to the left. In the shadows stood a lonely figure holding an arion by the lead rope. At his feet was a small creature, its eyes familiar yet chillingly cold. Disappointment shadowed their faces.

Tremi, Romi, and Sola.

"I love them too," Alcie protested. "That's not fair!"

If you had to choose?

"You can't make me!" Alcie told it. "I won't stop caring about them just because I'm going to save my family. I love who I love, and you can't stop that."

If you had to choose? The room persisted, moving around the people in the alley so that each of them

292

faced her, frozen in a dark tableau, their faces twisted with anger, accusing her of some terrible thing.

Alcie shrank back from the sight. "This isn't real," she told the room, but that didn't change the picture. Taking a deep breath, she stood up straighter.

What is it asking me? The room clearly wanted her to face these people, and to make a choice. She couldn't do it. *If I found the stones and stole them and it traced back to those I knew, Tion and Elly would likely die. If I take back my locket, Raka or I will die. And Tremi's been seen with me too often to be safe.*

Even if the Arkos never caught me, my friends would spend the rest of their lives in fear that someone might find out. Alcie sighed. Whatever she did, it would hurt the people she had grown to care for. *So what do I do?*

She looked at the people again; at the arion. The Caliarkos' words came back to her, about the gods having a larger plan. The people were hardly better off under the reign of the Arkos. The Grey Folk were still starving. People still lied, stole, were cruel to each other for no reason.

The Arkos's guards still punished people by law, as the King's guards once had done. The magians' mysterious presence warned others not to rise up in protest. So what had changed?

The Talaria.

She recalled how the Stabler had told her that the Arkos needed to get rid of the Talaria in order to get to the King. The Talaria had stood for a greater purpose than merely preserving the King's law. Without them, the land would have no protection from outside forces, few though they might be. And if the arion could not fly, they were of no use to guards or soldiers at all.

Is that my purpose? She looked at the arion – they had lost their wings that terrible night, when all of the Talaria were killed. Perhaps…

"If I went to Astraea, if I found my family, maybe there would be enough Talaria to bring back the arion's wings. But…why me? Why not Tion or Elly?"

I don't understand. All I want is to find my family. That doesn't have anything to do with the Talaria. So why am I suddenly so certain that it does?

The scene blurred, and Alcie returned to the room of the five windows. The noise was deafening, each of the scenes past the windows shouting at her. She rushed to the purple window. Elly's anguished voice screamed out from it.

"Mama! Papa!" he cried. "Ictor! Sofi!"

He was swept away in the onslaught of sound.

Another voice flooded in, level yet threaded with urgency. "We have to organize them, make them loyal to us, teach them. I had hoped not to need the arion so soon, but this is a more dire threat than even I imagined…"

That's the Arkos! He had some plan in mind for the arion – but what did their loyalty have to do with it? And what threat was he speaking of?

INTO THE SKY

"They will come from above," a clipped voice replied. "And we had better be ready. The others must be returned from the isles."

A voice from the blue window caught at her ear, tugging her to it. "We're not alone here anymore. They've been sighted as far south as the capital. If it falls, we're next."

From the green window, she heard a voice with the same thick country accent as the Stabler's exclaim, "They're in the trees! We'll not catch sight of 'em unless we can get above the forest somehow!"

She ran closer to hear, but the wind howling from the window that was the color of sunset suddenly drowned out all other sound. The voices that spoke a language she did not understand were shouting, arguing with each other. For the first time, she caught the sound of a word she knew. "Talaria!" shouted one man. An unintelligible burst of chatter came from others in the group, but the man kept repeating, "Talaria! Talaria!"

Exhausted, she moved to the beautiful window of many colors, straining to hear the sound of singing. But from this window alone, there was no sound at all. "Please," she called into the window, "Please, if you can hear me, make it stop! I can't think!"

The window began to glow, colors shooting out in twinkling prisms all over the circular room. Alcie closed her eyes and allowed the shining light to bathe her as the sound faded to silence.

"Alcione," a voice said, and she knew it was the voice of the room of trials. It was the voice of the Caliarkos; somehow too, it was the voice of her own father. "You will have to choose. The stones are a heavy burden. Have you the courage to do what must be done?"

Alcie felt her strength returning to her. She opened her eyes and looked directly at the iridescent window, despite not being able to see the voice, despite the burning light that made her want to squint. "Yes," she told it firmly. "I'll do whatever it takes to bring my family and the Talaria back. Just tell me where to start. I won't fail you!"

There was a sound of glass breaking, and the fragments of the rainbow window fell like a prism of tears. Another voice came to her, a girl – herself and yet not herself. "There will be sacrifices. Not only yours. Do you accept this?"

The purple window, just beside the rainbow one, glowed fiercely, and for the first time, she could see an image beyond it. It was the tableau of all of her new friends, standing together in Caulburne Alley. Dar and Tremi had come to stand beside Tion and Elly at the end of the show, laughing together. Sola's eyes, fierce but no longer frightening, caught hers for a long moment.

"I accept," she promised. "I said I'll do whatever it takes, and I will!"

"You have already begun," the room told her in a voice deep and resonant like the peal of a bell. "But you will not succeed alone. The stones await you."

She nodded, and reached a hand out to the purple window, touching her palm to it to seal the promise. All around her, everything was turning to light, and she felt a warmth from within, a quiet fire that started in her heart and tingled up her spine, spreading out from her like wings.

- CHAPTER 27 -
A Face That Does Not Move

S HE AWOKE WITH SOMETHING heavy upon her chest. "It appears you've made a friend, my daughter," said the Caliarkos.

The white ball of fluff with paws pressed to either side of her head stared at her. His deep eyes were solemn. *That's why you're here,* Alcie finally realized, reaching up to hug Sola. *You've been watching me, haven't you? I wanted a sign from the gods, a place to start, but it was beside me all along.*

"Thank you for letting me stay here," she said, getting out of the bed. "Would you like me to clean the bed, or fetch you some water?"

The Caliarkos' wide face creased into a smile. "No, but I thank you. Have you found what you were looking for?"

Sola hopped to the floor beside her. He had grown slightly larger, so much so that Alcie could now put a hand on his head without reaching down at all. "Not yet," she confessed, "and there's still a lot that I don't understand. But I think I'm on my way."

"You are doing your best," noted the Caliarkos, "and the gods reward those who care enough to try. Do not lose hope, my daughter. All will come right in the end."

Alcie made the sign of faith, and the Caliarkos repeated it back to her. "Go with grace," he said. "And please feel free to return here whenever you wish. If you want to speak with me, ask for Brother Fraitel."

Nodding, Alcie turned to go. Sola followed her. As the Caliarkos moved towards his bed, they passed each other and he placed a hand on Alcie's shoulder. She looked up at him. "May I know your name before you go?" he asked.

She smiled. She had nothing to fear from this man. "My name is Alcione," she told him. "Daughter of Pollinarus and Celandathia, Lord and Lady of Kayre Montelymnë in the north. I am a daughter of the Talaria, and I will always be proud of it."

The Caliarkos squeezed her shoulder in comfort, eyes sympathetic. "The gods have given you a hard road, Alcione. But I can see your heart is undaunted. I hope someday we meet again."

Before entering the stable in the Hollows, she checked to see who was there. It was far too early for most people to be awake, but she felt as if she'd gotten a full night of sleep. Elly was sleeping soundly in a corner of Romi's stall, hugging Flip to his chest.

Romi, standing watch over the curled figures, looked up at her. He sent her an image of an arion, laying on its side, unmoving. *Me?*

It took Alcie a moment to recognize what he was asking. *Of course not! I won't let them kill you!* She looked down at Elly. *I won't let them hurt you either. I'm going to get that crown, and then Sola and Romi and I are going to leave with no one the wiser. They'll never have a reason to suspect you or Tion.*

She left Romi with the comforting image of them soaring away, Sola carefully placed on the saddle in front of Alcie. The picture made her smile, a little. She did her chores quickly and silently, feeding and watering Romi, Sleepy, and Storm without disturbing the sleeping boy.

When she had finished, she returned to Romi's stall. She reached out to pet him, touching him with an image of the day before. *Why won't you let anyone ride you?*

Romi sent back a shiver of fear. *Control you once, control you always. Others say so.* The others were a picture of Welm, Inthys, and Ocne, her father's mounts. Her father had been a very good rider, but it had been the Stabler's job to care for the arion once they had done their job. There was little room for love or choice when there were orders to be followed.

Not me, Alcie insisted. *Not control — go together. You're bigger than me, but I give you food. I protect you. We take care of each other.*

INTO THE SKY

Romi did not reply, but she could sense that there was a part of his mind that was trying to understand. She left him thinking on it.

The time she spent on chores in Keecy Street went by rapidly. She tried to spend extra time with her family's arion, and sent them each as much love as she could through her thoughts. She had no idea if she could reach them the way she did Romi, but there was no harm in trying.

She didn't speak to Buske, only nodding when he gave her orders. Following his instructions, she mixed a de-worming paste together for Adrie. She poured it carefully into the vice flute Buske had gotten for the purpose, and brought it to the stall. Checking to make sure he hadn't been eating anything, she caught the tall arion by his halter and clipped on a lead rope.

She tied the rope to the hook in the stall and patted Adrie soothingly. He reached out to sniff the flute, then turned away in disdain. "Come on now, lad, buck up," Alcie told him, trying to sound reassuring. "Down the hatch!"

She caught his halter and brought the flute to his mouth. He moved his head higher, almost out of reach. In one fluid motion, she pushed it between his teeth and upended it down his throat. Some drizzled out, narrowly missing her hair, but most of it seemed to have gone to the right place.

"I wish I were taller," Alcie grumbled as she went to wash the gummy paste from her hands and the tips of her boots.

She flexed her hands at her side as she walked towards Shopkeep Square, curling them into fists and then uncurling them, trying to relax. Huin would be fetching new materials during dinner, and Raka would be taking her meal with Cormy, Yvo, and Tremi, likely all on Trifira Bridge since the weather was clear.

She stopped to buy a slice of quise from a vendor, and a few sticks of kert for Sola, and sat down in front of the shop to wait. She picked at her meal, too nervous to be hungry. The door was bolted shut. She looked up at the sky, one hand on Sola's head, and watched the clouds pass by, thinking of what to say.

Raka returned first, and upon seeing Alcione, her face darkened. "Why so early, rich girl?" she demanded. "Did you lose your other work? I'm so sorry." Her voice dripped with sarcasm.

"You wouldn't be a bit sorry," Alcie corrected. "But you will be if you don't give me back my locket."

Raka's eyes flashed. "And why is that?"

Alcie stood up and stared the other girl straight in the eye. "Because I'll tell Huin. She might not bring you to the guards, but she'll believe me. I don't lie and act mean, like you do. She might not throw you out for stealing, but she'll lose her faith in you."

INTO THE SKY

"She would never! I am her niece. Why should she believe you?"

Alcie stood her ground. "Call my bluff, then. I'm not afraid of you anymore, Raka. You're nothing but a big bully."

Raka turned wordlessly to go around to the back of the building. There was a small opening, so small that Alcie couldn't even imagine sneaking in despite being shorter than Raka, and the other girl used this to enter the building when it was bolted from the inside.

She came to the front and Alcie could hear the sound of the bar being set aside. The door opened, and Raka stood on the other side. In the shadow of the doorway, she seemed more like a spirit than a person, her skin blending with the drab of her blouse and the almost colorless homespun skirt. In one brown hand glinted the silver of Alcie's locket.

The first time Alcie had seen the locket was when she was very little. She had been enthralled with it, and had taken it from her father's study without asking. At first, there had been a thrill in doing something forbidden – not only the stealing, but in sneaking into the study in the first place.

When her father finally found out, she had expected him to yell, to punish her or send her to bed without supper. But he had merely looked at her with sadness and said, "I am much disappointed with you, Alcione."

The sting had stayed with her all those years, more than any day without supper, any lecture. And when her father gave her the locket a few days later, as a birthday present, it had become a part of the memory of the locket itself. Disappointing those you loved was its own punishment. Even Raka, it seemed, knew that.

Alcie took back her locket, carefully fastening it around her neck and tucking it under her tunic where no one could see. She stepped into the shop, pushing past Raka, and sat down on her stool. Looking up at Raka, she said quietly, "I won't tell anyone about what you did. But if you try it again, I'll have Sola bite you."

Beside her sat the pup, his gaze uncannily human as he stared down the girl who had upset his closest friend. Raka took up a swath of fabric and got to work. A moment later, Huin entered to find the two girls intent upon their mending.

"Elly says you did not come to bed last night, Alcie," Huin told her. "He was quite concerned for you. You should go to see Tion tonight after his show has finished. He spent some time looking for you."

"I…" She looked down, and then over at Raka. The other girl smirked, expecting her to lie. "I was in the Celestial Citadel quarter. I felt homesick, so I was speaking to Brother Fraitel to feel better. I'm sorry I worried everyone."

304

INTO THE SKY

Huin placed a hand on her shoulder, and Alcie looked up, afraid that Huin wouldn't believe her after all. "Brother Fraitel is a good man. I hope he has eased your heart. It is difficult for those who are not traders, who are unused to coming and going. I forget that sometimes."

Supper came all too quickly, and when it did, Alcie left to help Buske feed the arion. She checked on Romi, Sleepy, and Storm only after making certain that Tion wasn't lying in wait for her. Brother Fraitel or no, he wouldn't be happy that she had disappeared twice in only a matter of days. She didn't blame him; she knew he was truly only trying to protect her. And she didn't know what to say to him – his opinion of her had become so very important, and without meaning to she had made him worry once again.

When she was returning across Trifira Bridge towards Shopkeep Square, she felt something wet hit the back of her neck. "Girl!" called a familiar voice.

Alcie's heart sank. She turned to face Raka, looking at her feet to see the piece of brynza that had hit her.

Expecting to see Raka alone, she was surprised to find Tremi, Yvo, and Cormy standing beside her. "Do you eat stackers, or are you too delicate?" Raka jeered, but for the first time, there was a different look upon her face. She was baiting Alcie, but this time, there didn't seem to be malice but...

It took Alcione a moment to decipher the quirk of the eyebrow, the slight upturned jut of the chin.

Respect.

"Anything you can eat, I can," Alcie replied. "But are you sure my presence won't spoil your appetite?" This question she directed as much at Tremi as Raka.

Tremi didn't smile, but his eyes were fiercely assessing her. Cormy looked to Raka to see what she would do, while Yvo offered Alcie a gentle, encouraging smile.

"I think I will be...entertained...by your presence," Raka said slowly. "Perhaps I saw you once as a doll, with one face that does not move, and nothing behind it. It will be interesting to see if you can prove that I am wrong."

It was the closest she would ever get to an apology, or acceptance, but Alcie was more than gratified. She sat down next to Yvo, who handed her a stacker. She spoke little, listening as Cormy relived the errands he had run that day, and Tremi related gossip about the merchants on the bridge.

Tremi didn't look at her, but when she was finished with her stacker, he broke off a piece of his and handed it to her. "You're getting too thin," he murmured. "Never survive winter the way you look."

She smiled, and took the food. Perhaps he hadn't forgiven her yet, but he was getting there. She didn't want to leave with all of her friends angry at her.

INTO THE SKY

They talked until the sun began to set, washing the sky in red and gold. "You should return again, two-faces," said Raka, tossing a crust of bread at her feet for Sola. "There are too many men here otherwise."

Tremi, Yvo, and Cormy laughed, all knowing what was really behind her words. Alcie smiled. "Do they intimidate you, doll-maker?" she teased quietly.

Raka stuck out her tongue and flounced away. Cormy and Yvo, exchanging a bemused look, followed her to return to their homes in Shopkeep Square. Alcie stood with Tremi, feeling awkward.

They didn't stand there long. A voice from behind coughed, "Er-hem," and Alcie turned around, knowing that the happy respite of the good day had just run out.

"I'll let you two have a talk," Tremi said quickly, and waved a hand in greeting. He nodded, and bolted off for parts unknown.

Alcie looked up. It was worse than she'd planned. For it wasn't a furious-looking Tion who had come to fetch her, as she'd imagined he would.

It was Dar.

- CHAPTER 28 -
A True Rider

"**Y**OU KNOW, IN A WAY you're lucky he sent me to talk to you," Dar said without preamble. "Tion would have made you cry, because you care about each other. He would have been disappointed in you."

There was that awful word again. "I didn't mean to disappoint him," Alcie began, but Dar held up a hand to forestall her.

"I'm not actually interested in that. I saw you go to the Citadel – you weren't paying much attention, but I was…on an errand…that took me in that direction." He phrased it carefully, but Alcie knew that meant he had been working for the Arkos. "I let Tion know when I spotted you.

"You're not simply here because the wind swept you this way," His tone brooked no dispute. "You look up the hill too often. You hate him," Dar said of the Arkos, "understandably. But there's more.

You want to stop him. Tion hasn't seen that bit of you yet."

Alcie bit her lip. "How do you know that?" she asked. "I've never said anything. And doing something like that would get me killed." She kept her voice down, even though there were few passersby at this time of evening. "It wouldn't be logical to think that."

"Ah." Dar's musical voice made the syllable both question and answer. "But you're not logical, are you? Else you'd never have come to this city. This is the last place you ought to be."

"Maybe I stayed because of Tion and Tremi," she challenged. "They do fine here."

"And maybe you'd have stayed anyway, Tion or not, Tremi or not," Dar replied. "You've certainly cared little enough about them with the stunts you've pulled of late. Tion thinks you're just lashing out, angry about your family."

"I spoke to Brother Fraitel," she told him. "I was angry. Now I'm not." She tried to keep the fear out of her voice, the annoyance at his too-perceptive words.

Surprisingly, Dar laughed, the sternness of his expression melting away. "Young one, you impress me. It's a shame you're friends with Tremi, because you're a born liar. But walk with me – I didn't come here mainly to lecture you."

"Why did you come, then?" she retorted, wanting to get away.

"You'll see," came his maddening response.

As the sky turned deepening shades of blue, a few early stars began to twinkle above. Dar led her into the Hollows as people began to light the tiny street torches known as night-glows.

At the barn, Tion and Elly were waiting. "Dar told me you were at the Citadel," Tion said. "Are you all right?"

Alcie nodded, her throat tight. "No lecturing," Dar told his friend. "I think she's had enough for one evening."

Tion merely moved forward and patted her tentatively on the shoulder. She realized suddenly that he thought she didn't trust him anymore, and was afraid of saying the wrong thing. "I'm sorry," she said quietly. "I didn't mean to hurt you."

There was a tense silence for a moment, and Tion looked away from her. Finally, Elly came forward and locked his arms around her chest just below her heart, as far up as he could reach.

Tion came forward. Alcie looked at him, tears in her eyes. She thought she'd left all the tears behind in the Citadel last night, but it seemed she still had more to lose. He opened his arms tentatively and she and Elly rushed into them. "Please don't be mad at each other anymore," Elly whispered.

Glancing up, Alcie saw Tion look hard at Dar in the moonlight. The other man's expression was, as usual, unreadable.

The moment passed, and Tion stepped back, taking Elly with him. Alcie looked at them and then turned to face Dar, who was staring at her. "I have another errand to run tonight," he said. "If you're up to the challenge. I'm going to Trippleton. It will take us most of the night, even if we're moving quickly."

"Maybe I should give her Sleepy–" Tion started to say.

"No," Dar interrupted. "She'll learn on Romi, or she won't learn. It's not as if she'll have Sleepy to fall back on whenever times get rough. If Romi's her arion, she needs to learn to ride him."

"You'll take care of her?" Tion pressed.

"I will," Dar assured him. "You've trusted me on far more important matters than this."

Alcie wanted to ask what those matters were, but her joy at the prospect of riding again stopped her. "Tack up," Dar told her, "and meet me at the front of the barn."

She'd learned better than to rush, risking messing something up or overexciting Romi. He was already curious. *Ride at night?* he asked, giving a picture of the dark sky overhead.

Alcie sent back a picture of Trippleton. *Go there now.* She checked to make certain that her stirrups were even, and picked up her cloak from the hook in the tack room where she had left it that morning. It was chilly out.

Tion fussed over her like a mother hen, making her carry a ration of food in her old stone-pouch and

311

giving her a few extra coins, "just in case." Dar stood by impatiently, Stormweaver's dark coat making him near invisible in the shadows of the barn aisle.

"She's ready," Tion told him, handing her Romi's reins.

I could have said that myself! Alcie thought, but said nothing. She had already worried and angered Tion enough, poor payment for his care of her over the summer.

"Follow Dar's instructions," he told her, "and don't make trouble for him." He looked wryly at his friend for a moment, and then lowered his voice to a whisper. "Dar isn't one for outward kindness, but he's doing a good thing for you. Don't waste it."

She nodded. As she fell into line behind Dar and Storm, she looked over her shoulder. Tion stood, Elly's hand in his, under the dim light of a single lamppost. She and Romi turned a corner and headed out into the Hollows, Sola trotting quietly behind.

Alcie and Romi received strange looks as the guards went over Dar's paperwork. Alcie listened as they read one document aloud. "My messenger may proceed to do my work in whatever manner he sees fit," the guard spelled out slowly. "He is therefore permitted to pass through the gates of Ianthe with whatever aides he deems necessary." It was signed by the Arkos himself.

"The lad?" the guard asked.

"I cannot carry all of the baggage on my own saddle, and should I need to rest during the journey, the lad will be able to lead both arion forward until I wake," Dar replied casually.

"You can sleep," the guard jerked a thumb at Storm, "astride that thing?"

"If you are a messenger of the Arkos," he retorted sourly, "you learn to sleep where you must, to do his bidding."

The guard looked miffed, but he nodded. "Very well. Pass, both of you."

As the gate shut securely behind them, Alcie thought about the words. *Dar must be very important to the Arkos,* she thought, wondering not for the first time what exactly it was that he did when she didn't see him.

Dar took out a small item. It was too dark to see what it was, but Alcione recognized the sound of flint striking tinder. A small light sprang up from his hand.

"What is it?" Alcie asked as he reached forward to attach the light to Storm's bridle.

"A relic from the past," he said quietly.

She rode closer to see. The small object was circular, and made from iaspis. Inside was a small wick with a slowly burning flame.

"Why doesn't it burn Storm? And how does it stay lit?"

Dar rode forward. "I didn't invent it, so I have no idea. But the Talaria once used them for nighttime endeavors. Come on, we haven't time to waste."

He nudged Storm into a trot, and Alcie and Romi followed. The cold air was brisk – just enough to keep her awake without making her uncomfortable.

"If you want to ride, you can't let your fears lead you," Dar said, turning to look at her. "Bring Romi up alongside Storm. If he tries to bite, yank his head away and scold him. He can't get away with intimidating others, especially not you."

Alcie was nervous, and sent Romi a thought: *no-bite!* She couldn't tell whether he understood her, but she knew that he'd heard it. Carefully, she made her way towards Storm, nudging Romi forward with her heels.

When they came even with Storm's flank, Romi immediately snaked his head out. "No!" Alcie cried, and jerked hard on the left rein.

Romi tossed his head into the air and banked hard to the left. Alcie tipped in the saddle, unbalanced. She fell forward onto Romi's neck as he stopped dead and ducked his head to eat.

"Pull his head up," Dar instructed.

Alcie tried. She truly did. But Romi ignored her, both her thoughts and actions. He continued to graze serenely as she pulled fruitlessly at the reins.

"Heels down, back straight, shorten your reins, and pull! Not some halfhearted tug. You're not sewing a seam here, girl!"

It was the *girl* remark that did it. Alcie sat up as straight as she could, shoved her heels down to keep her balance, moved her hands up on the reins, and pulled. At the same time, she poked her heels into Romi's stomach. *Go!* She sent the thought at him as a yell.

Romi brought his head up, startled, and began to walk.

"Not bad," Dar approved. "But we still haven't conquered the initial problem. Try it again, and this time, keep your heels down. You're not dancing – if your toes are down your feet will slip in the stirrups."

His calm voice steadied her. She had been scared of falling when Romi put his head down so suddenly, but Dar's matter-of-fact attitude made it seem like this sort of thing happened all the time.

With care, she moved Romi forward into a trot and pushed him closer and closer to Storm. Every time he turned his head to the right, she gave the left rein a gentle tug, reminding him who was boss. Sola pranced alongside, looking bemused.

It seemed odd, the idea that a very small person could be in charge of such a large creature, but she remembered how the Stabler had explained it to her, so long ago. "They know they're bigger, but they don't understand things," he had said. "They fear them. They'd rather ye be in charge, 'cause they trust ye t' know what's what."

"I know what's what," Alcie murmured under her breath, reinforcing the words with a thought directly to Romi. If Dar heard, he didn't say anything.

Slowly, they gained on him and Stormweaver.

"If he bites my arion, you're walking the rest of the way," Dar warned. "Keep his head straight, and make him keep trotting. If you can't learn this, you'll never learn the rest. Immaturity is no excuse."

The tone of his words, if not the gist, kept her relaxed. She pushed Romi a bit farther ahead, and kept a steady hand on the reins. Storm acted as if they weren't there, and Dar sat straight and proud in the saddle, his crooked leg unnoticeable in the dark. *He looks like a rider,* Alcie observed. *He should have been one.*

Studying him, she realized that he was no longer the dark stranger in the shadows who had intimidated her so much when they first met. She still wouldn't want the brunt of his anger directed at her, but she saw now that underneath the gruff exterior was a kindhearted man.

"Whatever you're concentrating on, keep it up."

Even in the darkness, she knew she was blushing and prayed he hadn't seen. "I-I was just thinking that you know a lot about what you're doing," she blurted out. She wanted to clap a hand over her mouth, but dared not take her hands from the reins.

"Tion and I were childhood friends. Everything he knows, I know."

He fell silent, and they rode together for a time. Alcie let herself drop back, habitually following after Dar. The night was alive with sounds and scents.

INTO THE SKY

Kekkata chirped in the windlestrae, and she could hear the soft buzz that indicated the presence of halay. The warm smell of hay and arion-coat, even the slightly foul odor of manure, were welcome to Alcione. And in the vast black sky, the stars glittered like a jeweled curtain over the landscape. She felt alive, as she hadn't inside the city.

"I missed this," she murmured.

"Missed what?" Dar inquired after a moment. She hadn't realized she had spoken aloud.

"The countryside," she replied softly, sure he would laugh at her. "It's so noisy in Ianthe, so busy. Sometimes it feels like you can't hear yourself think for all of it."

"You don't belong in a city," Dar said. "Why did you come?"

This time, Alcie thought before she spoke. It would be so easy to reveal her ideas to Dar – and so easy for him to turn her in if he thought she posed a threat to the Arkos. "Because I had nowhere else to go," she told him. "My home was destroyed."

They continued on. After a while, Dar asked if she wanted to try a short canter. "Don't be too eager," he said. "I expect you to exercise control over your arion."

She agreed, and asked Romi with her inside leg, as she'd been taught. He needed no coaxing here; as soon as Storm began to move, Romi flowed into a canter beside him, his legs floating over the dirt road as if he yearned to leap into the sky.

One day, she thought to him. *One day we'll fly.*

Trippleton came into view sooner than she could have imagined. *When it was a caravan, we had to move slowly!* The realization made her smile. *You can move so much more quickly when you're just a few. You could even get as far as the gate at Skyreach if it was just you and an arion.*

Dar slowed Storm to a walk, the motion so graceful that she didn't notice until Romi had blown past the other arion. Alcie slowed Romi, circling him down to a walk and falling in beside Storm. Romi was puffing and snorting, and Alcie found herself taking short, quick gulps of air to catch her breath. Storm and Dar looked as if they'd never gone faster than a walk.

"You want to know why I brought you out here tonight."

It wasn't a question, but not quite a statement either. "Why?" Alcie asked, knowing it was expected of her.

"You have the skill to be a rider, and the heart. But you lack the focus."

"Focus?" It seemed all she could do was echo him.

Dar didn't speak for a moment. The breeze whistled between them, riffling their arion's manes. "Something drew you to the Kayre, to risk Tion's wrath – even possibly death. You're like an ysrei at a bone; you'll not let go. I don't care to know what it is, but when you're on Romi, put it away."

"I-I try," she stammered. "It's hard."

"It is," he agreed equably. "Do it anyway. Storm has thrown me twenty-seven times since first we met. The last time, he didn't throw me. He fell, and crushed my leg beneath him."

He said all this with no emotion, and Alcione stared at him. *Twenty-seven times!*

"Do you know why an arion listens to you?"

"Because they're frightened and want someone to lead them," Alcie replied, wondering what point he was trying to make.

"That's part of it, and whoever taught you was wise. But it's not entirely it." He pushed Storm back into a trot, and Alcie followed suit.

"An arion doesn't know stall from stall, kayre from city from town. They care nothing for where they start or finish. All they know is the journey, the ebb and flow into and out of it. They measure their lives not in time, but in feeling. And they're always feeling – the wind at their backs, the creak of fiddlebugs and wagon wheels.

"When you ride, you have to understand that. More, you have to feel it yourself. Be human to find your direction, human to sense danger and avoid it. Leave the rest. *That* is the mark of a true rider."

He spoke no more. Alcie turned his words over and over in her mind as the lone light that marked the edge of Trippleton came ever closer. *The mark of a true rider,* she thought. *I have to be like an arion when I ride. To feel what Romi feels.*

She looked at Stormweaver. *Can you hear me?* She sent the thought to him, but received no response. *I wonder if you can hear Dar, or he you? But you trust each other, and think the same thoughts even without that. How can that be?*

They drew up to the lone lantern all too soon. Dar disappeared into the inn, leaving her holding Storm's reins. When he returned, he beckoned her forward. "We'll head back in the morning," he told her. "For now, untack and brush them down. It's cool enough that they'll do without baths for the moment."

After rousing the stable boy and taking some papers and the iaspis sphere from the saddle, Dar left the two of them to care for Storm and Romi. It was some time before Alcie had finished preparing the arion to rest comfortably in their stalls for the night.

She stood with Romi for a moment before heading in. *Not control,* she told him, thinking of what Dar had said before. He meant for her to have control over Romi, but that wasn't what she wanted at all. Bullying Romi into doing what she wanted didn't feel like riding – it felt more like stealing someone's locket. *Go together,* she said.

She remembered how Dar had made Romi's neck and back arch all those days ago. In her mind, she replaced Dar's figure with her own. *Go together, and look beautiful.* She sent with it a wave of happiness, of light steps and warm breezes tickling the skin.

INTO THE SKY

She let him ponder the idea as she met Dar in the tavern. He waited for her in the front room, lit by the sphere's faint glow. "Everyone settled?" he asked.

She nodded. He led her to a room with two pallets on the floor. She made herself cozy on one, the thin blanket and her cloak more than enough covering, especially with Sola to warm her feet. Dar took the other pallet. Behind her, she heard him settle in. "Not bad, young one," he told her. "Sleep well."

Closing her eyes, she let herself dream of the journey back to Ianthe. Not what she would find when she got there, nor what awaited her in the morning, nor Dar's advice for the way home. She didn't even let herself think about the stones. There was just the sun on her face, and the feel of Romi's shoulder rippling underneath her hand as he moved.

The mark of a true rider...

- CHAPTER 29 -
Together

D AR WAS ABSENT WHEN Alcione woke the next morning, and she assumed he had gone off to do whatever his business entailed. When she had finished eating, she went out to the stable to groom Romi and Stormweaver.

"We'll be practicing leaps this morning," Dar said, startling her as he came into the barn. "Since the arion no longer fly, I've taken the liberty of developing a new method for shortening a journey. If there is an obstacle about the size of you," he pointed to her, "a large arion like Storm or Romi should be able to clear it."

Alcie tried to picture it, and couldn't. "Without their wings, how can they get enough height?"

Dar shrugged. "If they run up, they seem to stay balanced enough to get over. I've set up a small course deeper into the woods north of here, where no one should bother us. We'll go back to Ianthe near evening."

"Why?" Alcie asked, and then realized she needed to elaborate. "I mean, why are you taking the time to train me?"

Dar ducked his head a bit, looking almost guilty. When he spoke, it was in a softer tone than he usually used. "I know you're used to living in the city, but you can't stay. Before winter comes, you and Elly will have to leave. It won't be safe for you anymore, and Tion's got work of his own."

"What kind of work?" Alcie pressed.

Dar moved to take Storm's saddle and pads from the tack stand. "I can't tell you. I'm sorry. But when you go, you'll have to be able to control Romi on your own, and part of that means knowing what your limits are as a team. The leaps will test you both." With a tug, he cinched the girths tight. He gestured to Romi's saddle, and Alcie moved to get ready.

The woods north of Trippleton weren't nearly as deep as the Karya, and sunbeams dappled the ground with light. The clearing that they eventually reached had been set with fallen logs and other natural obstacles, but cleared of bracken and brambles that normally cluttered the woods.

"I'll take Storm over first, and we'll see if you can tell what I'm doing to make him leap," Dar told her. He spurred Stormweaver into a brisk trot and circled around the obstacles once to warm up.

Alcie watched carefully as Storm broke into a canter. She didn't even see Dar change the position of his hands or nudge the arion with his outside leg. It was as if…as if they were speaking to each other! Alcie wondered if it could be as Storm's long, graceful strides carried him rapidly around the clearing.

Do you think they understand each other? she asked Romi, trying to convey an image of their mind-to-mind speech. His response was confusion; he didn't understand what she was trying to ask.

All at once, Dar curved Storm sharply to aim for a low log. Alcie had seen arion take off before, from the high pastures at Montelymnë. Her father had used those fields to come and go from visits to Kayre Kymminthë.

But this she had never seen! Without wings, yet without hesitation, Storm gathered his hindquarters and sprang over the log. Dar stood and balanced over Storm's shoulders, taking the weight off the arion's front end and steadying him as he landed heavily on the other side. Storm's head ducked down a bit, and Dar leaned back to pull him up slightly, keeping him at an even stride.

"We haven't got it quite right yet," he explained as they came down to a trot, "but as you can see, we manage. Romi may do better, as he's smaller and more fine-boned than Storm."

"So, can I try it?" Alcione asked. *I know we can do it! Romi is every bit as good as Storm, and lighter too!*

From his high perch, Dar looked down his nose at her, brows drawing together in a forbidding frown.

"Let's start with the basics. If you can stay in the saddle, I'll consider it."

"But I thought you said–"

"Never mind what I said," Dar interrupted. "Taking a child over leaps isn't the best idea, especially when she and her arion are equally hotheaded."

"I am *not* a hothead!" Alcie snapped, barely restraining the urge to stick out her tongue. "Or a child!"

"Prove it," Dar challenged, a smirk lighting his face.

Inwardly, Alcie fumed as she stood upon the log and swung herself upwards into Romi's saddle. But she knew his game – if she lost her temper, he won. If she won, it would be because she was controlling Romi and doing exactly as he told them.

That meant not simply going over a leap and begging forgiveness after, which she hadn't been planning to do...mostly.

We'll be perfect today, she told Romi, showing him an image of themselves, moving around the ring and looking as straight and fine as Dar and Stormweaver. He didn't reply, but when she heeled him into a trot, he neither tugged the reins from her hands nor refused her request.

Dar put them through their paces, making her show that she could rise correctly at the trot, and coax Romi to lead with his inside leg at the canter. He made her halt with no warning, turn around and do every exercise in the opposite direction, and sometimes with her feet out of the stirrups.

It was grueling. By midday, she no longer even thought about leaps. She was so jounced around that she'd certainly land on her head if she tried.

Dar pronounced them finished when she'd ridden two laps around the ring at a trot, rising the entire time, without her stirrups. When he told her to walk and then dismount, she simply climbed out of the saddle and sat down. Romi looked curious as he regarded his worn-out rider. *Legs not work?* he asked.

"I'll never get up again!" Alcie announced, her head drooping.

A pale, long-fingered hand proffered a water skin. Alcione took it gratefully and drained it to the last drop. Handing it back, she took the arm offered and got wearily to her feet. "Come on," Dar said. "Not a bad job at all. We'll have dinner and see where we stand after."

"*If* we stand," Alcie corrected him, but her tiredness was fast receding in the knowledge that she and Romi had finally done well in his eyes. *Don't know why I should care,* she scolded herself. *Who needs his approval anyhow?*

They ate at the bar, a large bowl of Uger's best lentils between them, and a plate of dunking bread and brynza to share. Alcie drank glass after glass of mellonia, and even polished off an entire slice of fresh-baked bundleberry pie.

INTO THE SKY

After lunch, Dar left her briefly. She brushed out Romi's coat until he returned. "Mount up," he said curtly, "it's time for the other half of your lesson."

They tacked up in silence, Alcie standing on a bale of hay to make up for her lack of height. Once they'd cleared the barn area, Dar booted her into the saddle and mounted up himself. When they were on their way, Dar spoke again. "Are you still up for a leap?" he asked.

Alcie, who had been absorbed in the sway of Romi's mane in the breeze, looked up sharply. "Of course!"

Cutting to the left, they doubled back around to Dar's course in the woods, weaving through windlestrae almost as high as Alcie's head. This time when she rode close behind Storm, Romi didn't try to lean forward and bite the other arion. Her nervous energy was contagious, and he lifted his hooves a bit higher as he trotted along.

The course was as they had left it. "Focus," Dar reminded her, coming to a halt beside the lowest fallen log.

Walking around it, Alcie found that it only came up to Romi's knees. "That doesn't look too bad," she decided. "What do I do?"

"*We*," Dar corrected her. "You and Romi are a team, and you need to work together to succeed at this. For his part, Romi will need to learn to pick up his legs. We're going to take him over these bundles of branches to get him into the habit."

He gestured to where several small piles of branches stood in lines parallel to each other, only a few feet apart. "You're going to practice a new position." Lifting himself to a standing position in the saddle, he demonstrated. Leaning over Storm's neck, he balanced easily, his back curved, his arms crooked at angles as if he were holding a serving tray upon them.

"Your turn. Heels down, shoulders back, and don't lean too far forward or you'll land on Romi's neck."

At a halt, it wasn't too difficult. She wobbled backwards into the saddle the first time, landed clumsily on Romi's neck the next, but by the third time she had a shaky but definitely promising version of Dar's position.

"Not bad," he observed. "But everything needs to be sharper. Heels down and shoulders back aren't just for show. If you're leaning back, just a bit, you'll balance better over Romi. Right now, you look like a sack of salt laid over the saddle."

Frowning, Alcione tried to correct her position. She found that, as he'd said, leaning back improved her balance. She continued like that for a moment, adjusting here and there, and then looked up at Dar for confirmation when she was finished.

"Still needs work," he told her, "but it's a start. You'll take Romi over those branches in that position. You'll rise in the saddle and post with Romi's outside shoulder, circling to the left. As you approach the branches, get into position and stay there until you've passed the last bundle."

Alcie nodded. Turning Romi, she urged him to a trot. As they approached the branches, Dar stepped in front of the first pile and gestured to go around him. "You're posting to the inside shoulder. Switch it, and then come back around the circle."

Looking down, Alcie saw that he was right and inwardly scolded herself. Tion had taught her that weeks ago. *I can't get anything else wrong! Dar will never let me learn more if I can't master the basics! And if I can't get better, how will I ever make it all the way to Skyreach once I've found the stones?*

For a fleeting moment, Alcie wondered if this was what it might have been like for Hermion at Kayre Kymminthë. She was startled to feel Romi's mind pressing against hers as she rode around the circle, offering an image of Storm leaping the log and a frisson of excitement that was not solely her own.

If we work together, she told him, *maybe we can do that too!*

She could sense Romi's enthusiasm, and realized he was no longer expending energy on ways to fight her hold. Seeing Storm respond willingly to his rider's commands, and seeing the reward – the closest to flying he could get – he seemed to be learning that perhaps he needed a human's help after all, at least until his wings returned.

They went through the line of branches over and over, until Alcione lost count of how many times Dar had snapped, "Heels down!" or "Shoulders back!" or "Wrong diagonal!" The sun moved in an arc across the sky, changing the light dappling over the course as they went.

As the sun neared the horizon, Dar called them to a halt. Romi's neck was dark with sweat, as was Alcione's tunic.

"This is far later than I had planned to stay here, but you're making enough progress to warrant it," Dar said, surprising a smile out of her. "One leap, and then we're for home."

"What do I do?" she asked.

Dar strode over to the line of branches and gathered them together, making a pile half as high as the lowest log, and nearly as wide across. "I'm not sure you're ready for a larger obstacle, so you'll take this instead.

"Do exactly what you've done earlier, keep your balance, and let Romi do the rest. Urge him forward a bit, so you come out of the leap in a canter. It should feel natural."

Circling around the branches the first time to prepare, Alcie focused solely on making her form perfect. She was beginning to feel what Dar meant by, "the mark of a true rider." Maybe someday all this would be second nature but for now, moving together with Romi was taking up every ounce of her concentration.

INTO THE SKY

They approached the bundle of branches. Alcie nudged Romi slightly with her heels, made an encouraging clucking sound, and lifted herself out of the saddle into position. Romi accelerated, gathered himself, and sprang.

They were over!

Still in position, Alcie cantered around the circle with Romi. She could feel his joy, the lifting of all legs at once, and the barest memory of flight.

When they came to a halt in front of Dar, a hint of a smile creased his solemn face. "Well done," he told her. "I don't see the makings of a legend in you yet, but you're not the worst rider I've seen, either. Let's head back."

Turning Storm towards the exit to the clearing, he trotted off. Although a part of Alcie fumed inwardly at being dismissed so quickly, those thoughts were quickly banished by elation. *We did it!* she told Romi, laughing inwardly.

Fly soon? came his response, accompanied by a dizzying vision of the land as seen from far above. Patches of green and brown were broken up by a gauzy weave of clouds. She could almost feel his wings as if they were spreading from her own shoulder-blades, his hooves as if they extended from her own arms and legs.

Someday, she promised him.

It wasn't until they were well on the road towards Ianthe, the setting sun turning the sky into a canvas of fire and gold, that she realized the picture

Romi had sent her had been accompanied not only by the feeling of wings and hooves, but by the pressure of a small weight on his back, and two thin bands – legs – pressed tight around his sides.

- CHAPTER 30 -
Orfel and Geyende

THE NIGHT-GLOWS WERE burning brightly as they returned along the streets of Ianthe to Buske's stables. They put their arion away with no chatter, and Alcie walked between Dar and Sola towards Caulburne Alley for Rungilivanster's show, her thoughts turned inward.

Sometimes, Alcie mused, *it's hard to think of him as Rungilivanster. Even if not to the rest of the city, I feel as if he'll always be Tion to me.* She sighed. *Where will I go when he sends me away?*

She refused to feel sorry for herself, or give up the idea of finding the crown, but the question was never far from her mind. Dar's lesson had been a sign, a sort of last reprieve. Soon she and Elly would have to go. Before then, she was going to have to find a way to steal that crown.

That night, Tion brought out his well-worn puppet theatre, calling upon the children of the streets to help him tell tales of the heroes of old. In the third tale, she recognized with surprise the puppet clad in deep green, a silver circlet upon his head. Alcie gazed upon the miniature Orfel, and listened as Tion recited the list of his great deeds.

"He fought monsters, and slew great beasts," Tion pronounced, stabbing the puppet's sword against his other hand, clothed in the appearance of the Great Beast of Nyxe, last of the alanin. Red as blood, it stuck its forked tongue out with a wicked look in its eye.

"Indeed, he even rid the world of the very last alanin in his quest to win Geyende's favor. But her father did not want a simple hero."

His voice took on an odd, haunting tone. "The world had need of a different kind of man. People were hungry and cold, and the King did not see them. Orfel did not see them. But Geyende saw, and she wept." From behind the curtain, another hand appeared, wearing the figures of Geyende and her father.

What is he talking about? Alcie wondered. *I've never heard this before!*

"Geyende's father stole the crown from the rightful King, promising to give the people food and shelter. And for a time, this he did," Tion continued, effortlessly bringing out the puppet of a peasant without Alcie having noticed the alanin's disappearance.

"But soon Geyende's father saw the money being brought into the treasury, and his eyes filled with gold. With gold, he could buy wondrous gifts for his beautiful adored daughter. And he showered her with silk gowns and golden bracelets and ruby rings."

The peasant tilted its unhappy face down in sorrow and quietly sank back into the recesses of the theatre.

"Geyende refused to speak to her father until he saw the error of his ways. But he would not see. All he saw was an ungrateful daughter, who did not want his gifts. And so he locked her away in a magical tower."

The puppet of Geyende ascended towards the top corner of the stage, head bowed so her fair hair covered her lovely features, along with the lack of an actual tower.

"That is where Orfel found her." The puppet of Orfel took the opposite corner of the stage, looking up at his beloved. "From out the five windows of her tower, each colored with beautiful glass pictures of the world outside, she could not see him. But at last, hearing only the words of his beloved trapped in the tower, Orfel began to see the world that she could not."

Alcie gasped at the mention of the five windows from her dream. *That can't be a coincidence!* She listened intently as Tion continued the tale, feeling certain somehow that a vital clue to the stones was about to reveal itself.

"Speaking to him was painful, but Geyende told Orfel of the world she had lost, the world of kind people who wished only for food for their children and a warm place to sleep. Blacksmiths, tanners, dressmakers, each sharing the same world. She wanted them all to live in harmony, none lacking while others wore silk and rubies. Her heart heavy with the sorrow of it, Geyende died."

Some of the children looked near crying as Geyende fell from the invisible tower below the stage and her father vanished with her. The littlest girls clung to each other, hands gripped together in the darkness. The silence washed over them, and Alcie felt a tear slip down her cheek. *This isn't Orfel's story,* she realized. *It's ours. Tion is telling our story. But how does it end?*

"Prince Orfel was nearly destroyed by his grief. But he knew he had to find Geyende. He wanted her to see the world she had dreamed of in the tower. But his father and Geyende's were at war, and people were suffering. He knew he first had to find a way to free the kings from their hatred and blindness."

Orfel raised his head. A puppet of a crone came onstage opposite him. "He spoke to an oracle," Tion said, "who told him to search for five magical stones. They would bring him where he sought to go. And so he began his quest."

Orfel slowly, silently exited the stage, an oddly graceful and solemn figure. No one spoke, nor dared to clap. *Is that all?* Alcie wondered. *It can't be!*

INTO THE SKY

Tion came from around the back of the theatre, his hands bare and a grave expression on his face. "You will have to wait for next year to see the end of the story – I haven't thought up how best to tell it yet."

The twinkle returned to his eyes as he graced them with a small smile. "But you can make up your own tales over the winter and tell them to me when I return. I look forward to it. Thank you for sharing this summer with me.

"And now," the smile was back in full force, "a last bit of magic, and then toffin and luckle for all!"

Without warning, he launched into a complicated juggling routine, tossing three, then four, and then five balls that seemed to materialize from nowhere. Only Alcie noticed, out of the corner of her eye, Dar and Elly packing away the puppets in their trunks behind the stage.

When Tion had finished, he gestured to Elly to take the ever-present bags of candy around the crowd. As the children began to disperse back to their homes, one broke away and came towards her.

"You look different," Tremi said. His eyes raked up and down her frame. "Can't put my finger on it, though. Strange."

She gave him a brief smile. "It's just the change in the seasons. Summer is ending."

He scowled. "As if that makes sense."

She shrugged. "I didn't say it had to."

337

Tion, Dar, and Elly came over to them, the last of the children having scampered off.

"Dar tells me you've made great progress with Romi," Tion told her. "I'm very glad. Elly's already been told, but you ought to know that I'll be leaving for the south. I'll expect you to take Elly north for the winter, towards Elpis. It will be safer for you there."

Alcie nodded, then belatedly realized that she was not supposed to be taking the news so calmly. "I…I suppose that makes sense," she said, struggling to look like she was holding back tears. "After all that's happened, I suppose you might not want us here in the city."

Elly nodded. "The brothers in Elpis take in everyone, especially children. And in the summer, maybe we can come back."

"When do we leave?" Alcie asked, bracing herself.

"The day after tomorrow, early in the morning."

It was worse than she had feared. *But not unexpected. If he'd told me later, I'd only have waited out of fear.*

She nodded, unable to trust her voice. "I…I'm sorry," she told him, "about disappearing before. I promise I won't let you down again."

Tion met her gaze. She didn't know whether he searched for honesty or courage in her eyes, but evidently what he saw was acceptable to him. "I know you won't," he said softly. "You would never do anything to hurt Elly. Go get some sleep."

She, Elly, and Tremi walked back to the barn together. "We don't leave for the north until much closer to the winter snows," Tremi told her, "but we do stop by Elpis mid-season, to bring them supplies. We'll see each other then."

It occurred to her suddenly. "I'm really leaving."

Tremi nodded. "T'will be all right. You've made it this far."

"Yes," she said, her voice sounding small and distant to her own ears, "but there's a long way to go."

"There always is," Tremi told her. He laid a hand on her shoulder, but had nothing comforting to say. Squeezing her shoulder briefly, he let go and left her to her thoughts.

In the small hours of the morning, after the second chime of the night bells, she began to form a plan. She had failed so many times, but she couldn't afford not to succeed tomorrow night. As Elly snored softly, she put the pieces together. She smiled in the darkness. It was so simple, she couldn't believe she hadn't thought of it before.

In a way, it was oddly fitting. Everything would hinge on one hope, one guess: if there was any chance to steal the crown from the Arkos, it would come only because of her memories of home.

- CHAPTER 31 -
Last Chance

S HE DIDN'T SEE DAR or Tion all day. Tremi told her they were packing for their new assignment, and then nudged her to keep her focus on selling halay. Who knew when the extra coin might come in handy?

She couldn't concentrate all through the afternoon and found her mind drifting to the days ahead. How was she to travel alone with Elly, with no Tion or Tremi or Dar to guide them, unsure of whether she'd ever see them again?

"Tremi, what's Elpis like? Is it far?" she asked as she met him for supper.

He shrugged. "Not awful far. You follow the Trifira north until it reaches the mountains. After you get past the Karya it's rough going for a bit, but if you know how to forage it's easy not to starve. Gets cold, though. Winter comes earlier up there."

She shuddered at the thought of starving. "I wish you were coming with us," she said softly.

INTO THE SKY

He didn't reply. Alcie tried to smile, to brighten the mood. "I'll be looking forward to seeing you, though!" she said as she purchased two stackers, one for herself and one for Sola. "I expect you'll have lots of new stories to bring me."

Dar stopped by just as they were finishing up their meal. "I've secured a permit from the Arkos for the bearer of the message to be left to go about his business. It was intended for me, but no name is mentioned, so you should be fine as long as you don't draw too much attention. After Trippleton, the road to Elpis is fairly empty at this time of year, so you shouldn't have much trouble. You'll be a few days behind the Nirval caravan, so any bandits about should be focused on them."

"How will we travel without arion?" she asked, not sure she wanted to hear the answer.

He smiled gently. "You wouldn't. As usual, little one, you owe Tion your thanks. He's freed Romi from Goso for you. He got that pony – Moti, was it? – for you as well, to carry your packs. Try not to dash yourself and Elly to pieces falling off."

Her eyes lit but she couldn't quite bring herself to smile, though days ago the news would have filled her heart nearly to bursting. "I really do owe him," she agreed. And then her heart twisted with sorrow. "I wonder if we'll ever see each other again."

Dar shrugged. "I suspect you will. The world is more changeable than it was. Anyway, I'll have the permit for you in the morning."

Alcie nodded, preoccupied. "Alcione?" he prompted, and his voice shaped her name in a way it never had before, like he was saying it for the last time.

She looked up. "Be safe," he said shortly. "May you journey with the wind at your back."

It was the traditional blessing riders gave before heading off to do the King's bidding, and she thought that much like she, he would have heard it many times growing up with Tion's family. It brought to mind the night when he'd told her about being a true rider. It seemed burned into her memory, like something from a vivid, long ago dream instead of only two days ago.

She nodded, throat constricted, and left.

She didn't see him for the remainder of the evening, joining Tremi and the others for one last batch of stackers. Elly munched contentedly, sitting on the floor beside Sola. In between bites, he asked Yvo what Ianthe was like in the winter. Raka berated Cormy for not finding suitable berries for the pie Huin intended to make, while Tremi and Alcie sat silent and watched the people on the bridge go by.

At length, Tremi asked, "Do you think you'll come back in the spring?"

Alcie turned to him. "I don't know. If Rungilivanster's not there to watch over us, it would be much harder to stay. Maybe it would be best for Elly and me if we just…disappeared."

INTO THE SKY

Tremi snorted. "He might be gentle enough to do that. But I don't see you for a lifetime among the monks. Too much trouble for them."

"Hey!" she protested, but without much heat. He was right.

"She has plenty of time to decide. The journey to Elpis is only a few weeks. They will be there through the winter," Raka said, without looking up.

Cormy stopped arguing for a moment to chime in. "I've never seen Elpis before. What's it like?"

"We've never been anytime but in winter," Tremi told him, "but it's fair nice with the snow falling on it. It's deep in the mountains, so there's only one slim path for the caravan to travel. The monks are kind, and always buy extra to give to those in need in the villages below."

Below. Remembering the map in her father's study, she tried to picture it. Elpis was nestled in the mountains on the far side of Karya. Would Montelymnë have been one of the villages in need? What would the villagers have done, without coin from her family's treasury with which to survive? She was ashamed to realize the thought had never crossed her mind before. *Perhaps I'll have the chance to help...*

"You'll be able to go sledding," Tremi was telling Elly. "There's a big hill, and the monks use the sleds to make the descent quicker."

It struck her suddenly that the Stabler had mentioned a brother in Elpis. Would he be there?

She was still angry, but found she missed the sound of his voice despite his betrayal. The thought troubled her.

"I think I'm going to stop by the Citadel," she told the others. "I'll see you all in the morning."

Tremi cocked his head in an unspoken question. "I'm already starting to miss this place," she told him. "I just...want to think about it on my own."

He nodded. "I'll let Tion know. Will you be staying overnight?"

She tried to smile, but the corners of her mouth seemed too heavy to lift. "I think so. Tell Tion not to worry."

"Alcie?" Elly looked at her, worried. "You will come back, right?"

"Of course," she soothed him. "I won't leave you alone, Elly."

His smile was honest, and bright. *I have to keep my promise,* Alcie thought as she walked away towards the Citadel, Sola trotting silently at her heels. *No matter what happens with the crown tonight, I won't let him and Tion down again.*

She stopped first by Romi's stall, to explain her plan. She gave him images of the Kayre, and how she planned to get in and out. She showed him the path to Trippleton, and tried to show, using an image of the sun rising, that they would be leaving tomorrow.

He seemed to understand, and looked pensive – for an arion – as she finished communicating. *If you hurt,* he told her, returning the image of the Kayre, *I find you.*

The sky was beginning to darken as she stopped by the Citadel. Brother Fraitel was speaking with another of his order when he spotted Alcione. He waved his companion on and then approached her.

"My daughter, what brings you here tonight?" he asked.

Her smile was tentative. "I just thought I'd stay here a bit. I'm leaving tomorrow, and wanted...well..."

She didn't have to finish the thought. He nodded and placed a hand on her arm. "I understand perfectly. You may sit wherever you wish. Be at peace, daughter."

The hours passed in a restless blur as she went over her plan again and again. She kept a hand in Sola's fur, and he made no sound as she rose at last, ready to move beneath the full cover of night.

Brother Fraitel was speaking to a man at the altar. His back was to Alcione as the man, agitated, gestured wildly. She caught the words "my wife" and "lying" and was glad for the distraction. She and Sola slipped out the side door of the Citadel into the alley, and disappeared into the darkness.

- CHAPTER 32 -
Betrayal

THE PASSAGE BY THE wall remained unguarded. Troops walked the battlements above, but Alcie wore the dark tunic and leggings Huin had given her to replace the ones she'd destroyed the last time she'd been in this place. She would blend in perfectly with the long shadows cast by the Kayre walls.

She looked at Sola. "Stay," she told him, and he nodded. His coloring would give them away instantly. His eyes locked on hers, and something passed between them in that moment. A prayer for luck or safety, a promise of friendship, Alcie didn't know. But she accepted it for the approval that it clearly was.

She listened for the sound of footsteps, and waited until they passed over her and faded away before she darted across the field. Almost too late, she realized that someone occupied the gazebo, a faint light emanating from within.

INTO THE SKY

She ducked down by the bushes below and glanced around. The light illuminated a face, a nose pressed up to what appeared to be a book. Alcie waited. A page turned.

In the shadow of the gazebo, she looked around. The guards had raised no alarm. Alcie heard a slight yawn from behind her, and glanced up sharply as the figure put down the book. When it moved, Alcie rocked back on her heels, nervous.

But the figure only made to extinguish the light. Alcie saw its head duck down as another yawn followed. An eternity passed before she finally heard the sound.

Snoring.

Tiptoeing along the hedge, Alcie aimed for the kitchen door. Nearly everyone would be asleep at this hour, and she planned to take advantage of that. This time, she did not intend to try and find the trapdoor in the study. The Caliarkos had said treasures were found at the top of the tower, so she'd eliminated that possibility. It must be in the secret tunnel. In the darkness, finding the trapdoor in the study would be impossible. There was only one other way in.

The kitchen was guarded this time by a night maid – probably preparing the morning meal for tomorrow, but Alcie could see her flirting with one of the palace guards a little ways away. She watched for an opportune moment.

When their lips met in a kiss, Alcie rushed to the kitchen and darted inside, grateful that they had left the door ajar. Standing still behind the door, Alcie listened and heard more snoring. Another maid was in the kitchen, but this one was sound asleep.

Alcie stepped quietly to the door leading to the inner ward. The maid was off in a corner. Her head lolled against a bag of flour, and her mouth was wide open as she slept. This would be the first test.

She studied the situation carefully. The best course would be to find a place for the bolt – but how to move it without raising suspicion when the other maid and her beau returned?

Alcie let the plan take shape in her mind. Cautiously, she began to slide the bolt from its perch. Feeling the dampness on her palms, she was grateful once again. This door had been recently oiled; it would not squeak so easily.

The maid stirred. Alcie paused with the bolt in her hands, heart pounding in her chest so loudly she wondered if the girl had heard it. So loud it almost sounded like footsteps. The maid rolled over and fell back to sleep. There was no other sound.

Afraid to breathe, Alcie made her way over one perilous step at a time. When she stood near the flour, she gently lowered the bolt to the floor, propping one side up on a fluffy sack. When the girl's eyes remained closed, Alcie returned, again a step at a time, to the door. Pushing, she let out the tiniest sigh of relief when it opened soundlessly into the inner ward.

This time, she did not make her way towards the study in the corner of the main castle. In the shadow of the outbuildings, she walked along the far wall of the Kayre, and the ayrlea that sloped up towards the sky. For the briefest instant she dreamed of the magic of soaring from that field over the wall, the beautiful wings of an arion dappled in starlight as they took the air.

Two torches illuminated the main entrance to the Kayre and the four guards who stood at attention above her, barring the way.

Turning away from the main entrance, Alcie squinted into the darkness for what she sought. *There!* A small door, barely noticeable, but moonlit just enough for Alcie to see it. Looking up, she nodded and made her way to stand directly opposite the door.

When the moon passed behind a cloud, the ward was plunged into darkness. Alcie trotted straight across. She kept her hands out in front of her until they touched the smooth surface of the door. Reaching down, her hands found the latch and lifted it effortlessly. She pulled it open and slipped inside.

She gulped in the pitch darkness. This was the leap of faith she had made: that Kayre Montelymnë had been built on the same lines as Kayre Ianthe. She knew that originally it had been constructed to be identical, but that was two hundred years ago. Much could have changed.

She walked blindly to the left, keeping one hand on the wall. There was no light, no torches in the empty sconces her hand passed, to show her the way. Just the hope that somehow, this servants' corridor would take her where she wanted to go.

The darkness was palpable. She could feel her breath growing louder, heavier, as she continued. It seemed almost as if others breathed with her, and the sound amplified until she couldn't help coming to a stop, sure at last that she was lost for good.

A harsh breath broke the silence, and Alcie gasped.

It was not her own.

"Curse it," came a voice. Her heart leaped into her throat at its familiarity. "Alcie, you got any idea where we're going?"

She didn't have to reply. Another voice, solemn and determined, answered for her. "To the audience chamber."

Her mind whirled. "How?" she stammered out.

Tremi's voice shot back to her, moving closer with each word. "I know you too well. I can't fathom what you're doing, but I don't mean for you to get killed after all this time. When Elly shot out after you, I followed him and nipped him at the boxes. He said he'd scream murder if we didn't go in after, so I had no choice."

With a disgusted snort, he reached out and touched her arm, causing her to jump. "What in Tanatos' name are you thinking, coming here after the last time?"

She couldn't think how to answer, she was so stunned. Elly had gone after her? And Tremi? *I have to turn back! I can't risk getting them hurt!*

"She's got a good reason," Elly came to her defense. "You know she must. Right, Alcie?"

The silence enveloped them for a moment. *I suppose I owe them the truth, after all this.* She sighed.

"I've come for the Crown of Orfel."

"What?" Tremi's voice was an urgent whisper. "Are you mad?"

Elly said nothing. And then, "Of course. To get to Astraea."

She felt Tremi shift. "You mean to tell me you've come all the way here to find a way into the Land of the Dead?" He growled. "There are quicker roads. You should know. You've tried nearly all of them!"

His grip tightened on her arm. "This is what you've been after this whole summer? What you got yourself beat for? Nearly killed for?" The hand on her arm reached up to her shoulder and shook her. "You idiot!"

"She's right, Tremi."

Alcie turned towards the sound of Elly's voice. "She doesn't want to stay in Astraea, she wants to bring her family back from it. If we can find the crown and the door, we can find my family too. And we can stop the Arkos!"

"Stop him? You're *both* mad! There's naught to be done now. And why's he even need stopping?"

"He murdered hundreds," Alcie whispered furiously. "I don't care what he's done now. If he'd kill parents and children by the score, he'd kill anyone. Who'll be next, if we don't stop him?"

"What do you care, so long as it's not you? You'll stick your neck out for a myth, but it's not only your neck on the block anymore! I've no love for the Arkos, but I've also no aim to see Makaria's domain for a long while yet."

"I didn't ask you to come!" Alcie hissed back at Tremi, knocking his hand away. "Go back. I can do this alone."

"No, you can't," came Elly's surprisingly firm voice. "I know where the crown is."

His footsteps moving forward ended the discussion. Tremi pushed past her to follow him, and Alcie scrambled to keep up. Elly's soft footfalls were determined, as if he knew exactly where he was going.

At last, a faint light appeared at the end of the corridor. Alcie knew it to be the back way to the audience chamber, so servants could deliver refreshments unobtrusively. The flickering torch in its sconce marked the end of the corridor, and was placed well away from the curtain that backed the chamber.

INTO THE SKY

A few steps from the torch, they drew up together. Elly peered around the corner. "There's no one in the back, but someone's at audience."

Without warning, he moved forward. Alcie and Tremi followed as silently as they could.

They crowded into a small alcove set back and aside from the curtain separating them from the audience chamber. Meant as a spying nook for castle guards, it looked out onto a sliver of space between the curtain and the wall, giving extra guards a way to judge guests' intent while remaining hidden from their view. The guards standing in front of the dais were meant to deceive visitors into believing this was the only security protecting the lord and lady of the Kayre.

When the conversation and its speakers at last came into focus, Alcie bit her lip and struggled not to speak. Through the curtain she could see a tall, crooked man with piercing blue-violet eyes, focused on someone speaking from just out of view. Dar.

Her throat went dry, and Elly's hand found hers as they listened.

"I think you will find Cathatiur quite to your liking, Mat Vanisterai," came the Arkos's voice. Alcie could almost picture him, his slight frame dwarfed by the girth of the lord's chair.

King's chair, she reminded herself, picturing something even grander. "Your varied talents will make you much at home there."

"And your orders, Arkos?" That voice was Tion's, Alcie was sure of it.

"Nothing too taxing. You've given me valuable intelligence on the state of the capital this summer, but I've since found capable replacements who shall aid me in your stead. However, none of them is as…shall we say, adaptable?" He drew out the thought.

"I want to know the nature of my people's feelings in Cathatiur and Turan, not just here in Ianthe. You are most suited to glean this information for me."

She couldn't see, but expected Tion's nod in the silence. As Rungilivanster, he ran frequent errands for the Arkos, but he was also trusted by the locals. His friendliness and ability to entertain would fast gain him the trust of those around him, wherever he might go. It was that same charm that he had used to protect her and Elly from suspicion. But what was the name that the Arkos had called him by just now?

"As for you, Mat Ferrinore," the Arkos continued. The name tugged at her, but she couldn't figure out why. Dar looked up, revealing that it was he the Arkos had addressed. "You are more useful to me elsewhere. I want to see you at Kayre Kymminthë before the week is out."

Alcie fidgeted. *Kymminthë? What in the world could the Arkos be doing with the riders' training ground?*

"I thought that the project there was well underway, sir?" Dar replied evenly.

"It is. But I am confident that your aid would speed the pace of progress."

Tion spoke up, his tone wary, "May I inquire as to the nature of this project, sir? I had no knowledge of any faction of yours at Kymminthë."

Dar remained expressionless, unmoving, as the answer came. "I am glad you asked, for you might also be able to aid me in this endeavor. I have asked Mat Ferrinore to go to Kayre Kymminthë to aid in the creation of a new fighting force. A group of children, to be trained in the ways of the Talaria."

Alcie bit the inside of her lip, and Elly's hand crushed her fingers as both of them tried not to show their shock. *New Talaria! No!* It was an affront to all that her family stood for, that the Arkos should steal the greatest honor from those he had murdered.

Tion's tone, when he spoke, was harsh in a way that Alcie had never heard before. But he did not address his rebuke to the Arkos.

"So, my friend, you would train this force, these false Talaria?"

Dar's nod was almost imperceptible.

"After all that was taken from you, you would still do this for him?"

Tion's tone indicated the Arkos, but the man in question did not interrupt. Tion's words alone echoed through the grand chamber.

"And can you find peace, knowing how deeply you betray your dead family?"

The pain in Dar's gaze flashed for only a moment, but the look on his face was so horrible, it seemed that of a man fatally wounded. Alcie ached at the look in his eyes, until her mind caught up. In an instant, all the pieces fell together.

Ferrinore. A name mentioned in Hermion's letters. A dead family. An arion who trusted Dar with familiarity gained over years. A man who knew better than even Tion the way of a true rider. A betrayal of family honor.

Because Dar was no groomsman.

He was a noble.

Like her.

"No!"

Her anguished whisper lashed out into the silence, and Alcie knew she had doomed them all.

- CHAPTER 33 -
Leave the Rest

"**G**UARDS!" THE ARKOS COMMANDED.

Elly held her hand tightly as the guards ran behind the curtain, coming up short when they peered into the darkness and saw only three small figures. With a stern grip on her shoulder, Alcie was marched out to stand before the Arkos.

Tion gasped when his eyes met hers, but it was not his gaze she sought. Her eyes burned into Dar's. He did not flinch. His face was fiercely expressionless, and he neither blinked nor looked away as she passed.

She turned to the Arkos. He sat up straight in the grand chair, looking intrigued. "Spies? Hmm."

He tapped his fingers on the armrest. "They're lamentably young. I'd hate to put children to death, but this information can't get out."

"You don't care about killing children!" Alcie spat. "You murdered my family! Better to die here than live like you!"

"Ah." A look of enlightenment passed his face. "You're one of *them*."

"Arkos, please," Tion interjected, "They're only children—"

The Arkos held up a hand. "I know you would see them spared, Tion, but I'm afraid that even for you I could not show leniency."

He beckoned to the guards. "Bring them here."

"Sir," Tremi stammered. "She's no nob. She's me sister – addled in the head she was, and the riots made her worse. And me little brother—"

"You look nothing alike," the Arkos snapped. His stern expression softened. "But it was well-meant."

Alcie followed Elly's gaze to a place behind the throne as the Arkos beckoned a guard close and commanded him to search the rest of the passage.

Lying on the floor was a dusty portrait, the canvas slashed through. The line bisected the King's proud face, and it seemed a travesty, with the Queen's kindly expression untouched beside him. Her auburn curls were similar to that of the eldest prince, while the next youngest boy had the darker hair of his father.

As Alcie looked at the final face in the picture, the right side of the face shredded, she caught her breath and froze. The boy had curly red ringlets, and mischievous blue eyes. A ball of copper fur with two large eyes peeked out from over his small shoulder. It was a younger face, but one she knew. A face that had looked back at her every day for weeks, and slept peacefully beside her every night.

Elly. Or rather, His Highness Prince Elistroyn.

She turned sharply back to the Arkos as the guard returned, grateful no one seemed to have noticed. But she saw quickly that Dar had, as he met her eyes once more with an imperceptible nod.

The Arkos looked at her, assessing her up and down. "Poor girl," he said, looking at the mud-colored tunic, the ragged clothes. "Perhaps it will be a blessing to return you to the arms of your family."

He motioned to the guard.

"Please," Tion begged, as Alcie was dragged to her knees before the Arkos.

"We cannot know what they have heard," the Arkos reminded him. He addressed the guards. "Make it brief and painless."

Alcie stood up as the captain of the guard drew near. Beside the Arkos, the magian had seemingly appeared from thin air. His cold eyes pinned her, but she forced herself to look away. She faced the Arkos as the guards closed in.

"This doesn't end tonight," she told him softly. "Someone will stop you."

He met her gaze evenly and did not respond.

Tremi struggled in the grasp of another guard as the captain drew near. Elly was fighting to get to her, but time had slowed almost to a halt for Alcione. As she bent her head to the floor, she felt a pressure in her mind. *Romi,* she thought, praying her words could reach him, *I failed. I'm sorry.*

Her eyes were closed when she thought she heard Romi's piercing whinny, seemingly echoing through the entire chamber. At least he would survive. A small smile crossed her lips.

And then something pierced her inner thoughts, as a hand grabbed hers and pulled. Her eyes shot open. The sight that graced them was impossible.

Arion were flooding the audience chamber.

Alcie was riveted to the sight before her eyes, ignoring Tremi's efforts to drag her away. Welm, Ocne, Adrie, Inthys – all the Montelymnë arion had come galloping into the chamber. With them came more familiar faces – all of the Hollows arion, and those from the barn on Keecy Street. And more still! It seemed as if every arion in the city had come.

They thundered across the marble floors and swarmed around the guards like a tide. A sea of dun and chestnut, bay and grey and black surged over them, knocking the guards off their feet and forcing the Arkos to retreat. The magian threw up his hands and suddenly the arion were thrust away by an invisible barrier, shielding the magian and his leader.

In the commotion, Alcie searched for Romi but couldn't find him. There was no time. Tremi dragged her back into the shadows, Elly dogging their heels.

"This way!" Elly shouted, darting forward towards the opposite end of the curtain behind the stage. He fumbled against the wall, and then the groan of moving gears was heard. A stone passage heaved open, and Elly was gone. Tremi shoved her after him, and followed after grabbing a torch from the nearby wall.

They ran like shadows through the darkness. Alcie could barely see the outline of her own hands as she reached forward to find the walls. Elly seemed to know exactly where he was going, and kept urging, "This way! Hurry!"

The passage wound down and down into the depths, and Alcie saw the vague shapes of wine casks forgotten in the bowels of the cellar. Elly's voice pressed them onwards. They followed as he ran beyond the casks and piles of rotting vegetables to a door so narrow she nearly missed it, and so short she had to duck her head to get through.

Even with the torch, the darkness was nearly absolute as they moved forward. The passage was barely walkable with its low ceilings, and Alcie could imagine that an adult might have to crawl to fit. The cacophony of the audience hall had died back into a dull roar from far behind them.

Tremi cursed from behind her as he stumbled. The torch hit the floor beside him. He picked it up, but not before Alcie spotted the object that had tripped him. "Wait!" she called to Elly.

She snatched the torch from Tremi, nearly burning her hand. Bending down, she knelt to view the tarnished metal shape nearly embedded in the rocky dirt path.

It didn't look fit for royalty, smudged and dented as it was. The points atop the crown were twisted, and one had broken cleanly off. In her free hand, Alcie looked at the five indented spaces adorning the broken crown.

Elly turned back and took the crown from her. "What's it doing here?" he asked breathlessly. Alcie snatched it back and turned it around over and over in her hands, hope shriveling inside her chest. She was so cold.

The stones were gone.

All the fight went out of Alcione as she sank to the ground. "It can't be," she murmured. "It can't have all been for nothing. It can't. It can't!"

Tremi knelt beside her. "Come on," he said roughly. "We've still got our lives."

She handed the torch back to him, her other hand dropping to the floor. Something brushed against it. Out of habit so ingrained her hand moved by itself, she lifted the rock to examine whether it would fit her collection.

Polished and cut so that even torchlight reflected its radiance, it shimmered in the dim glow. "You found one!" Elly murmured, desperately searching the ground for the others. But a quick sweep with the torch revealed nothing more.

"Well and good," Tremi said, breaking the silent spell of the moment. "But we've got to go! Now!"

INTO THE SKY

Alcie got to her feet, slipping the stone into her pouch and leaving the crown where it lay in the dust.

Elly led them to a trapdoor. He tried to open it with no success. Tremi nudged him aside and handed the torch over. His wiry strength slid the door aside with a thump. Taking the torch back and handing it to Alcie, he boosted Elly up into the study. Then he threw the torch to the floor to burn out in the dirt.

Before she could protest, Tremi shoved her up. Elly's small hands closed around her wrist and pulled. She landed in a heap on the floor as Tremi pulled himself up beside her. In a flash, he had pulled the door haphazardly back into place.

"Let's go," he whispered, and they crept together towards the door to the outside. The study window provided the only light – a barren patch illuminated by an unsteady moonbeam.

They could hear shouts in the distance, coming from around the other side of the castle. "The gates will be impossible now," Tremi said. He sounded scared for the first time Alcie could remember. "And I can't imagine us getting back to the garden from here."

A snort sounded beside them and they were still, huddling in the dark.

A moment later, a silhouetted muzzle attached to a long, graceful neck intruded through the window. "Romi," Alcie murmured, feeling the warmth of his mind touching hers.

Found you, he said. *We go together.*

"Together," she whispered back to him, sending the words to him in her mind as well. She got to her feet and unbolted the door. "Now and always."

They came to stand beside him outside. Although he was wearing no tack, Alcie reached up to grab his mane and, with a push from Tremi, dragged herself over his back to sit astride him. Elly followed suit.

Tremi looked concerned. He darted back inside and returned with a small stool. Standing on it, he put one foot on the windowsill and used it to leverage himself on behind the others. "We've all lost it," he muttered as he clung desperately to Alcie's waist, Elly between them like cheese in a stacker.

Romi needed no guidance as he turned towards the back of the Kayre. Alcie held tight to his mane as he burst into a canter. Tremi prayed softly beneath his breath. Sound seemed amplified here, and Alcie looked around, expecting to see soldiers swarming them from every side. But no one was there.

The moon loomed above as they rode up the hill. Up the ayrlea, Alcie realized.

The ground was more level but still rising as they approached the wall. It was lower from this side, but still at least eight feet off the ground. Even at full gallop, they couldn't hope to clear it. Alcie heard a shout from behind, and watched as the guards crested the foot of the hill.

INTO THE SKY

Romi thought a question to her. *What now?* Alcie gazed at the wall. The wind stirred at her back and her heart caught in her throat.

Dar's words thundered in her ears. *Be human to find your direction...leave the rest.*

Leaning forward, burying her hands in his mane, she clucked to him, communicating an image with a certainty she'd never had before in her entire life. "Hold on!" she shouted.

Romi galloped a full circle as the guards stumbled towards them, picking up speed as he turned squarely to face the castle wall. Alcie closed her eyes. She saw as Romi saw, and felt a tingle run out through her fingertips. A crackle of energy arced along her spine, flowing down her arms and Romi's back and up, and out.

Romi sprang off the ground. Tremi gripped them in terror. Elly's hands reached for a lower part of Romi's mane. Alcie felt it as if he'd touched her instead. And she saw, through eyes not her own, guards skidding to a halt behind them in wonder.

The wind caught them, bearing them up beyond the wall, and out of the Arkos's hands. It seemed to cradle them, and Alcie felt like the stars were rushing past, filling them with light. The ground was so far below. The Kayre grew distant. There was only the night sky, and the wind, and the stars all around them.

Without wings, without feathers, they flew over the castle wall to freedom.

They landed in the windlestrae, the impact sending them tumbling to the ground. Tremi was the first to rise, groaning but still able to stand. Elly looked dazed. "We flew," he whispered excitedly. "We really flew!"

The castle lay miles behind them. Romi had taken them to the trees at the edge of the practice field. Alcie had no concept of how long they had flown, and how they had come to be there. She was stunned by the mere fact of it. "We made it!" she murmured.

Tremi shook his head in bemusement. "Mad," he told her. "You're completely mad." But he didn't look angry anymore. She couldn't fathom the look he gave her.

Carefully, she got to her feet. Romi grazed peacefully a few steps away. *How?* she asked him.

She felt a mental shrug, tingles of pleasure and pride. He had no idea what had happened, or how, but it was awfully nice to have flown once more. *Again?* he asked.

Soon, she replied. *As soon as I figure out how it was possible the first time.*

Looking into the distance, she marked a solitary oak tree standing adjacent to the windlestrae, far from the road to Trippleton. "That way," she said.

They settled by the foot of the tree, not speaking. Tremi sat back against the trunk and shut his eyes. After a few moments, Elly sat beside him.

INTO THE SKY

Chilled and shaking, he snuggled close when Tremi draped an arm over his thin shoulders.

Alcie listened for a while, wondering why no one pursued them. As the moon shifted and the hours passed, it became clear that, whatever the reason, no one would.

With bated breath, Alcie pulled the stone from her pouch. It glistened in the moonlight and warmed and grew brighter as she touched it. Somehow, she knew that in the light of day it would be violet so deep it was almost blue, as bright and pure as the window in her dream. And as deep as a certain pair of eyes that haunted her even now.

"Where do we go?" she asked it.

There was no response.

I'm not afraid, she told it. *Not anymore. And I'll never give up. Even if you don't show me the way, I'll find it somehow. I'll never stop looking.*

Eyes closed, she gripped the stone. *I know now,* she thought. *I'm meant to do this.*

The stone sizzled in her hand. Opening her eyes, she saw spears of violet light erupting from her closed hand. Holding it aloft, she watched as a clear, burning line illuminated the windlestrae, pointing past Trippleton, towards the nearly invisible wall of the mountains in the distance. Towards Elpis.

As the line faded, she leaned back against the tree and smiled, awaiting sunrise.

Epilogue

ALCIE OPENED HER EYES to see Dar and Tion before her, just as she had expected. She had stayed awake for hours, watching over her friends in almost a waking dream, seeing but unseeing. Shivering, but not feeling the cold. Sola had arrived in the night, and she had accepted his presence in silence, placing a hand on his fur as he settled beside her.

She rose, and her eyes cut to Dar's fearfully. He held up a hand. "I'm not here to do you harm," he said quickly. Tion held up a hand to forestall any further protest.

Behind them stood Stormweaver, Sleepy, and Moti, along with Sola and Flip, who scurried from Sleepy's saddle onto his favorite place under Elly's ear. Tremi waited to one side, eyeing Dar warily.

The sun had yet to rise, and the sky was purple with the promise of the coming dawn. A few trees stood like black towers against the horizon, and the windlestrae danced in the gentle breeze. No one spoke.

INTO THE SKY

At last, Tion broke the silence. "Everything was chaos after you jumped," he said. "The guards thought you had magic."

Do you? Was the unspoken question. Alcie shook her head. "We had to get away," she said slowly. There was no other explanation she could give.

Tion seemed to understand. "They'll pursue you this morning. Superstition only fuels fears in the nighttime. If you returned to Ianthe, they'd certainly kill you all." He looked at each of them in turn, but the longest at Tremi. "And the Arkos will have them out in full force. He had long enough to look at you and memorize your faces. Whatever it is you're looking for, you won't find it now."

Alcie looked down at her feet. Tremi wouldn't be able to return to the traders now, and it was her fault.

"We found what we were looking for," Elly said. "We'll go to Elpis now."

Tremi pointed to Moti, who was wearing a saddle and loaded down with bulging packs. "Did it have to be him?"

Dar quirked an eyebrow. "Less noticeable. And the distance to the ground is shorter. You're not exactly an expert."

Tremi sighed. "I suppose you're right."

Tion locked eyes with Alcie. "It won't be easy out there, especially now that you're being hunted. Word will spread, and it might catch up to you one day. I expect you to take care of each other."

Leading Moti forward, he helped Tremi into the small arion's saddle. Dar pulled supplies from Storm and from the large pack on his own back. Wordlessly, he tacked Romi. He lifted Elly into the saddle, and turned to offer a hand to Alcie.

She didn't take it. "You're helping the Arkos," she accused. "Even though you're one of us!"

He didn't deny it. His eyes locked on hers, and she wondered what was behind them.

Tion came over to them. "He's helping us right now, Alcie. And whatever he may do for the Arkos, I trust his reasons. I trust him."

"Why?" she asked, her voice small against the wide expanse that loomed around them.

Tion shrugged, and the corners of his mouth turned up slightly, despite the sadness in his expressive gaze. "He's still my best friend."

She reached out and slipped her hand into Dar's, accepting his help. His grip was strong and warm. He studied her as he helped her into the saddle, slipping her foot into the stirrup. "Heels down," he reminded her with a slight smile.

Stepping away, he mounted Storm and stood beside Tion and Sleepy. Alcie felt Elly behind her, the fuzz of Flip's muzzle nestled into the crook of her left shoulder. At her feet, Sola looked up at her expectantly. And to her side, Tremi struggled to hold Moti's reins properly, looking back and forth to see what the others were doing.

Tion and Dar turned to go.

INTO THE SKY

"Wait," Alcie said, looking at Dar. "Why?"

He didn't ask, *why what?* She wanted to say, *why are you working for the Arkos?* Or, *why are you helping us instead of turning us in?* But what she wondered most of all, and understood least, was this: *why teach me? If you're training new Talaria, if you truly believe that the Arkos is right, why keep my secret all that time?*

Without a word, he understood it all. Smiling, he said quietly, "Because you're a rider."

Clucking to Storm, he urged the arion into a gallop, Tion and Sleepy following. The others waited with her until the figures faded against the faraway wall surrounding the city they were leaving behind.

In a brilliant bloom of color, the sun speared into the sky. Alcie held the stone aloft, freeing its violet glow once more. The line of light arrowed forward. Tremi looked at her and grinned. Behind her, she could feel Elly sitting up straighter, ready to go. Flip's wet nose sniffed at her neck. And faithful Sola stood alongside her as always, ears pricked towards the light. She nudged Romi forward, turning away from Ianthe.

"Let's ride," she told them. "We've got a long journey ahead."

Thank you for buying this book! Looking for more of Alcione's adventures? Visit my webpage at www.ericaconverso.com for news about future books, contests, and giveaways between book releases. Sign up for my mailing list for more information about Alcie's world and new releases.

About the Author

Erica Converso is a former librarian, and forever champion of great stories. She holds a Master's degree in Library Science, with an emphasis on young adult literature. *Into the Sky* was begun as an independent final project for her dual-degree in English Literature and Creative Writing, but has evolved into so much more. Erica lives on Long Island with her husband Chris, their hyperactive cat, Aria, and their adorable rabbit, Shadow.

Acknowledgements

Into the Sky had an eight-year journey to print, and many people have had a hand in helping it get there. First, I want to thank William Flesch of Brandeis University, who sponsored my independent study project, resulting in the novel's first draft. His mentorship was invaluable.

Many thanks to my brilliant editor, Jen Blood, who turned a rough first draft into a beautifully polished novel, while also helping me improve as a writer. Her enthusiasm for *Into the Sky* guided me through every part of the editing process. Profuse thanks to Ewan A. Dougall, my earliest editor. Beta reading your work inspired and challenged me to improve my own, while your sharp critical eye alerted me to my weak spots without ever discouraging me. I can't wait to see your books in print!

Over the years, my friends have helped me polish the novel to perfection – special thanks to Vicky and Kat for your constant encouragement.

Thanks to the extended Converso and Greenblatt families – your cheerleading has always pushed me to do my best. Thanks to my grandparents for your steadfast confidence in me. And my deepest gratitude to my parents, who always believed in and supported my dreams, and to my siblings, Ken and Michelle. You are the best! Lastly, thanks to Chris, my loving husband and best friend. You made *Into the Sky* what it is today. Words can't express what you've done for me. Thanks for everything.

Made in the USA
Middletown, DE
12 June 2016